Jenny Cooper Has a Secret

The Housekeeper

Cul-de-sac

All the Wrong Places

The Bad Daughter

She's Not There

Someone Is Watching

Shadow Creek

Now You See Her

The Wild Zone

Still Life

Charley's Web

Heartstopper

Mad River Road

Puppet

Lost

Whispers and Lies

Grand Avenue

The First Time

Missing Pieces

Don't Cry Now

Tell Me No Secrets

See Jane Run

Good Intentions

The Deep End

Life Penalty

The Other Woman

Kiss Mommy Goodbye

Trance

The Transformation

The Best of Friends

Home Invasion—a special project designed to encourage adult literacy

JENNY COOPER
HAS A SECRET

JENNY COOPER HAS A SECRET

A Novel

Joy Fielding

BALLANTINE BOOKS

NEW YORK

Ballantine Books
An imprint of Random House
A division of Penguin Random House LLC
1745 Broadway, New York, NY 10019
randomhousebooks.com
penguinrandomhouse.com

LIBRARY OF CONGRESS CATALOGING-IN-PUBLICATION DATA
Names: Fielding, Joy, author.
Title: Jenny Cooper has a secret : a novel / Joy Fielding.
Description: First edition. | New York : Ballantine Books, 2025.
Identifiers: LCCN 2025014956 (print) | LCCN 2025014957 (ebook) |
ISBN 9780593873175 (hardcover) | ISBN 9780593873199 (ebook)
Subjects: LCGFT: Detective and mystery fiction. | Novels.
Classification: LCC PR9199.3.F518 J46 2025 (print) |
LCC PR9199.3.F518 (ebook) | DDC 813/.54—dc23/eng/20250409
LC record available at https://lccn.loc.gov/2025014956
LC ebook record available at https://lccn.loc.gov/2025014957

Printed in the United States of America on acid-free paper

2 4 6 8 9 7 5 3 1

First Edition

Book design by Alexis Flynn

Title page background art: stock.adobe.com/Krakenimages.com

The authorized representative in the EU for product safety and compliance is
Penguin Random House Ireland, Morrison Chambers, 32 Nassau Street,
Dublin D02 YH68, Ireland. https://eu-contact.penguin.ie

For Warren,
    Shannon and Eric,
    Annie and Courtney,
        Hayden and Skylar,
        Remy and Foxy Cleopatra

JENNY COOPER
HAS A SECRET

CHAPTER ONE

"Psst . . ."

The word pings against the back of my ear like a well-aimed pebble. I turn toward the sound, see nothing but the long corridor stretched out behind me. There is no one there.

I shrug, take another step.

"Psst . . ."

Really? I stop, my eyes scanning the area. Is someone crouched behind one of the plush purple velvet sofas in the nearby lounge? And if so, aren't we a little old to be playing such games? "Hello?" I say, more question than greeting, my body twisting toward the empty visitors' lounge to my right, then over toward the deserted nurses' station on my left, ultimately completing a full circle. I am about to throw up my hands, as if to say, "I give up," when I see her.

No wonder I missed her, I think. She is tiny, her skin almost the same shade as the concrete pillar her frail body is leaning against, her uncombed hair a perfect match for her ghostly pallor. *If she were any less substantial, she'd be invisible,* I think, then laugh, wondering if that's how the younger generation sees *me.* Or *doesn't* see me. I'm no spring chicken, after all. Seventy-six, as of a month ago. Well past the age when women become invisible to most of the outside world.

And this woman is at least a decade my senior, I estimate. Although that could be just wishful thinking, I'm forced to concede.

"Are you talking to me?" I ask, hearing echoes of Robert De Niro's famous line from the movie *Taxi Driver* as I take a few trepid steps toward her. *And how long has it been since that movie came out? Twenty, thirty years? Longer?*

I stop, startled to realize that I'm nervous, although I have no idea why. What can this frail old woman possibly do to me? She can't weigh more than ninety pounds, and I'm easily a hundred and thirty-five. Okay, closer to a hundred and forty, according to the last time I got weighed, although I'm still considered slim for my five-foot, nine-inch frame. Okay, five feet, eight and a quarter inches. I've lost almost an inch since the last time I was measured. Pounds gained; inches lost. Getting shorter and wider. "Nothing to be concerned about," my doctor has assured me. "I'm not worried."

And why should he be? At barely fifty, he's years away from his best-before date. I, on the other hand, am circling cautiously around mine. Yes, everyone says I look much younger than my age; I exercise, have regular facials and the odd chemical peel, my hair is a fashionable lightly streaked bob that keeps the ever-encroaching grays at bay, my wardrobe is current and designer chic. Still, the body knows.

The body definitely knows.

Can anything be more ego-destroying than growing old?

It beats the alternative, my best friend, Carol, used to say.

If we have to grow old and die, I would counter, only partly in jest, *could we not at least get better looking?*

She'd laugh, dutifully.

She doesn't laugh anymore.

So, what's there to be nervous about? I wonder. I'm standing in the middle of the fourth-floor hallway of the upscale oceanfront memory care facility that calls itself—with not the slightest hint of irony—*Legacy Place.* Outside the sun is shining, as it does with monotonous regularity here in Jupiter, Florida. There are nurses and orderlies scattered throughout the six-story gleaming white structure. A simple shout would bring them scurrying down the hall. Not to mention that one halfhearted push would surely send this ancient crone flying. Still, I stop several feet away from where she is standing. "Can I help you?" I ask, hating the tentativeness clinging to the edges of my voice.

"I have a secret," she tells me. Her own voice is surprisingly strong, no tentativeness there.

I say nothing.

"Do you want to hear it?" she presses.

"Do you want to tell me?"

"I don't know," she says. "Who *are* you?"

"I'm Linda. Linda Davidson," I add when it becomes clear from her silence that she is expecting more.

Her mouth twists from side to side, as if she is literally ingesting this information. "Linda is a pretty name," she says finally. "You don't hear it so much anymore."

I nod. She's right. Names like Linda have pretty much disappeared from the lexicon in recent years, like the Gertrudes and Ethels before them, giving way to the current crop of Britneys, Skylars, and Briannes.

"I'm Jenny," she says. "Jenny Cooper."

"Nice to meet you, Jenny."

"Is it?"

I'm not sure how to respond, so I say nothing.

"Who are you?" she asks again.

"I'm Linda."

"Linda is a pretty name," she says, as if for the first time. "You don't hear it so much anymore."

"No, you don't," I agree.

"I'm Jenny. Jenny Cooper."

I don't bother to repeat that it's nice to meet her, wishing to skip a third go-round of the same conversation. Instead I offer up what I hope is a kind smile. "I should get going . . ."

"Where?" she asks.

"Where?"

"Where are you going?"

There is no point telling her that this is none of her business. "To see my friend. Carol. Carol Kreiger," I continue, to avoid her having to ask. "She's in room 403. Down the hall." I point in what I think is the general vicinity of Carol's room. This is only the second time I've visited in the weeks since Carol took up residence, so I'm not altogether sure. Room 403 could be down the opposite corridor.

Some things are too painful to remember.

"That's a nice outfit you have on," Jenny remarks of my canary-yellow sundress.

"Thank you."

"I normally don't care for yellow. Where'd you buy it?"

"Saks."

"Sex?" she demands, sudden alarm flashing through her watery blue eyes.

"Saks," I correct quickly.

"That's very rude."

"I'm sorry," I mutter, eager now to get away. Even Carol's hopelessly blank stare will be better than this. "I really should go . . ."

"Don't you want to hear my secret?"

"Maybe you'll tell me another time."

"I kill people," she says.

"What?"

Behind me, I hear footsteps approaching and turn with relief toward the sound.

"Is everything all right here?" the nurse asks.

Jenny turns around abruptly, scurrying away with surprising speed.

"I'm sorry. Was she bothering you?"

"No," I answer. "She just . . . she just . . . She's obviously not all there," I manage to spit out.

"I'm afraid so. Dementia is a terrible thing." The nurse smiles, a gesture as unexpected as it is unsettling. "Can I help you with anything?"

"Room 403?"

"That way." She points down the hall. I nod and start walking.

"Psst . . ." I think I hear as I approach the door to Carol's room. I swing around. But this time, there really is no one there.

CHAPTER TWO

I knock.

No one answers.

"Carol?" Slowly, I push open the heavy oak door, stepping immediately into a small sitting area containing a salmon-colored love seat, two comfortable-looking matching chairs, a small fridge, and a round coffee table, its surface littered with the popular celebrity magazines she used to love. Lorne must have brought them, I think, picturing Carol's husband of eight years. A third marriage for both of them. Companions for their later years.

Poor Lorne, I think.

Carol is standing in front of the large window that takes up most of her bedroom's east wall, staring out at the ocean below. She's wearing a pink quilted housecoat over a pair of striped pajamas. A duvet-covered twin-size bed sits against the wall behind her. Paintings of pastel-colored flower gardens in various stages of bloom hang on the walls.

"Carol, hi," I say, closing the door behind me.

The smile that turns to greet me is wide and genuine, childlike in its openness. "Hi," she says.

She was always a beautiful woman. Shorter than me by two inches, with high cheekbones, piercing green eyes, and wavy brown hair that used to be long and dark but is now short and graying noticeably at the roots. The Carol I knew would be horrified. She was always so fastidious about the way she looked.

But this is no longer the Carol I knew.

"Is it lunchtime?" she asks.

"No," I say, understanding that she has mistaken me for one of the nurses. "You've already had lunch."

Her once full lips turn down in obvious disappointment.

"It's me, Linda. Your friend." *Your best friend since forever.*

"Of course it is. I know."

Do you? I wonder. Although the better question is, *Who are you?* "How are you feeling?"

"I'm well. You?"

"I'm good."

"That's good."

Good. We're all good, I think. *Are we?*

I strain to think of what to say next.

This is not how it used to be, and definitely not the way it was supposed to be. Carol and I have been inseparable since the fourth grade. She was new to Florida and new to our school, assigned to my class. She used to delight in reminding me that the first words I ever said to her were "Get out of my seat!"

We used to laugh about it.

We used to laugh about a lot of things.

"Come sit," I say, sitting down on the love seat and patting the cushion beside me. She quickly obliges, arranging her body so that we are facing each other, her knees brushing against the cotton of my sundress.

"What a pretty dress," she says. "Such a lovely color."

"*I normally don't care for yellow,*" I hear Jenny Cooper say.

I shake my head to clear it.

"*I have a secret,*" Jenny persists.

"What have you been up to?" I ask my friend.

"*I kill people.*"

"Oh, you know," Carol answers. "This and that."

Our lives, the richness of all our experiences now reduced to three vague words: *this and that. How can this be?*

I search for the answer in her once-vibrant eyes, but I see nothing. I am as much a stranger to her as she is to me. *How can this be?* I ask myself again.

We were there for each other through all the important milestones: high school proms and college graduations, virginities lost and identities found, miraculous first loves and gut-churning heartbreaks. I was your maid of honor; you were mine. You cried in my arms when your first husband left you for another woman; I cried in yours when my husband of forty-five years succumbed to his cancer and died.

It's two years now since I lost him, and almost that long since I started losing Carol.

It began slowly. The loss of one everyday word, then another. A name forgotten, a set of keys misplaced. *Happens to all of us,* we commiserated, laughing it off. And then a missed lunch date, a forgotten phone call. You got lost driving over to my house, a place as familiar to you as your own. Then one afternoon you found yourself driving along I-95 with no clue where you were headed. It happened a second time, and then again. *Brain fog,* you said, waving away growing concerns. Eventually you stopped driving, citing too much traffic, too many bad drivers on the road. I sighed with a relief that was all too short-lived. You'd get better, I told myself. You wouldn't leave me.

And then that awful night at the Kravis Center, where we'd gone to see the latest touring production of *Hamilton,* and you suddenly started screaming—that you didn't know where you were, that you didn't recognize the people you were with, that you didn't know, you didn't know . . .

We used to laugh about the ever-increasing indignities of growing old, the sagging flesh and aching backs and too-frequent trips to the bathroom.

"It beats the alternative," you used to say.

What would you say now? I wonder.

I suspect that you would choose a quick death over this steady drain of everything that once defined you, this slow descent into a black and merciless void.

Even madness might be preferable, I think, picturing Jenny Cooper.

"The strangest thing just happened," I tell Carol. "I met this woman . . ."

"Yes?"

"Jenny Cooper. Do you know her? I think she lives down the other hall."

"Yes," Carol says again.

"You know her?"

"Yes. Of course."

"Tall woman, heavyset, bright red hair," I venture, deliberately misrepresenting Jenny's appearance. A test. Waiting—hoping—for Carol to correct me.

"Lovely red hair, yes," she says instead.

I sigh audibly. "She told me she kills people."

"Does she now?"

Tears fill my eyes. "She said it's a secret."

"Of course it is."

"The nurse says she has dementia."

"Dementia. Yes," Carol says.

"Yes." I pick up an issue of *People* magazine from the coffee table, and we spend the next twenty minutes mulling over the lives of the rich and famous—more accurately, I mull and she agrees—before Carol jumps to her feet. "Such a beautiful day," she says, going to the window and resting her forehead against the glass.

"Would you like to go for a walk?"

"I don't think so. No."

I feel guilty when I realize I'm more relieved than disappointed. Carol and I used to love going for long walks on the beach. We'd talk about anything and everything, solve the world's problems along with our own. There was nothing we couldn't talk about. Now there's nothing to say. Not even Brad Pitt elicits more than a word or two.

"So handsome," I say.

"So handsome," she repeats.

"You have to understand that the person you knew as Carol doesn't exist anymore," her husband tried to explain after my last visit.

But the idea that my lifelong friend no longer recognizes me, that she no longer recognizes *herself,* is too much for my brain to accept. "I know you're in there somewhere," I tell her as I join her at the window, taking her in my arms for a lingering goodbye hug.

Come out, come out, wherever you are . . .

I cling to her, to the memories we used to share, now mine alone, until she wriggles free from my suffocating embrace. "I'll come again soon," I tell her.

"That would be lovely."

She stays by the window, staring out at the ocean, as I open the door. I take a quick peek down the long hall, half expecting Jenny Cooper to lunge out at me, to pin me against a wall and accost me with her secrets.

Should I tell the floor nurse what she said? I wonder as I approach the elevators. *And have her think I'm just another in a long line of peculiar old ladies?* I say to myself, answering my own question.

Jenny Cooper is clearly not in her right mind. I don't really believe she killed anyone.

I enter the empty elevator.

Jenny Cooper's secret is safe with me.

CHAPTER THREE

I hear them arguing as I leave my car in the driveway and approach my front door, a slight breeze carrying their voices beyond the open living room window of my neat three-bedroom bungalow into the humidity-heavy air, depositing the harsh words at my feet like so many bird droppings.

I take a step back, wondering if the open window could be the source of the argument. My daughter likes fresh air, regardless of the outside temperature, while her husband prefers the comfort of air-conditioning. This has become a bone of contention of late, another addition to the ever-growing pile.

"How do you expect me to sleep in this heat?" I heard Mick shout in exasperation the other night. I was having trouble sleeping myself and had gone into the kitchen to see if there was any rhubarb pie left over from dessert. The kitchen is on the same side of the house as their bedroom, so even with their bedroom door closed, it was easy to hear them.

"Please don't make it freezing cold," Kleo pleaded, giving in.

I tiptoed back to my bedroom on the other side of the house. The next morning, everything seemed fine, although I could tell from the puffiness around Kleo's eyes that she'd been crying. I debated asking her if everything was okay, then decided it was best not to interfere.

"Please don't turn on the TV when I'm trying to talk to you," I hear Kleo say now.

"We're done talking," Mick counters as the TV roars to life.

For a moment, I consider climbing back into my car and driving aimlessly around the neighborhood, give them some time to cool off, hopefully resolve whatever is bothering them. I could head over to Publix, pick up something for dinner. Although even that simple task has become fraught of late, my daughter favoring fish, my son-in-law insisting on his preferred diet of red meat.

Has it always been this way? I wonder, thinking back to when they first moved in, just over a year ago. My husband had passed away the previous summer, and I was lonely, feeling more than a little lost.

"You shouldn't be alone," my daughter had insisted.

"This is too big a house for you to manage on your own," her husband had concurred. "Let us help you."

That may very well be the last time they agreed about anything.

I fish around in my purse for my cellphone, deciding to call the house, announce my imminent arrival, and give the warring couple time to get their shit together—yes, old ladies swear, too—but nothing happens when I press in the numbers, and I realize that the battery is dead. Once again, I've neglected to charge the damn thing, just as I'm always forgetting to charge the Apple watch they bought me for Christmas.

Or maybe I don't forget. The truth is that I hate all these so-called smart devices. I resent being told it's time to stand up or that "you can do it." The last thing I need is a pep talk from my watch.

"Shit," I mutter, dropping the phone back into the bowels of my too-large, floppy leather purse, unsure how to proceed. If I could just think of the right thing to say, a few words of hard-earned wisdom that would put an end to these pointless squabbles. *Think,* I tell myself.

But my words disappear into a maze of conflicting thoughts. I don't want to chance saying the wrong thing and making things worse. Better to say nothing.

In the forty-five years Bob and I were together, we rarely fought. Oh, we bickered from time to time. But there were never any long drawn-out battles, no nights when we clung to opposite sides of the bed, no days spent in angry silence that I can recall. If things ever threatened to get heated, we waited till cooler heads prevailed, then talked it out peacefully.

Maybe it was the fact that we'd both been high school teachers for much of our lives, a career where patience is more a necessity than a virtue, or maybe it was because I was determined not to subject our two daughters to the kind of verbal vitriol with which I'd been raised. Whatever it was, at the first sign of trouble, one of us always gave in or backed away.

Usually me, I think now.

"Do you think you could move your ass so I can see the screen?" I hear Mick say, and I jump, thinking he's talking to me.

Not that he would ever talk to me that way. Mick has never been anything but polite with me.

"I thought you said you had all this work to do," my daughter says.

"And I'll get to it when I get to it."

"Leave it alone," I whisper.

"You keep saying that," Kleo persists, ignoring my warning. "You're going to lose this client, too, if you're not careful."

"Damn it, Kleo. Would you just lay off!"

"Damn it," I repeat, returning to my car and opening the front passenger door, then slamming it shut with as much force as I can muster, hoping it's loud enough for them to hear.

The front door opens almost immediately. "Mom, hi!" Kleo says, and I marvel, as I always do, at how pretty she is. At almost forty-seven, she looks barely thirty, her light brown hair pulled into a high ponytail, not a trace of makeup on her flawless skin. She's wearing a white T-shirt and a pair of cut-off denim shorts that showcase an exceptional pair of legs. How I produced such a beauty is beyond me, although Kleo has never considered herself such. "How'd it go with Carol?" she asks.

"Not great."

"I'm sorry."

"What's my wife sorry about?" Mick asks, joining Kleo in the doorway, his arm falling easily, even tenderly, across her shoulder. He's a handsome man, several inches over six feet, with a full head of sandy brown hair and an impressive set of biceps. Together they are an almost blindingly attractive couple.

If only they could just get along.

"Things didn't go great with Carol," Kleo says, reaching up to pat the back of her husband's hand.

He kisses her forehead. She looks at him, adoringly.

If I didn't know better, I'd swear these two had just climbed out of bed.

"Her Alzheimer's getting worse?" Mick asks.

"Hard to tell."

"I think someone could use a drink," he says. "What do you say, Linda? It's almost five o'clock. A shot of whiskey? A glass of Chardonnay?"

"I'd love a cup of tea," I say.

"Tea, it is. Kleo? You gonna make your mom a cup of tea?"

Kleo smiles and turns toward the kitchen at the back of the house. Mick gives her backside a playful slap as she wiggles away.

"Come tell me all about it," Mick says, guiding me into the small den off the central living room and quickly turning off the TV. We sit together on the white sofa, our knees touching, much like mine and Carol's did earlier.

"Nothing much to tell. Although a kind of weird thing happened." I tell him about my encounter with Jenny Cooper.

"She told you she kills people?" he repeats.

"Shh," I admonish. "It's a secret."

He laughs. "Who'd she kill?"

"She didn't say."

"You didn't ask?"

"I didn't get the chance."

"Didn't get the chance to do what?" my daughter asks, entering the room and handing me a mug of steaming-hot tea.

You don't even have to boil water anymore, I think. It comes boiling hot straight out of the tap. I lift the mug to my mouth as my watch pings, congratulating me on having completed the second of three exercise rings. I have no idea what it's talking about.

Mick repeats the details of my encounter with Jenny Cooper.

"Of course, she's nuttier than a fruitcake," I remind them.

"Doesn't mean she isn't telling the truth," Mick says.

CHAPTER FOUR

I step off the elevator at Legacy Place the following Monday morning to a scene of barely controlled chaos. The corridors are crowded with people: nurses and orderlies rushing here and there; a few of the residents standing around, watching, the fear in their eyes disturbing their otherwise blank faces.

"What's happening?" I ask one of the nurses as she hurries past me down the hall.

She ignores me.

"What's happening?" I ask the nurse at the nurses' station. The name tag on the front of her white uniform identifies her as Selena.

She lowers her head, whispers out of the side of her mouth. "I'm afraid that one of the residents died this morning."

"Oh, my God! Carol . . . ?"

"No, no," she assures me. "Mr. Oscar in room 409."

"*I kill people,*" I hear Jenny Cooper whisper in my ear.

Don't be ridiculous, I think. "How did he die?" I ask, warily.

"How?" Selena asks, as if she doesn't quite understand the question.

"He wasn't . . . murdered, was he?" *Did I really just ask that? Am I an idiot?*

"Murdered?" Selena looks scandalized. "He was almost a hundred years old and died peacefully in his sleep. We should all be so lucky." She is about to turn away, then stops. "Why on earth would you think he'd been murdered?"

"I kill people," I hear Jenny say again.

I push Jenny's preposterous assertion aside. "Watching too much *Dateline*," I say.

Selena offers a weak smile, then hurries off.

It's then that I see her.

Jenny Cooper is perched on the edge of a purple velvet sofa in the visitors' lounge, her gaze directed at a distant wall. But even in profile, one thing is clear: she is smiling.

Her smile sends shivers down my spine. "Definitely watching too much *Dateline*," I mutter, moving quickly toward Carol's room, my shoulders stiffening, as if my body is preparing to be hit by another *Psst*. But none comes, and if I'm being honest I'm a little disappointed. At the very least, I might have had an interesting anecdote to share with Kleo and Mick when I got home.

I sigh. Fortunately, it's been a relatively quiet week. No fights that I'm aware of, nothing to be overly concerned about. Although as a mother, you're always concerned.

"Should I tell her she'll never have another worry-free moment for the rest of her life?" I asked my husband when our younger daughter, Vanessa, announced she was pregnant with her first child. Vanessa and her husband live in Connecticut with their three children. She keeps begging me to move up there so I can spend more time with my grandchildren, but what can I say? I'm a dyed-in-the-wool Floridian. Besides, Kleo is here, and my best friend is . . . *was* . . . here.

And she may yet come back, I tell myself. Miracles do happen. Although any hope I once had of miracles died along with my husband.

I proceed down the corridor. Most of the residents have returned to their rooms, although a few still linger in open doorways. I note absently that all the rooms are decorated in much the same way.

"Hello, Ada," an old man calls from a wheelchair. Spindly fingers wave in my direction.

There's no point in telling him he's mistaken, so I wave back and continue walking, pass another open door.

Two women occupy the salmon-colored love seat in the small sitting area in the room across from Carol's. Probably a mother and daughter, judging by the obvious similarities in their appearance, both thin and pale and blond. I have no idea how old they are. I can't tell anymore. I glance at the frail, white-haired man in the chair beside them. Probably the older woman's father.

The woman smiles at me as I go by; her daughter frowns. Poor thing looks as if she'd rather be anywhere in the world but here. *Welcome to the club,* I say silently.

The man laughs, as if I've voiced this thought out loud. His daughter smiles. Her daughter scowls. Someone screams from behind a closed door at the end of the hall.

What nightmares are they revisiting? I wonder.

I recall reading that some Alzheimer's sufferers who survived the Holocaust imagine they're back in the camps and are forced to relive past horrors over and over again. How is that fair?

I shake my head. Do I really expect life to be fair? Have I learned nothing in my seventy-six years?

The door to Carol's room is closed, as it is most days. Too much noise upsets her.

She used to love noise. The more chaos the better, she used to say. Probably why she had five children. All of them boys. Three from her first marriage, two from her second. One lives in Miami. The other four are scattered around the globe: one in London, another in Spain, the oldest in California, the youngest in New York. They take turns coming to visit. Sometimes Carol remembers who they are; more often, she has no idea. "Such a nice young man," she commented after one recent visit.

So why do I keep expecting her to remember me? Why am I always setting myself up for disappointment?

I knock, about to push the door when it opens.

Lorne Kreiger stands before me, a surprisingly handsome man despite his almost eighty years. *How is it that some men get better-looking with age?* I wonder. His light brown eyes have lost none of their sparkle, and the wrinkles lining his deeply tanned face somehow make him appear more distinguished, more *consequential,* than he ever did in his youth. "Linda," he says, leaning forward to kiss my cheek. "It's nice to see you."

"You, as well," I say, sounding strangely formal. "How is she today?"

"See for yourself." He stands back to let me enter.

Carol is standing in her usual spot by the window, and if she heard me come in, she gives no sign.

"Carol," Lorne says, closing the door after me. "Carol, honey. Look who's here."

Carol looks at me and smiles, says nothing.

"It's Linda, honey."

"Linda," she repeats, the word a foreign object on her tongue. "How are you?"

"I'm fine. How are you?"

"Right as rain," she says, an expression I've never heard her use before. "It's so nice of you to visit."

"Why don't we sit down?" Lorne suggests, and we do, although Carol remains standing at the window. "Carol, sweetheart? Come join us." He pats the seat beside him.

Carol arranges herself beside her husband. She is wearing the same housecoat over the same pair of pajamas that she had on when I visited last. She tucks an imaginary hair behind her ear and smiles at me expectantly.

"How's Kleo?" Lorne asks. "And Mick, is it?"

"They're good," I say. "Mick's having a little trouble getting his new business off the ground."

"What business is it exactly?"

"Something to do with digital sales and marketing." I shake my head. I have no idea what this means, which means I have no idea what it is that Mick actually does. Not that he hasn't tried to explain, but I tend to tune out the minute I hear words like "digital" and "marketing." Together, they're a deadly combination.

"And Kleo, still working on her PhD?"

"She's hoping to have her dissertation done by Christmas."

I glance toward Carol, who seems to be listening intently. *Is any of this getting through to her?* I wonder, as Lorne and I continue exchanging small talk for the better part of the next hour. "I should go," I say finally, checking my watch.

"I'll walk you to the elevators," Lorne says, leaning in toward his wife. "I'll be right back, honey."

Carol smiles and continues staring at the space we just left, her expression unchanging.

"Thanks so much for coming," he tells me as we approach the elevators.

"Is that your boyfriend?" someone suddenly shouts.

I know without having to look that the voice belongs to Jenny Cooper.

"Linda has a boyfriend! Linda has a boyfriend!" she hollers.

"Oh, my God!"

"Do you know her?" Lorne asks.

"I met her last week. I can't believe she remembered my name."

"Linda has a boyfriend! Linda has a boyfriend!"

"Okay, Jenny," Selena says, rising from her seat at the nurses' station and walking quickly toward her. "That's enough."

"Is he your *lover*?" Jenny persists, all but smacking her lips. "Are you going to *fuck* him later?"

"Oh, dear God," I say, wishing that the earth would just rise up and swallow me whole.

"Fuck, fuck, fuck, fuck, fuck," Jenny repeats, each "fuck" more emphatic than the one before.

"Sorry about that," Selena says, taking hold of Jenny's arm, the obscenity bouncing off the walls as she guides the reluctant woman down the opposite hall toward her room.

One final *"Fuck!"* and she's gone.

"Well, that was . . . different," Lorne says, smiling.

"That it was."

"She certainly likes that word."

It's a good word, I think.

The elevator doors open, as if on cue, and I step inside. "Fuck," I whisper as the doors close. "Fuck, fuck, fuck, fuck, fuck."

CHAPTER FIVE

I haven't had sex in three years.

This is what I'm thinking as I pull my car into the parking lot at Legacy Place a week later. In truth, I've been thinking of little else since my last visit, the word *fuck* continuing to bounce around my brain like one of those silver balls in a pinball machine.

Do they still make pinball machines? I wonder. Or have they gone the way of stereos and CDs, replaced by videogames and games you play on your phone? I maneuver my large cream-colored Mercedes into the first available spot, a series of shrill beeps warning me I'm getting too close to the cement parking block in front of the car's fancy front tires. Bob purchased the car, which came with an alarming number of such bells and whistles, immediately following his cancer diagnosis. "Might as well enjoy the drive to the hospital for my treatments," he reasoned.

As it turned out, there wasn't much time left to enjoy much of anything.

I shut off the car's engine and lean back against the headrest. I can still smell traces of Bob in the creases of the car's leather interior. Or maybe I just think I can. Which is likely why I've been reluctant to trade the damn thing in, even though it's too much car for me. I was the same way when it came to Bob's clothes. It wasn't until Kleo and Mick moved in that I finally agreed to take his old suits and golf shorts over to Goodwill. I still keep a few shirts hidden in the back of my closet, occasionally donning one when I have trouble falling asleep.

You're not the only one with secrets, I think, picturing Jenny Cooper.

The word *fuck* once again fills my brain. "Thanks a lot, Jenny." I open my car door, the unseasonably oppressive April heat almost knocking me back into my seat. Somehow, I'd managed to relegate thoughts of sex to the back of my mind, where they'd remained comfortably hidden for the past two years, like Bob's shirts at the back of my closet. Jenny's shocking outburst had brought them vaulting back.

Sex with Bob had always been so good. We'd discovered that what one loses in stamina over time, one can make up for in technique. And while neither of us maintained the desire, or the patience, for lovemaking sessions that lasted half the night, over the years we'd learned what worked and how to get there with surprising—and surprisingly satisfying—speed.

And for the first few months after he was diagnosed, nothing changed. We continued to enjoy an active sex life, and I was able to convince myself that, despite Bob's terminal diagnosis, he wouldn't actually *die.*

Not until we stopped having sex.

Then I knew.

I told myself I didn't miss it. I resigned myself to the knowledge that I wouldn't be one of those happy seniors you occasionally read about who enjoy sex well into their nineties.

Do such people really exist? I wonder now, walking toward the front entrance of Legacy Place.

Maybe, I think, entering the comfortably air-conditioned lobby and walking into a waiting elevator. As with almost everything in life, you have to be lucky.

I'm luckier than a lot of people, I remind myself. *Luckier than Carol,* I think, exiting the elevator and proceeding down the corridor. I take several long, deep breaths in front of her door, bracing myself for the blank stare about to greet me.

But when I push open the door, it's not Carol I see.

It's Jenny Cooper.

She's standing beside the bed, staring down at Carol, who is lying motionless on top of the covers.

Is she breathing? "Oh, my God," I gasp, all but vaulting across the room to her side.

"Careful," Jenny cautions, taking a step back. "You'll wake her up."

I sigh with relief that Carol is, in fact, asleep. *Did I really think—even for a split second—that Jenny might have harmed her?* I spin toward Jenny. "What are you doing here?"

"I came to visit."

"Well, I think you should go now," I tell her.

Jenny heads for the door. "What's *your* problem?"

I watch her leave, willing my breath to return to normal. Jenny's surprise visit has unsettled me. What was she doing here?

"I kill people," I hear her say.

"You do not," I say out loud, collapsing into one of the salmon-colored chairs.

After ten minutes, it becomes obvious that Carol isn't going to wake up anytime soon. And even if she does, it won't make much of a difference, despite what I keep hoping for.

I wait another five minutes, then approach the bed. "Goodbye, Carol," I whisper. I bend down to kiss her cheek, then think better of it. What if she were to wake up and find me standing over her, much like Jenny Cooper earlier? Would she scream in terror or attack me with her fists? Lorne had confided in me that she occasionally got violent, although I find this hard to believe. Carol was always such a gentle soul. "I'll come back in a few days," I say, straightening up. "Watch out for yourself," I add, again picturing Jenny looming over her.

I walk toward the nurses' station, wondering if I'll find Jenny perched on the end of a sofa in the visitors' lounge waiting for me.

But the lounge is empty, and I'm surprised to realize I'm disappointed.

"Did you know that Jenny was in my friend Carol's room earlier?" I ask Selena.

"Yes," she says easily. "She often visits with the other residents. Calls it 'making her rounds.' It's kind of cute, really. She didn't take anything, did she?"

"I don't think so, no."

Selena smiles and returns her attention to her computer.

"Do you think it would be all right if I go see her?"

"Jenny? I'm sure she'd be thrilled."

I nod and turn toward the far corridor, then stop, turn back. "I'm sorry. What room is she in?"

"Four fifteen. You're sure you want to do this?"

"No," I admit.

"Well, have fun," she calls as I proceed down the hall.

Why am *I doing this?* I wonder. Why spend more time than I have to with someone who is obviously not of sound mind, a woman who hurls obscenities at me and claims she kills people? Why am I so intrigued by her? Is the world not a dangerous enough place without actively looking for trouble?

And then it hits me: I don't have anything else to do.

And truthfully, I don't want to go home.

Three adults living together under one roof isn't easy at the best of times, and this is definitely not the best of times. Kleo and Mick have been arguing again, and while they try to keep their voices low, it's hard not to feel the tension. It seeps through the walls, slithers across the floor, climbs up on the furniture, surrounds me like a poisonous mist, stirring up painful memories.

Maybe Carol is the lucky one after all, I think, stopping in front of Jenny's door, taking several deep breaths before I knock.

"Who's there?" comes the familiar voice.

"It's me. Linda Davidson."

The door opens only slightly, a sliver of ancient face peeks out. "Linda Davidson," Jenny repeats. "You were very rude to me before."

"I'm sorry."

"What do you want?"

"I thought we could visit for a while."

"Why?"

"I honestly don't know."

Jenny Cooper opens the door wider, staring at me as if I'm the one suffering from dementia, not her. *And perhaps she's right,* I can't help thinking.

I turn to leave. "Sorry I bothered you."

"Well, you're here now. You might as well come in."

Don't do it, a little voice shouts in my ear. *Run while you have the chance.*

But as is so often the case when your curiosity overwhelms your common sense, I ignore the little voice and step inside.

CHAPTER SIX

Jenny Cooper shuts the door after me, motions me toward the pair of corduroy chairs. "Who'd you say you are again?" she asks.

"Linda Davidson. We met a few weeks ago."

She nods, although her vacant blue eyes tell me she has no memory of any such meeting. She pushes some long gray strands of hair away from her forehead and lowers herself gingerly into one of the chairs, motioning me to do the same.

"You told me you had a secret," I venture as I sit down.

A slight spark enters her pale blue eyes. "Did I tell you what it was?"

"You said that you . . . that you . . . kill people."

"I did?" She laughs, a disarmingly girlish giggle. She pulls at the buttons of her white blouse, wipes the palms of her hands across the lap of her gray slacks, giggles again.

Is she playing with me? I wonder.

"Are you with the CIA?" she asks.

"What?"

"The CIA. Did they send you to spy on me?"

"What?"

"Why do you keep saying, 'what'?" Are you deaf?"

This was definitely not a good idea. What in God's name was I thinking? "I should go," I say, half out of my chair as long, bony fingers reach for my arm.

"Stay," she directs.

I sit back down.

"Who did I kill?"

"I don't know. You didn't tell me."

"Did I say how many people I killed?"

"You didn't."

"Huh," she says. Then again, as if settling the matter once and for all. "Huh."

I watch her face as her thin lips twist from side to side. A hint of blush appears on her pale, almost translucent skin.

"Four," she says.

"What?"

"Four people."

"Are you saying that you killed four people?"

"Are you with the FBI?" she asks in return.

"The FBI? No, of course not."

"The police?"

"I'm not with anybody."

"Never married, or a widow?"

"What?"

"You said you're not with anybody. Are you a spinster or a widow?"

A spinster? How long has it been since anyone used that word? I wonder, my focus momentarily diverted. "I'm a widow."

"Guess you're lucky either way," she says.

"Lucky?"

"Husbands are nothing but colossal pains in the backside. I know. I had several of them."

"Did you kill them?" I ask, recognizing that this conversation is becoming more surreal by the moment. I also recognize that I'm kind of enjoying myself, and I feel instantly guilty.

"What a question!" Jenny exclaims. "Did you kill yours?"

"What? No, of course not."

"Then why would you think I'd kill mine?"

"Because you said that you kill people and that husbands are colossal pains in the ass."

"I believe I used the word 'backside.'"

"Yes. Sorry."

"I never cared for the word 'ass.' It's quite rude. Don't you think?"

Truthfully, I'm at a loss for words. So I say nothing.

"I may have."

"You may have . . . what?" I broach warily. "You may have killed them?"

"I may have killed them," she agrees.

"You're not sure?"

"Sure of what?"

"If you killed them or not."

"Killed who?"

"Seriously?" *For sure she's playing with me,* I decide. "Did you kill Mr. Oscar?" I broach cautiously.

"Who's Mr. Oscar?"

"Mr. Oscar in room 409. He died last week."

"Why would I want to kill him?"

"I don't know."

"You're not very bright, are you?" Jenny says.

Probably right, I think. "I should probably go."

"Oh, my God," she shouts, jumping to her feet.

"What is it?" I ask, on my feet now as well.

"There's blood."

"What?"

"Blood! Blood!" She starts pulling at the front of her blouse.

I become aware of a quarter-size brown circle in the white cotton of her blouse, below her left breast.

"Blood!" she keeps shouting. "Blood! Blood!"

"It's not blood," I say, trying to reassure her. "It looks more like a coffee stain. Did you have coffee this morning?"

"What have you done to me?" she demands, ignoring my question, her voice dangerously close to a shriek.

"I haven't done anything. Jenny, you have to calm down. Please . . ."

"You stabbed me!"

"*What?* No! Of course I didn't stab you . . ."

"Help me! Somebody help me!"

"Jenny, please. Nobody touched you. It's not blood."

"You're trying to kill me!"

"It's just a coffee stain."

She stops screaming. "A coffee stain?"

"Did you have coffee this morning?" I ask again.

She pulls open her blouse to reveal the graying camisole beneath. There is no sign of blood.

"You see? You're fine. There's no blood."

"A coffee stain," she says.

The door opens. Selena pokes her head inside the room. "Is everything all right in here? I thought I heard screaming."

"Everything's fine," I tell her, as Jenny fusses with the front of her blouse, trying to close it. "She just got a little confused."

"Maybe you should come back another time," Selena suggests. A suggestion I'm only too happy to take her up on.

"Sure thing."

"Wait," Jenny cries as I head for the door. "Please, Linda Davidson," she says, my name on her lips stopping me in my tracks. "You'll come back, won't you?"

I hesitate.

"Please. I'm sorry I said you weren't very bright."

"I'll try." *What else can I say?*

"The next time you come to see your friend, Carol," she says with a clarity that almost takes my breath away. "You'll come see me, too?"

Is her reference to Carol some sort of veiled threat? I wonder. "I'll try," I say again.

"I'd like that."

I follow Selena into the hall.

"We have so much to talk about," I hear Jenny say as the door closes behind me.

CHAPTER SEVEN

"You're not seriously considering visiting her again!" Kleo's hazel eyes are wide with disbelief. We're sitting at the round white table in my small kitchen, having finished our dinner of poached salmon and grilled vegetables. Mick is enjoying his weekly night out with "the guys."

I'm not sure why Mick gets to enjoy a night out every week, especially since he's always harping on Kleo to cut back on her spending, but truthfully, I'm happy for some alone time with my daughter.

"She accused you of stabbing her, for God's sake."

"I know, but . . ."

"What buts? There are no buts. She tells you she killed four people and then she accuses you of trying to kill *her*? You are not going back there."

"Of course, I'm going back there. Carol is there."

"Okay, you can see Carol. But you're not going anywhere near this . . . this . . . person . . ."

"Jenny Cooper."

". . . this Jenny Cooper person again. She's certifiable."

"Which is why she's there," I remind her, smiling.

"Which is why you stay away from her. What is it you told me when I was little and I stopped to gawk at that man who was taking off his clothes in the middle of the street? 'You don't stop for crazy,' you told me."

"She's just confused," I say, understanding that dementia is a little more than simple confusion. "I don't think she gets any visitors. She's probably just lonely."

"Yeah, well. That's what happens when you kill all your friends."

I laugh. "She didn't say she killed her friends . . ."

"No. Just her husbands."

"Well, to be fair, she wasn't sure . . ."

Now we're both laughing. My earlier guilt returns. It's not nice to laugh at someone else's misfortune. Still, if you can't laugh . . .

"How'd she end up in Legacy Place anyway?"

"What do you mean?"

"I mean, it's not exactly a state-run institution. Those apartments are pretty expensive. Somebody must be paying for it."

I consider the choice oceanfront location, the twenty-four-hour medical and support staff, and the three-meals-a-day service that Legacy Place provides. Lorne has confided that it's costing him an arm and a leg to keep Carol there. "It's not cheap," I agree.

"So, who's paying her bills?"

I admit that I have no idea.

"At any rate," Kleo continues, "the woman is clearly unstable. And she's not your problem. You can't save everyone, Mom."

I nod and start clearing the dishes from the table.

Over the years, I watched my father succumb to heart disease and my mother die of a stroke. Five years ago, I lost my older brother to prostate cancer and three years later, my husband to pancreatic cancer. Now I stand by helplessly while my best friend disappears before my tired eyes.

The truth is that I've never been able to save anyone.

"I'll do that," Kleo says, taking the dishes from my hands and stacking them in the dishwasher. "You sit. You've had a trying day."

I do as directed. "What about you?" I ask. "I've been doing all the talking. Tell me about *your* day."

She shrugs. "There's nothing much to tell."

"How's your dissertation coming along?"

Another shrug. "Not great," she admits. "You want some tea?"

"I better not. I'll be up all night, peeing."

She laughs.

"Come on back." I pat the tabletop, knowing something is wrong. Kleo has been working on her PhD for the past three years. She's on a year's sabbatical from teaching to complete her dissertation, and she's always loved talking about her work. "What's the problem?"

"Just having a bit of trouble concentrating these days, that's all." She returns to the table, plops back into her chair. "Sometimes I think I should just scrap the whole damn thing and start over."

"Well, I'm sure it hasn't been easy, moving back home with your mother," I offer. "I know you worry about me, and you really don't have to . . ."

"It's not you. You've been a godsend. Being able to take the year off, not having to worry about rent . . ."

"Then what is it, sweetheart?" I ask, although I already know the answer. "Is it Mick?"

A long sigh fills the space between us. "He's having a hard time, what with quitting his job to start his own business and the two of us both working from home. It's a little too much togetherness and too little money coming in. He thinks we may have bitten off more than we can chew."

"It's a lot," I agree. "How's the business going?"

"Not as well as he hoped it would. He lost one important client and it's looking like he won't be getting this other one he was counting on, so . . . He says that maybe I should go back to teaching until his business gets on its feet, that now probably isn't the best time for me to be worrying about 'The Rise of the Self-Conscious Heroine in Modern American Literature.' "

"Maybe this wasn't the best time for him to quit his job to start his own business," I counter. "This was supposed to be your year . . ."

"Yeah, well . . ."

I bite my tongue to keep from saying something we'll both regret. "You're a smart girl," I tell her instead. "You'll figure it out."

"Thanks, Mom." She smiles. "I love you."

"I love you, too."

"I love you more," she teases, a game we used to play when she was little.

"Impossible," I say.

Our smiles fill the room.

I fall asleep to *Dateline,* a not uncommon experience. I don't think I've ever made it through an entire episode. In fact, despite its often horrifying recounting of real-life murders and betrayals, I'm usually asleep before the start of its second hour.

Tonight's episode was about a middle-aged woman who murdered her husband and children because her lover had convinced her they were zombies and she'd be doing the world a big favor by getting rid of them. Not surprisingly, the world disagreed, and she was currently on trial for murder.

Unfortunately, I fell asleep before the verdict was rendered, so I have no idea whether she was found guilty or not. Maybe one day they'll do a story about Jenny Cooper.

Could she really be a cold-blooded killer?

Amazing how much space Jenny takes up in my mind these days, I vaguely remember thinking as I nodded off.

The sound of someone pounding on the front door jolts me awake at just past midnight. I jump out of bed, throwing my bathrobe over my nightgown, opening my bedroom door just as Kleo is opening the front door to her obviously inebriated husband.

"Mick, for God's sake!" she cries as he stumbles inside. "It's okay, Mom. Go back to bed," she tells me, tossing the words over her shoulder as she guides Mick toward their bedroom.

"Is he all right?"

"He's fine. I'm really sorry."

"She's really sorry, Linda," Mick agrees, a dopey grin on his handsome face. "Go back to bed. Sleep well," he adds as their bedroom door closes behind them.

Unfortunately, *Dateline* isn't on to lull me back to sleep, and while I know there's a way to bring it up *on demand*, I'm too tired to figure it out. So I lie there until morning, thoughts of zombies, alternating with images of Jenny Cooper, dancing across my brain.

CHAPTER EIGHT

"You came back!" Jenny says, surprise lighting up her pale blue eyes.

She's not the only one who's surprised, I think, as I settle into the corduroy chair across from her. *What the hell am I doing back here? Didn't I promise Kleo I'd keep my distance?*

Well, no, I think, answering my own question. I didn't actually promise. *You just let her assume . . .*

"I didn't think I'd see you again," Jenny says.

"No? Why is that?"

"The look on your face when you left the last time," she replies without hesitation.

I confess to being caught more than a little off guard by her answer. She's far more observant than I realized. "How did I look?"

"Scared."

"I looked scared?"

"You looked terrified."

"I looked terrified?"

"Why do you keep repeating everything I say?" she asks. "It's very annoying."

"It's annoy—?" I start to ask, then stop myself. "I'm sorry."

"You don't have to be sorry. Just stop doing it."

I nod.

"Have you been to see your friend Carol?" she asks.

I feel an unwelcome stab of anxiety. "Yes. Have *you*?" I ask, warily.

"Why would I go to see her? She's your friend, not mine. She wouldn't even know who I am."

"She doesn't really know who I am anymore either," I admit.

"Does that upset you?"

"It does."

"So, why do you keep visiting?"

"Because she's my best friend."

"And that man I saw you with," Jenny says, leaning forward in her chair. "Who was he?"

I'm both surprised and not surprised by her question. "That was her husband. Lorne."

"Lorne," she repeats, her tongue darting between her lips, as if she has tasted something unpleasant. "Are you fucking Lorne?"

Oh, God. Here we go again. I jump to my feet. *I should never have come. What the hell was I thinking?*

I was thinking that anything would be better than my visit with Carol, I realize. I was thinking that even madness would be better than the nothing I see in Carol's eyes.

"Oh, sit down," Jenny instructs, waving me back into my chair. "I didn't realize you had such delicate sensibilities."

I shrug. I've never thought of myself as someone with *delicate sensibilities,* but maybe I'm wrong. I'm wrong about a lot of things these days.

"He's a very handsome man, your Lorne," Jenny says. "I like handsome men. All my husbands were handsome men."

"Is that why you killed them?" I ask, only half in jest.

She laughs. "Hah! You're funny. That was a good one. Are you a cop?" she asks suddenly. "Are you here to arrest me?"

"No to both questions."

"Then why are you here?"

"I don't know. It was obviously a bad idea."

"No, it was a good idea. I truly appreciate your coming to see me." She smiles in gratitude. "Did I tell you that my father killed my mother?"

"What?"

"There's that look again," she says. "Am I scaring you?"

"You think your father killed your mother?" I ask, ignoring her question to voice my own.

"I don't *think*. I *know*. I saw the whole thing."

"You saw your father kill your mother?"

"You're doing it again," Jenny admonishes. "Repeating everything I say."

"I'm sorry. It's just a lot to take in."

"That's a very pretty dress you have on," she says of the shapeless blue cotton shift I'm wearing. "You like dresses, don't you?"

Just go with the flow, I tell myself. "I do, yes."

"You wear them to show off your legs."

"What?"

"Do you wear them to show off your legs?" she asks, turning her earlier statement into a question.

"I guess I used to," I admit. "Not so much anymore."

"Why not? You have very shapely legs. You *should* show them off."

How are we talking about my legs? "You said that you saw your father kill your mother," I remind her.

"Oh, that." She crosses her arms across her chest. "I don't want to talk about that."

"Oh. Okay." I'm disappointed, I realize, wondering what kind of person this makes me, that I'm so intrigued by the ravings of a deranged old woman.

"Maybe I'll tell you about it the next time you visit," she says, the twinkle returning to her eyes.

Is she scattering tidbits of her past, real or imagined, like so many breadcrumbs, to entice me to come back? And is it seriously working?

"I'm tired," she says. "You should go now."

I've been dismissed, I realize. I nod and stand up, walk toward the door. I turn around to say goodbye, but Jenny Cooper's eyes are closed, and the soft and steady sound of her breathing tells me she's already asleep.

CHAPTER NINE

"Are you okay?" Selena asks as I approach the nurses' station.

"Fine," I tell her. "Why do you ask?"

"You look a little pale."

"Can I ask you something?"

"Sure."

"What's the story on Jenny Cooper?"

"I'm afraid I don't know a whole lot," Selena says. "She was here when I started five years ago. Not sure where she's from originally. Some little town in California, I think. Morro Bay, maybe? But, like I said, I'm not sure. One of the nurses told me she used to be a pharmacist." She shrugs. "No friends or family. As far as I know, you're the only person who's ever come to visit her. Which is really nice of you, by the way. Especially after that outburst last week." She giggles. "Who'd have thought a sweet old lady even knew words like that, right?"

You'd be surprised at what old ladies know, I think. *And who said anything about sweet?* "So, who's paying for all this?" I ask, my eyes sweeping up and down the halls.

Selena shrugs. "Your guess is as good as mine."

I turn to leave. "See you in a few days."

"Take care."

The elevator arrives and I'm about to enter just as Carol's husband, Lorne, is exiting.

"Linda!"

I step back into the hall, taking a wary look around, in case Jenny is lurking. I'm not up for a replay of last week.

"How is Carol today?" he asks.

"About the same." *Haven't I already had this conversation once today?* "What about you?"

"About the same." He chuckles, but it is a sound without mirth. "Not doing so great, actually," he qualifies. "Listen, if you're not busy, maybe we could grab a cup of coffee? I shouldn't be too long."

"Sure," I say. "There's a Starbucks over on Indiantown Road."

"I know the one. I'll meet you there in . . ." He checks his watch. "Say, half an hour?"

"Meet you there," I agree, pressing the button for the elevator.

"Linda . . ." he says, as the elevator arrives.

I stop, hold the doors open.

"You're a good friend," he says.

I'm not so sure about that, I'm thinking, as I wait for Lorne to arrive. It's going on forty minutes since I left Legacy Place; I'm on my second mochaccino and starting to feel a slight buzz. Also, I'm feeling a familiar tug on my bladder, but I don't want to risk leaving my seat to use the facilities and missing him.

I could call him, I think, reaching inside my purse for my cellphone, realizing I've left it at home. "Goddamn it." I decide to give Lorne fifteen more minutes.

You're a good friend, I hear him repeat.

Am I?

Does he know how hard it's become for me to visit my lifelong friend, the disappointment and outright anger that I feel toward her condition, that I feel toward *her,* and the guilt I carry for feeling this way? Would he still consider me a good friend if he knew

the depth of my resentment, the rage I can barely suppress when-
ever I confront the glazed look in her eyes, the unstated fear I
carry of ending up the same way?

What kind of friend is that?

Lorne is a good man. Carol had been lucky to find him. After
two failed marriages, she'd always considered their meeting to be
something of a miracle. "A gift from God," she used to say, even
though she considered herself agnostic.

I remember the day she called me, breathless from what I first
assumed was her daily afternoon jog. "I just met the most fabulous man," she told me, barely able to contain her excitement.
"His name is Lorne and he's a retired doctor, and he's just so, so
handsome . . ."

"Just so-so?" I teased.

"So . . . so . . ." she repeated with a laugh. "So, what do you
think? Should I marry him?"

"You absolutely should marry him," I said.

And we laughed at the sheer lunacy of the idea. But six months
later, she did just that.

We laughed a lot in those days. Even when we cried, we laughed,
I think now, recalling those long-ago nights when I sat with her
while she bemoaned her first husband's betrayal. "How could he
just throw it all away like that?" she cried, brokenhearted.

"Because he's an idiot," I answered, truthfully. "And a moron,
and a jackass and a jerk. Should I go on?"

"Please."

"And a scumbag and a lowlife and a no-good cocksucker."

"Wow! Cocksucker! I like that. Continue."

And I kept going until there were no words left.

How was I to know there'd come a time when there would be,
literally, no words left?

I take a long sip of my coffee.

Is that what draws me to Jenny Cooper? I wonder. That she is
so full of words, even if half the time they don't make a whole lot
of sense? That even if everything that comes out of her mouth is

nothing but gibberish, the delusional ravings of a mind lost to dementia, it's still preferable to the vacant stare that has replaced the laughter Carol and I used to share?

Do I think for one minute that there is any truth to the "secret" Jenny has confided in me, that she is, in fact, capable of having murdered four people? And what of her latest confession, that she witnessed her father murder her mother?

Despite my doubts, I must admit that Jenny Cooper has aroused my curiosity. Is she really a cold-blooded killer? Did her father really murder her mother?

And has my own life become so boring that talking with an obviously unbalanced old woman is fast becoming the highlight of my day?

Am I losing my mind, along with my waistline and my once-prominent upper lip?

We lose so much of ourselves as we get older, I'm thinking as the door to Starbucks opens and Lorne Kreiger appears.

"Sorry I kept you waiting," he says.

"No problem."

"Can I get you another one of those?" He motions toward my now empty cup.

"I think I'm good."

"No question about that," he says with a smile. "Be right back."

I watch him walk to the counter to place his order.

I just met the most fabulous man, I hear Carol say.

I smile at the memory. Then I burst into tears.

CHAPTER TEN

"Dear God, what happened?" Lorne asks, returning to the table with his coffee to find me sobbing uncontrollably.

I shake my head. "It's nothing."

"It's obviously something," he counters.

"I just feel so stupid." I grab a tissue from my purse and dab at my eyes, but the tears keep coming. "They won't stop!" I wail.

Lorne pries the tissue from my fingers and gently pats my wet cheeks. "Please, Linda. Tell me what's wrong."

"There's nothing wrong. Well, no. That's not true. Everything's wrong."

"Could you be a little more specific?" A smile creeps into his warm brown eyes.

And suddenly I'm laughing, laughing so hard that the tears are coming even faster. "Oh, God. What's wrong with me? I think I'm losing my mind." My words echo back at me, smacking me across the forehead with such force, I almost fall off my stool. "Oh, God. I'm so sorry," I cry, thinking of Carol. "I didn't mean . . ."

"I know you didn't," Lorne says. "It's okay, Linda. I understand."

"It's just so hard, seeing her this way."

"I know."

"I keep hoping . . ."

"I know. Me, too."

"Do you visit her every day?" I ask, swallowing the last of my tears.

He nods. "Pretty much."

"I should visit more often."

"I'm grateful that you visit as often as you do."

"I just wish . . ."

"That things were different?"

"I'd settle for having more control. Did we really get to be this age only to lose everything?"

Lorne smiles sadly. "What is it they say? 'Getting old isn't for sissies'?"

It beats the alternative, I hear Carol chime in.

We sit for a few moments in silence.

"So, what else is wrong?" he asks, taking a long sip of his coffee.

"What else?" I repeat.

"You said that everything is wrong. What else besides Carol?"

I tell him about the growing tension between Kleo and Mick. "Hopefully, it'll blow over."

"Hopefully," he agrees. "Any more run-ins with that woman? The one with the interesting vocabulary."

I shake my head. "Jenny Cooper. No." I decide not to tell him about our subsequent conversations. Or finding Jenny at Carol's bedside.

Why give the man anything more to worry about?

"Probably a good idea to stay out of her way," he says.

"But you won't, will you?" Jenny whispers in my ear. *"You'll come see me again. I know you will. You're too curious not to. And you know what they say about curiosity, don't you, Linda?"*

"You don't think she'd actually hurt anyone, do you?" I hear myself ask.

"Hurt anyone?" The shock on Lorne's face mirrors the shock in his voice. "What makes you think she'd hurt anyone?"

I shake my head, offer my familiar excuse about watching too much *Dateline*.

"So," he says, after a moment's silence, "are you seeing anyone?"

"Are you serious?"

"Why wouldn't I be?"

I remind him that I'm seventy-six years old.

"Almost a teenager by Florida standards. Not to mention, you're smart, you're funny, you're beautiful."

I turn away to hide the blush I feel spreading across my cheeks. It's been a long time since a man told me I was beautiful. It sounds good, I realize, feeling my blush deepen. "Seen any good movies lately?" I ask when I can't think of anything else to say.

"No," he says. "And I miss it. Carol and I used to go every week."

"Yeah, it's not the same, watching them on TV."

"We should go one day," Lorne says.

"What?"

"One afternoon, maybe. We could take in a movie, maybe grab something to eat afterward."

"Sure," I agree. "Sounds nice." I glance at my watch. "I really should get going . . ."

"Of course." He quickly downs the rest of his coffee and jumps to his feet. "See you soon," he says as we reach the door.

"See you soon," I echo.

CHAPTER ELEVEN

"So, wait a minute. Let me get this straight," Mick is saying, spearing the last of the steak on his plate with his fork and lifting it into the air. "You're telling me that your best friend's husband is hitting on you?"

"What! No! That's not what I'm saying at all. Of course he wasn't hitting on me."

"Sounds like that's exactly what he was doing," Mick insists, depositing the piece of rare meat into his mouth and chewing vigorously, followed by a long sip of beer.

We're sitting at the kitchen table, Mick enjoying his steak, Kleo and I playing with our lemon sole. Truthfully, I'd have much preferred a steak, but Kleo insisted that sole was the healthier option, and I felt she could use the support. A show of solidarity, as it were, although I think the point was lost on Mick.

"He wasn't hitting on me," I say. "He was just suggesting that since we both like movies, we go see one together one afternoon. That's all."

"Sounds like a date to me."

"It's not a date," Kleo argues. "He's a married man, for God's sake."

"When has that ever stopped anyone?" Mick pushes his plate

into the center of the table, drains the rest of the beer from his mug.

"He's married to Mom's oldest and closest friend."

"Who barely recognizes either of them anymore."

"He's just lonely," I insist.

"Which only underlines my point."

"We're just friends."

"Right. Does he know that?" Mick asks.

"Of course he knows that," Kleo says, taking the words out of my mouth. "They've been friends for years."

"Except things are different now," Mick says, as Lorne had said earlier. "He might as well be married to a piece of asparagus." He motions toward the vegetables sitting untouched on his plate.

"What a horrible thing to say!" Kleo says.

"Just calling it as I see it."

"Yeah, well, you're being ridiculous."

"I'm being ridiculous? *I'm* being ridiculous?"

"And mean," Kleo adds.

Mick swivels toward me. "You think I'm being ridiculous, Linda? You think I'm being mean?"

I struggle to find the most diplomatic way to respond.

"Okay. I'm mean and I'm ridiculous," Mick says before I can find the right words. "But I'm also a man, and I'm telling you, he's hitting on you." With that, he throws his napkin on the table and walks from the room.

Seconds later, the front door slams shut.

I wake up at two in the morning, knowing instantly that it's one of those nights when I won't be able to fall back to sleep. My brain is working overtime, Carol, Lorne, Kleo, and Mick taking turns tap-dancing across the insides of my eyelids. Normally, I'd just lie there, hoping to fall asleep, praying they'd tire themselves out, but judging by the spunk I see in their steps, I know this isn't going to happen. Besides, I read recently that the better option, as Kleo would say, is to get up and do something, *anything*.

I decide to clean out my closet. Admittedly, not the most rational of decisions. But it's two in the morning and I don't want to watch TV or read a book. So, I climb out of bed, turn on the overhead light, and start pulling clothes from their hangers, wondering whatever possessed me to buy most of them in the first place.

I make two piles—one for the items I like and the other for those I don't. This grows into two more piles, one for the clothes I've worn in the past two years, the other for the clothes I haven't. This necessitates the need for yet another pile, clothes I haven't worn in two years but like enough to hope I'll wear again. Now my entire bed is covered with piles of clothes and I couldn't climb back in if I wanted to.

So, I do what is arguably the most logical or the most insane thing I've done so far, which is to start trying things on. I pull my nightgown over my head and slip on a white knit dress that Bob used to love. He said it showcased my curves. *What would he say now?* I wonder, staring at my reflection in the full-length mirror hanging on the inside of my closet door. Where once it might have showcased my curves, now it highlights my every bulge. "What the hell is that?" I ask the heavy-lidded woman staring back at me. She grabs at the roll of flesh circling her waist. "When did this happen?" I turn to examine my profile, catch sight of my no longer flat stomach.

Stop slouching! Stand up straight, I hear my mother say. *Stomach in, chest out.*

Immediately, my shoulders straighten and my stomach muscles contract. "Why is nothing happening?" I moan. When I used to hold my stomach in, it disappeared. Now, no matter how hard I try sucking it in, it's still there. "Not fair, not fair!" I pull the stupid dress back up over my head, fling it to the ivory carpet at my feet.

"I used to have a waist," I remind the old woman in the mirror.

"I used to have an upper lip. And whose fucking arms are these?" I shout, bending them at the elbows as I lift them into the air, grimacing at the crepey flesh I see. The same thing is happening to my legs, I know without having to glance down, the elasticity of my skin having all but disappeared.

At least you don't have to shave your legs so often, my reflection reminds me. *Or your underarms. Or anywhere else, for that matter.*

And it's true. Hair growth lessens with age.

"Except then it starts popping up on your chin," I cry, pressing my forehead against the mirror in defeat. Immediately, a new series of fine lines appears around my eyes, each one a symbol of my encroaching mortality, an unnecessary reminder that my time on earth is not only limited but running out.

There is a light tapping on my bedroom door.

"Mom?" Kleo peeks her head inside the room. "What's going on in here? I heard yelling." She glances at the bed. "What in God's name are you doing?"

"Just getting rid of a few things." I say this as if it's the most normal thing in the world to be cleaning out one's closet at two in the morning. Not to mention, doing it stark naked. I reach for my nightgown, slip it over my head. "Sorry. Did I wake you?"

"I wasn't asleep."

"Everything okay?" *Please say yes,* my eyes plead.

"Everything's fine," Kleo obliges me by saying, although *her* eyes say otherwise. "So, what are you going to do with all this stuff?"

"Bundle it up, take it over to Goodwill."

"Everything?"

"Pretty much."

"Well, it'll have to wait till morning," she says, tossing the clothes from the bed, one pile at a time. "Get in," she directs, and I do as I'm told. She pulls the top sheet and blanket over my shoulders and kisses me on the cheek. "You look great naked, by the way."

I laugh, close my eyes.

"Good night, Mom," she says. "Love you."

"Love you more."

"Impossible."

I'm asleep before I hear the bedroom door close.

CHAPTER TWELVE

I wait four days before returning to Legacy Place.

I tell myself that there's no need to go more often, that Carol won't know the difference, that Jenny Cooper can foist her insanity on some other unsuspecting visitor, that I have too much else to do, other friends to see.

But the truth is that I have very little to do. I quit my bridge group when my husband's condition worsened; I left my book club around the same time. And while I could probably find another bridge group, another book club, the truth is that I have little concentration these days for either bridge or reading. Nor do I have the patience, the interest, or the wherewithal to seek out other activities online.

As for friends, their number has been shrinking every year. Soon I'll be the last one standing, I think, pushing the real reason I haven't gone back to Legacy Place to the back of my mind, only to feel it push back even more forcefully. *You can't fool me*, it says in Mick's voice. *You haven't been back because you're afraid of running into Lorne.*

"Linda's got a boyfriend!" I hear Jenny chant. *"Linda's got a boyfriend!"*

"Don't be ridiculous," I chide as I walk toward the entrance to Legacy Place. "He hasn't even called," I say, only realizing I've said the words out loud when confronted by the startled looks on the faces of a man and woman exiting the building.

And am I relieved or disappointed not to have heard from him? I wonder as I cut across the white marble lobby. Which is when I see Lorne departing one of the elevators, and I spin around abruptly, ducking into the nearest glass-walled office before he sees me. *This is stupid. You're acting like an idiot.*

"Can I help you?" a male voice asks.

The man behind the voice is about fifty, with thinning hair and a pleasant smile. He sits at a large black marble desk, half-hidden by his computer. The nameplate on the desk identifies him as HENRY MARSHALL, DIRECTOR. "Why don't you have a seat," he suggests, motioning to the chair across from him.

I glance toward the lobby to see Lorne walking my way, so I quickly drop down into the chair, my shoulders slumping forward, trying to make myself as small, as invisible, as possible.

"Are you okay?" Henry Marshall asks.

"Fine," I assure him. *What the hell is wrong with me? Lorne visits his wife almost every day, for God's sake. He is clearly not interested in me, except as a friend. This is all Mick's fault. He's the one who put these stupid ideas in my head.*

"Is there something I can help you with, Mrs. . . . ?"

"Davidson." *"Linda Davidson!"* I hear Jenny Cooper shout. "I was just wondering . . ."

"Yes?"

"I was wondering . . ." I say again, trying to organize my thoughts. *What the hell was I wondering?* "About the process . . ."

"The process?"

"I have a friend," I offer, trying a different track. *Really? A friend? That old chestnut?* "She's a widow and she's starting to have memory issues, and she heard about Legacy Place, and we were wondering just how it operates . . ."

"Certainly." Henry Marshall smiles and hands me a brochure. "This can probably answer most of your questions, but if there's anything in particular you're concerned about . . ."

"How does it work as far as money goes?" I ask.

"Well, we're a privately run, for-profit institution, so we operate the same way as most assisted-living facilities. Residents or
their guardians sign a lease, authorize an automatic monthly with-
drawal from their bank account, pretty standard stuff. It's all in
the brochure. Unfortunately, there are no vacancies at the moment, but if your friend would like to fill out an application, we
can certainly arrange for an interview, get the ball rolling—"

"What happens if the money runs out?" I interrupt.

Henry Marshall seems uncomfortable with the question. "Well,
as I said, we're a privately run, for-profit facility, so if a resident
can no longer afford to stay here, then, well . . ." He leaves the rest
of the sentence dangling. "We would obviously do whatever we
can to help that person find more suitable accommodations . . ."

"I understand. Thank you." I push myself to my feet.

*So, either Jenny or someone close to her signed a lease and au-
thorized automatic monthly withdrawals from her bank account,*
I'm thinking as I leave Henry Marshall's office. Which means that
she obviously has enough money to afford to be here.

*Did that money come from one of the people she claims to have
killed?*

Do I really believe that nonsense? I wonder as I enter the elevator, pressing the button for the fourth floor. *Whatever I believe, it's
not my concern,* I remind myself as I see a woman running to
catch the elevator before the doors close.

My watch pings, telling me, *You can still do it!*

"What the hell can I still do?" I snap, stretching to hold the
doors open.

The woman stops dead in her tracks. "That's all right," she
says, waving me on my way with a too-big smile. "I'll take the
next one."

Jenny is waiting as I exit the elevator. She's wearing a red cotton
dress, and her hair is neatly combed away from her face, as if she's
been expecting visitors.

"I knew you'd come today," she says, in greeting. "I told the nurse, Linda is coming to see me today. Didn't I, Selena?"

"You did," Selena agrees from behind her desk.

Jenny laughs. "Your boyfriend was here before. You just missed him."

"He's not my boyfriend."

"Oh? Too bad. You look so good together."

"If you'll excuse me . . ." I start to move away.

"Carol's asleep," Jenny says.

"How do you know?" *Has she been in Carol's room again?*

"Because I heard your boyfriend tell Selena that she was asleep when he left. Didn't he, Selena?"

"He did," Selena confirms.

I breathe a sigh of relief.

"So, you might as well come visit with me for a while." Jenny grabs my elbow, her long fingernails digging into my flesh. "Carol can wait."

"Jenny," Selena admonishes, "I think maybe you should leave this nice lady alone."

Tears instantly fill Jenny's eyes. She releases her hold on my arm, her body shrinking into itself, as if she's been physically struck.

"That's okay," I tell Selena. "I guess I can visit with Jenny for a little bit."

Jenny's tears immediately disappear. "See?" she shouts in Selena's direction, her eyes remaining focused on me. "I told you she'd come to see me today."

"Yes, you did."

"My room's just down the hall," she says, as if I don't know. Her hand returns to my arm, guiding me down the long corridor.

"Be good, Jenny," Selena calls after us.

"What's the fun in that?" Jenny calls back.

CHAPTER THIRTEEN

"So, tell me all about yourself," Jenny says as we take our seats.

I laugh.

"What's funny?" she asks, arranging the skirt of her red dress around her like a fan.

"Just . . . Nothing. Sorry."

"What are you sorry about? Did you do something wrong?"

"No."

"Then why are you sorry? What's your name, anyway?"

Oh, dear. "Linda. Linda Davidson."

"Linda's a pretty name. You don't hear it so much anymore."

Just go with it. Humor the poor thing for a few minutes, then beat it. "No, you don't."

"My name's Jenny. Jenny's kind of a classic, don't you think? It's always popular."

"Yes, I guess it is."

"I was named after my mother. *Her* name was Jenny. Were you named after your mother?"

"No. My mother's name was Anne."

"She still alive?"

"No. She's been dead a long time."

"How long?"

"Over twenty years."

"How'd she die?"

"Stroke."

Jenny's eyes narrow in concentration. "What about your father? Is he still alive?"

"No. He died a few years before my mother. Heart attack," I offer before she can ask.

"How old were they when they died?"

"My father was eighty. My mother was maybe a year older than that."

"What do you mean, maybe? Either she was or she wasn't. Which is it?"

"She was eighty-one when she died."

"Huh. How old are you?"

"I'm seventy-six."

Her eyes narrow again, as if she's contemplating how many years I likely have left. "How old do you think *I* am?"

"I honestly have no idea."

"Take a guess."

"Eighty-seven? Eighty-eight?"

"I'm eighty-two," she says. Her lips tremble, as if she is about to cry.

"I'm so sorry," I say quickly.

She throws her head back in a raucous laugh. "Hah! I'm not eighty-two. I'm ninety-two! Hah! You should see your face."

"You're ninety-two?" I repeat, when what I really want to say is "What kind of game are you playing?"

"My mother was thirty-four when she died," Jenny says, her voice falling to a whisper, so that I'm forced to lean in closer.

"That's so young," I say, wondering if she's still playing with me. "How did she die?"

"I told you," Jenny says, impatiently. "My father killed her."

I hold my breath, wondering if this could possibly be true.

"How . . . how did he kill her?"

"He put his hands around her throat and choked the life right out of her."

"That's terrible."

"Yes, it was," she agrees.

"And you saw him do it?" I broach carefully.

"Yes," she says simply. "Not a very nice thing for a child to see."

"How old were you?"

"Five. I was five."

I watch a faraway look fill Jenny's eyes, as if she is staring directly into her past. *Is she remembering something that actually happened or just imagining it?* I wonder. Whatever the case, I have to admit that I'm hooked. I want to hear more. "How did it happen?"

"I was playing hide-and-go-seek in the backyard with my brothers," she begins, her voice growing smaller, younger with each word, so that it almost feels as if I'm listening to a child. "My brother Tommy, he was it, and he was counting to ten. We were supposed to stay outside but I didn't want to be it, so I ran inside the house, into the kitchen. I knew a secret place under the sink where there was just room enough for me to squeeze in between the pipes. I used to go hide there sometimes, when my parents' fighting got too loud."

She stops, starts pulling at her hair.

"And?" I prod. "You were hiding under the sink . . ."

She nods. "I kept the door open a little bit, so I could breathe. I could hear my parents fighting upstairs. They'd been fighting all day. My dad was calling my mom a bitch and a bunch of other really bad names, and she was crying that she was gonna take us kids and 'leave his ass.' That's what she said. 'Leave his ass.' I never liked that word. Do you?"

"Not really, no. What happened then?" I press, not wanting to be waylaid by a tangent.

"Well, they came into the kitchen. They didn't know I was there. And she's screaming, 'Get away from me.' And he's yelling, 'Nobody leaves Dan Prince!' That was his name—Dan Prince. Handsome name, don't you think?" She continues before I have time to formulate a response. "And then he put his hands around her throat, and she was trying to get them off, she was kicking and punching at him, but he was too strong. And then it suddenly got real quiet, and she stopped struggling. Stopped moving and went all limp, like one of my rag dolls." Tears fill Jenny's eyes. "And Daddy picked her up and threw her over his shoulders, like a big sack of potatoes, and took her into the garage."

"Oh, my God."

"And I ran out of the house, right into Tommy's arms. *I found you!* he shouted. *You're it!*"

"Oh, my God," I say again. What else is there to say?

"Daddy told us he was going out for a while, but he'd be back soon, and we'd all go out for dinner. Then he drove off, came back about an hour later, took us kids out to the local diner, like he said he would. My brother Jake asked him where Mommy was and Daddy said she'd gone to visit her sister. We kept asking when she'd be back, and he'd always say, *Soon*. But, of course, she never did come back. After a while, we just stopped asking."

"And you never told anyone what you saw?"

"I was five," she reminds me.

"You poor thing." I reach for her hands. "And nobody ever found out?"

"No." She covers my hands with her own, as if she is the one comforting me and not the other way around. "But it's all right. You know what they say—'What goes around, comes around.'"

CHAPTER FOURTEEN

After I leave Legacy Place, I go for a walk on the beach.

There's a breeze coming up from the ocean, and the sand by the water's edge is hard and relatively easy to walk on. I need to clear my head before I go home, to digest the things Jenny told me, decide if any of it could be true.

There must be some way of finding out, I think. Although I have no idea how to go about it. Maybe Mick might be able to help. Unlike me, he's very tech-savvy. Maybe he could find out something on the Internet.

Nobody says "on the Internet," I hear Kleo chide.

What do they say?

They say "online."

I'll need a little more information, Mick interrupts, prolonging the conversation in my head. *All you've got is a name, and "Jenny Cooper" isn't going to get me very far. Do you even know where she's from?*

I shake my head. "California. Possibly Morro Bay." I look around to make sure no one is within earshot. But even if someone hears me, they'll likely assume I'm talking on my phone.

Which, of course, I've left in the car.

But it's almost five o'clock on a weekday afternoon, and the beach is relatively empty: a few people gathering their belongings and pulling up their umbrellas; a row of surfers still hoping to catch the perfect wave; some teenage girls in barely-there bikinis soaking in the day's last rays; a middle-aged couple walking toward me, directly in my path, clearly not about to give ground.

"Sorry," I say, stepping into the water to avoid a collision and scraping my foot on a small rock.

"Why are you sorry?" I hear Jenny demand.

The man and woman say nothing, offering up not so much as a smile as they stroll past. I'm left wondering if they've even seen me.

The water is relatively warm for April, and it feels nice as it curls around my ankles, then retreats. Back and forth, back and forth. Steady and soothing. *Just what the doctor ordered,* I think, giving myself over to the rhythm of the surf, feeling my shoulder muscles gradually uncramp, the tension in my neck start to release.

My watch pings, disturbing my newfound serenity. I lift my wrist to my eyes, squinting to decipher the message on the watch's face.

It looks like you're working out, it says.

"Oh, fuck off!" I fight the almost overwhelming urge to throw the damn thing in the ocean.

"Time to get you into the twenty-first century," I remember Mick saying soon after they moved in.

Getting me into the twenty-first century meant replacing the perfectly adequate old-school TV in the den with one of those big-screen, so-called smart TVs. The TVs in the bedrooms were also quickly tossed aside. "No stupid TVs in this house," Mick announced.

My old stereo system was soon replaced by something called "surround sound"; we got a new, self-cleaning barbecue; a sleeker, more up-to-date microwave; some special kind of stovetop that requires special pots, the special pots requiring their own special utensils.

"Don't worry, Mom," Kleo assured me. "You won't have to

use any of these things. Mick will do the barbecuing and I'll do the cooking. In exchange for, you know, you paying for everything," she added, a sheepish smile on her lovely face.

I didn't object to footing the bill. Bob had invested wisely and, along with small inheritances from both sets of parents, I was left comfortably well off. I could afford the cost of moving into the twenty-first century. And I was more than happy to help them out in any way I could.

And for a while, everything progressed as planned. Except that as time went on, Mick seemed to be doing less and less while Kleo took on more and more.

Mick commandeered the bungalow's third bedroom, originally intended for Kleo to use while working on her dissertation. "It makes much more sense for me to have a separate office and for Kleo to set herself up on the dining room table," he argued persuasively. "I obviously need a space for my new business where I can just shut the door and I'm not in everyone's way and nobody has to tiptoe around me. And it's not like we really need a dining room. We eat in the kitchen and we don't entertain. If we do have company, we can eat on the back patio. Kleo's dissertation will be finished soon anyway," he added, almost as an afterthought. "So, don't you think it makes more sense for me to have the bedroom?"

Like they say, it seemed like a good idea at the time.

But now Mick's new business is struggling, and Kleo's dissertation is stalled and she might not meet her deadline, and they're always at each other's throats.

"He put his hands around her throat and choked the life right out of her," I hear Jenny say.

Could this possibly be true?

"Shit," I mutter, as the breeze picks up, carrying Jenny's words off to sea. *What happens to love,* I wonder, *that it can so easily slip into hate?*

I glance at my watch. "No answer for that one?" I ask it.

But my watch stays silent, offering up only the time. I stop, turn around, and march purposefully back toward my car.

I wake up at just after seven the next morning, after a night of unpleasant dreams in which Jenny Cooper played a starring role. Not that I can remember enough of these dreams to share with Kleo and Mick at breakfast, which is probably a good thing. Other people's dreams are never as interesting to anyone else as they are to the dreamer. *Rather like one's childhood memories,* I decide, climbing out of bed, my back so stiff that it takes several seconds before I'm able to stand up straight.

Unless they're Jenny Cooper's childhood memories, I remind myself.

I hobble toward my en suite bathroom to use the toilet, feeling the pull of yesterday's beachside stroll on my calves and Achilles tendons.

"What goes around, comes around," I hear Jenny say.

What does that mean, anyway? I ask myself as I return to the bedroom.

That her father was one of her victims?

I retrieve my yoga mat from beside my dresser, catching sight of my tired face in the mirror above it.

Do I really believe this seemingly harmless old lady is capable of killing anyone? That anything of what she's told me is true?

"I will not spend one more minute worrying about Jenny Cooper," I tell my reflection. "I have enough to worry about."

I unroll the mat and lie down, take a deep breath, and begin my morning exercises.

Another voice suddenly intrudes, as sharp as it is unexpected.

You really think those exercises are going to make a whit of difference? I hear my mother say, scorn dripping from every word.

I shake my head, trying to will her away.

But her ghost lies down beside me, effortlessly mimicking my exertions. *You've put on weight,* she chides. *What happened to my "Skinny Linny"?*

I fall back, my mind racing to find a suitable retort, the right combination of words that will banish her to the deep recesses of my mind.

But my mother refuses to be so easily dismissed and, as was usually the case when she was alive, words fail me.

CHAPTER FIFTEEN

My earliest memory is of my mother screaming.

Not in pain. Not in surprise. Not in horror.

In anger.

I grew up in an angry house.

My father had inherited a successful import-export business from his parents and, not being much of a businessman himself, successfully ran it into the ground within ten years.

My mother never forgave him.

"Why does your mother yell all the time?" Carol asked me one afternoon. We were maybe ten years old, and she'd come over after school to work on a science project we were doing together.

I shrugged. "She's frustrated," I answered, repeating a word I'd heard my grandmother use.

"What about?"

I shrugged again. "Everything."

I used to lie awake at night, trying desperately to think of what I could say or do that would ease those frustrations. If only I could come up with a funny story that would make her laugh, the right words to soothe her when she cried. Anything that would make her happy, make her proud, make her look at me with something other than profound disappointment.

In those days, we had dinner with my maternal grandparents every Friday night. I used to dread those dinners. My older brother, Peter, and I were expected to impress our grandparents with something new we'd learned during the week. Peter always had something to relate. "Fun facts," he called them, statistics dripping from his lips like breadcrumbs, along with a seemingly endless supply of amusing anecdotes. His contribution to the evening was always met with smiles and approval.

I, on the other hand, would stumble repeatedly over my inferior offering, despite having memorized it and rehearsed in front of Carol until she pronounced it "flawless."

"Really, Linda. With everything that's going on in the world, is that the best you could come up with?" I recall my mother saying on more than one occasion.

My best was never good enough.

I spent my teenage years agonizing over everything: how I looked, what I wore, whom I dated, and second-guessing every decision I made. No matter how much thought I poured into something, no matter how carefully I weighed the pros and cons of each and every situation, I always fell short in my mother's eyes. She never approved of my becoming a teacher. She approved even less of my marrying one.

I thought that once she became a grandmother, she might change. While I never expected her to morph into the kind of granny who baked cookies and volunteered to babysit, I harbored hopes she might, at the very least, soften. But she proved as critical of my girls as she'd been with me.

She was especially tough on Kleo, always the more sensitive of the two, the more fragile. Vanessa was tougher. Whereas Kleo emerged from the womb with her eyes tightly closed and barely opened them for the first three months of her life, Vanessa came into this world with her eyes wide open. I remember when she was maybe three years old and my mother was yelling at her over some minor transgression. "Don't *yell* at me!" Vanessa shouted right back.

How proud I was. How I wished I'd had that courage.

My mother used to call me "Skinny Linny" because I was so thin. That was one of the reasons I named my own daughters Kleo and Vanessa, names that couldn't be shortened and used against them. Names she hated. Hadn't my brother named his firstborn Anne, after her? "What kind of name is Kleo?" she demanded when I informed her of our choice. "You think she's some sort of Egyptian princess?" She was no less scathing regarding Vanessa. "So pretentious," she pronounced, dismissively.

"She's a real piece of work," Carol said to me one day, after I'd cried on the phone to her about another one of my mother's mean-spirited pronouncements. "I don't understand why you're so nice to her."

"She's my mother," I told her, as if this was explanation enough. *I'm used to her,* I thought. *I can take it.*

What I couldn't take was her treatment of Kleo, which got worse the older Kleo got.

There were nights I lay in bed, wishing my mother would just disappear. Not that I wanted her dead, exactly.

Just gone.

Of course, then I'd feel immediately guilty, and would determine to be even more understanding.

"Why is she so mean?" my daughter, then in her early twenties, asked me one afternoon, tears falling the length of her pretty face.

I felt my chest immediately constrict. "What did she do now?"

"She said I dressed like a Salvation Army reject and asked how I ever expected to catch a man if I didn't start wearing makeup. She said I should take a page out of Vanessa's book, that she had real 'style,' and I should follow her example if I ever wanted to land a husband."

I felt my anger rise, bile fill my throat. This was typical of my mother—pitting one child against the other. She'd done it with Peter and me, the main reason we'd never been especially close. She was doing it with Kleo and Vanessa. *She's an idiot!* I wanted to shout. *Tell her to go to hell!* Instead I took a long, deep breath, and said, "She's from a different generation. Just ignore her."

I remember reading somewhere that women either turn out like their mothers or become their exact opposites. I had long ago decided to be the latter. I would not criticize; I'd keep my opinions to myself; I would not play favorites. I would strive to see both sides in any disagreements between my daughters, between my daughters and their respective mates. I would listen. I would think before I spoke. I would be loving, fair, understanding, and above all, kind.

But that afternoon with Kleo, I'd been none of those things. What I'd been was cowardly.

My job as a mother was to protect my children, and I'd failed. I hadn't protected Kleo; I'd let her down.

And while she claims not to remember the incident, it is seared in my memory forever.

I think of my last visit with Jenny Cooper, and wonder what she would have said in my place.

She winks. *"What goes around, comes around,"* she says.

CHAPTER SIXTEEN

I wait a few days before returning to Legacy Place.

Will Jenny be there to greet me? I wonder. *Will she have any memory of the things she told me? And why am I thinking about Jenny when it's Carol I'm supposedly here to see?*

A wave of guilt rushes toward me as I exit the elevator onto the fourth floor. *How can I be more eager to visit with some demented old woman I've only recently met than with my oldest and dearest friend?*

The answer hits me like a slap to the face.

Because staring into Carol's sweet but empty eyes has become a form of torture, and Jenny's ravings, be they true or total fabrications, are at the very least . . . entertaining.

God help me, I want to hear more.

What kind of person does this make me?

I head for the visitors' lounge, sinking into one of the purple velvet sofas and taking a series of long, deep breaths. "Definitely watching too much *Dateline*," I mutter into my lap.

"I'm sorry," a voice says from somewhere beside me. "Did you say something?"

I look up to see a skinny girl, early twenties, with a long, pale face and shoulder-length, light reddish-blond hair. I recognize her as the young woman I sometimes see with her mother, visiting the old man in the room across the hall from Carol.

"Are you okay?" she asks.

"I'm fine," I assure her. "Just taking a moment. You?"

"Waiting for my mom. She's still with my grandfather. Ralph McMillan, room 418?" she asks, as if she isn't altogether sure. "I can only tolerate it for so long."

"Yes," I agree. "I know how hard it can be. I'm sure your mother appreciates you being here. I'm Linda, by the way. Linda Davidson."

"I know." She smiles. "I think the whole floor knows. '*Linda Davidson!*'" she cries, doing a passable, if quieter, imitation of Jenny's voice. "I'm Shannon."

"Nice to meet you, Shannon."

"Amazing, isn't it?" Shannon says, after a pause of several seconds. "How they can just forget."

"Well," I offer. "It's not like they have a choice."

"You sure about that?"

I shake my head, her question catching me off guard. "I'm not sure about anything."

"It's not fair," she says, tears filling her eyes.

"No, it isn't. I'm so sorry. You and your grandfather were obviously very close."

She laughs. But the laugh is harsh, unpleasant. "Not exactly."

I'm not sure how to respond to that, so I say nothing.

"If you want to know the truth, I hated that old man's guts. Still do," she adds, swiping at her tears. "I'm not crying because I'm sad," she continues after another, lengthier, pause. "I'm crying because I'm angry."

I nod, realize I'm holding my breath. I can tell that she's about to confide something I'm not sure I want to hear. *What is it about me,* I wonder, *that encourages people to share their deepest confidences? Has someone pinned a sign on my back? Don't they know that there are only so many such confidences a person can take?*

"I'm so angry I could burst," she continues, her eyes connecting with mine, as if pleading with me to ask why.

"What did he do to you?" I ask instead.

"You can probably guess." Once again, her eyes fill with tears.

I nod. Over the years, I've seen too many young girls like Shannon, with those same wounded eyes. They'd sit in my classes, rarely raising their hands to answer a question or offer an opinion, robbed of their childhoods, their youth, their confidence, their voices. By the very men who were supposed to protect them: their fathers, their uncles, their brothers.

Their grandfathers.

"My father left us when I was a baby—he and my mother were never married—so we had to move in with my grandparents," she volunteers without further prompting. "The abuse started when I was about three. My grandpa would pull me onto his lap, give me hugs and kisses, tickle me, tell me how pretty I was. And at first, I admit I liked it. But gradually, the hugs got tighter and tighter. The kisses moved from my cheeks to my mouth. I could feel his tongue worming its way between my teeth." She breaks off, forcefully wipes the memory of that kiss from her lips. "When no one was around, he'd slip his hand down my pants. When I was about six or seven, he started sneaking into my room at night."

Dear God. Please don't tell me any more.

"Does your mother know about any of this?" I ask.

"I tried to tell her once, but she accused me of making the whole thing up. Said I had to keep those stories to myself or we'd get thrown out of the house and then where would we be?"

"I'm so sorry."

"Yeah, well, I couldn't blame her really. I had a pretty active imagination in those days, and I *did* make up a lot of stuff. I was a kid, for God's sake. And I kind of blamed myself, thought I must be sending him some kind of signals. Anyway, I never mentioned it again. Then, when I was eleven or twelve, he had a stroke that deprived his brain of oxygen for a few minutes, and he developed something called 'aphasia,' which eventually turned into Alzheimer's, and he turned into this sweet, loving old man who wouldn't harm a fly. Never came near me again except to say he loved me and I was his sweet little angel. So, I tried to forget. I tried to forgive. I really did. But tell me," she says, "why is it that he gets to forget the terrible things he did to me and I have to live with those memories for the rest of my life? Where's the fucking fairness in that?"

I move to her side, take her in my arms, let her cry on my shoulder.

"Jenny!" Selena calls out suddenly. "What are you doing there?"

I look up, see Jenny hiding behind one of the nearby pillars. *How long has she been standing there?* I wonder.

Jenny scurries back down the hall without saying a word as Shannon's mother approaches from the opposite corridor.

Shannon quickly composes herself and jumps to her feet. "Ready to go?" she asks her mother.

"Ready to go," her mother agrees.

"It was really nice meeting you, Linda Davidson," Shannon says. "Have a good day."

"You, too."

Shannon and her mother walk to the elevators. I glance back down the hall toward Jenny's room. She's standing in front of her open door, her eerily familiar smile stretching across her cheeks.

CHAPTER SEVENTEEN

"What do you mean, Jenny's missing?" It's Friday, three days after my conversation with Shannon, and the first time I've returned to Legacy Place since then. "How could she be missing?"

"We have no idea," Selena confesses, her voice a whisper as she leans across her desk toward me. "One minute she was in her room, the next minute, she was gone."

"Maybe she's in the garden," I offer.

"Believe me, we've checked everywhere. More than once. You wouldn't have any ideas where she might go, would you? I mean, you've spent more time with her than anyone these last weeks . . ."

"Have you checked under the kitchen sink?"

Selena looks at me as if I've lost my mind. "Why on earth would we check under the kitchen sink?"

"Jenny told me that she sometimes used to hide there when she was a child."

Selena picks up the phone, her eyes still firmly on mine, as if I, too, might just suddenly vanish into thin air. "Check under the sink in the kitchen," she instructs whomever answers. "Don't ask."

"I can't believe she would just take off," I say, feeling a stab of guilt that I didn't visit Jenny after talking to Shannon. I wonder if she's gone looking for me.

I shake my head, ashamed of my self-absorption. When did everything become about me?

Selena's phone rings. "Okay," she says. "Thanks for checking. It was a long shot." She returns the phone to its cradle. "Any more suggestions?"

I admit I'm all out of ideas.

Which is when the phone on Selena's desk rings again. She picks it up before it can ring a second time. "Whew," she says after a minute's pause. "That's great news. Thank you." She smiles up at me. "We've found her."

"Well, hello, Linda Davidson!" Jenny cries as she steps off the elevator approximately twenty minutes later, a burly young orderly close behind. She rushes toward me, surrounding me with surprisingly strong arms. She's wearing a heavy jacket, despite the outside heat, and her forehead is bathed in sweat. "Have you heard the news?"

"What news?"

"I won fifty-two Pontiacs!"

"What?"

"You heard me, Linda Davidson. I entered a contest at the drugstore and I won fifty-two Pontiacs! And I'm going to give you half! Half of fifty-two is twenty-six. Twenty-six Pontiacs!"

"I'm not sure I understand." I look toward Selena, who is struggling to keep a straight face.

"What don't you understand?" Jenny demands. "It's pretty straightforward. I entered a contest at CVS and I won. Fifty-two Pontiacs! I went there to collect them but they told me they hadn't arrived yet."

My mind is racing. The nearest CVS is at least a mile away. Could this frail old lady really have walked over a mile in this heat?

Are they even making Pontiacs anymore?

"Jenny," Selena says, leaving her desk to join us. "I think you're a little confused, sweetheart. You've had a very eventful morning and you must be exhausted. Why don't you let Lance take you back to your room so you can lie down for a while?"

"Why don't you go fuck yourself?" comes Jenny's swift response. "And don't call me 'sweetheart.' I'm not your goddamn sweetheart."

"Okay, Jenny. I'm afraid I'm going to have to insist that you go back to your room."

"I'm afraid I'm going to have to insist that you go back to your room," Jenny mimics.

"I need you to calm down."

"I need you to calm down."

"Lance," Selena instructs the orderly, "can you please escort Jenny to her room?"

"I'm not giving him any of my Pontiacs!"

"He doesn't want your Pontiacs. Now, please, Jenny. Go with Lance."

"Don't you come near me," Jenny warns the young man.

"Jenny . . ." Selena says.

"I want Linda. Can Linda come with me?"

"Maybe in a little while. After you've had a rest."

Jenny sighs. "I don't like you," she tells Selena. "You're a meanie-poo. No Pontiacs for you either."

"Jenny . . ."

"I'm going. I'm going." She turns to go, then stops. "I'm hungry."

"I'm afraid you missed lunch, but I'll see what I can drum up . . ."

"You know what I'd like?" Jenny interrupts. "A raspberry croissant."

"A raspberry croissant?"

"Isn't that what I just said?"

"I don't think we have any raspberry croissants."

"What kind of place is this?" Jenny shouts.

"How about I bring you some the next time I visit?" I interject.

"What good will that do? I'm hungry now."

I can't help smiling.

"What are you smiling about?" Jenny demands.

"Lance," Selena directs, "please take Jenny to her room."

Lance takes a step toward Jenny.

"Don't you touch me!" she warns, cowering. "Please, Linda. Don't let him touch me. I'm sorry. I'll be a good girl, I promise. Don't let him touch me."

"Lance isn't going to hurt you," Selena says.

"Please, Linda. Don't let him touch me."

I see the terror on Jenny's face, the pleading in her watery eyes. "I can take her to her room," I say.

"I don't think that's a very good idea . . ."

"Honestly. I can handle it."

"Please, Linda," Jenny cries. "Please, please, please, please."

"You're sure you want to do this?" Selena asks.

No, I think. "Yes," I say. "Is that all right with you, Jenny? Will you let me take you to your room?"

"Yes, please take me to my room. Don't let him touch me."

Moving almost in slow motion, so as not to startle her, I drape my arm across Jenny's heavy jacket and lead her down the hall, her feet shuffling along the tile floor.

"Will you stay with me till I fall asleep?" she asks as she climbs onto her bed, securing her jacket tight around her and curling into a fetal ball.

I sit down in one of the chairs. "If you'd like."

"And you won't let Lance touch me."

I glance toward the open door, see the orderly hovering nearby. "I won't let Lance touch you."

She closes her eyes. "I changed my mind about the Pontiacs. You can have them."

"Thank you."

"You're welcome," she says.

·   ·   ·

"What's this?" Jenny asks, opening her eyes to find me sitting in basically the same position I was in approximately an hour ago. Except that now I'm holding a small brown paper bag containing two large raspberry croissants.

"They're the croissants you wanted. I went shopping when you were asleep and picked some up. There's a little bakery not far from here . . ."

Jenny pushes herself into a sitting position. "What are you nattering about?"

I ignore the edge in her voice, attributing it to her barely wakened state. "Your raspberry croissants. Try one. They're nice and fresh."

She takes the bag from my hand, sticks her fingers inside, lifts one out, and takes a large bite. Then promptly spits it to the floor. "What the hell is this?"

I'm instantly on my feet. "It's a raspberry croissant . . ."

"Why the hell would I want a raspberry croissant? I hate raspberries. They taste like dog poo and those stupid little seeds stick in your teeth. Are you trying to poison me?"

"What? No! Of course not."

She throws the bag at me, and I have to move quickly to avoid being hit. "Who are you anyway? What are you doing in my room? Somebody help me!" she screams toward the open door to her apartment. "Help me!"

"Jenny, for God's sake. Calm down. It's me, Linda."

"Help! Help!" she continues to holler.

"I'm going," I assure her, moving quickly toward the door as Selena and Lance come running down the hall.

"And take your damn croissant with you!" Jenny hurls what remains of the croissant in her hand at my head.

"What is it they say about no good deed?" Selena asks me as I flee the room.

CHAPTER EIGHTEEN

Two days later, Ralph McMillan is dead.

"What?" I ask Selena. "How can that be?" Around me, I hear the buzz of the residents grappling with the news.

"Looks like he choked on something and then aspirated."

"Oh, my God."

"It happens. Especially with Alzheimer's patients. They forget how to eat, how to swallow."

I watch several orderlies disappear into Ralph McMillan's room.

"They're preparing the body," Selena says before I can ask. "The family's on their way over now."

I picture Shannon and her mother, feel Shannon crying in my arms, her tears dampening the cotton of my blouse. And I see something else—Jenny lurking behind a nearby pillar, that eerie smile.

"It was Jenny who found him," Selena says, as if reaching into my brain.

"What?"

"Jenny found his body."

"Jenny found his body?" I repeat, numbly. "How is that possible?"

"I'm not sure, exactly," Selena admits. "It was just prior to my shift. Apparently, she was 'making her rounds' and she found him lying on the floor."

I picture Jenny hiding behind the pillar in the hallway, listening in on my conversation with Ralph McMillan's granddaughter. Is it possible that Jenny killed him? That Shannon's confession re-ignited the murderous impulses inside Jenny's tortured mind?

What the hell is going on here? I wonder, trying to organize my thoughts. *Am I seriously thinking that Jenny could have had anything to do with Ralph McMillan's death? How is that even possible?*

"Will there be an autopsy?" I hear myself ask.

Selena looks startled. "An autopsy? What on earth for?"

"To determine the cause of death."

"The man basically choked to death," Selena says succinctly, tilting her head to one side, dark eyes narrowing. "Are you all right?"

Lance comes out of Ralph McMillan's room, closes the door behind him, and approaches Selena's desk. "All done," he tells her, as the elevator doors open and Shannon and her mother appear.

"Perfect timing," Selena mutters under her breath. "Ms. McMillan . . . Shannon," she says, coming around her desk to greet the two women. "I'm so sorry for your loss."

"Thank you," Shannon's mother says, swiping at her steady flow of tears.

Shannon glances toward me, her eyes dry.

"What happened?" her mother asks.

"It looks as if he choked on something he was eating and then aspirated," Selena tells them, as she told me moments ago.

Or he was murdered by the old lady in room 415.

"It's not uncommon with people with Alzheimer's. They forget how to eat, how to swallow."

Or he was murdered by the old lady in room 415.

"Can I see him?"

"Of course."

"I don't want to see him," Shannon whispers.

"Are you sure?"

Shannon nods.

"Okay," her mother tells her. "You wait here. I won't be long."

I take a step toward Shannon. "Would you like to sit down?"

I guide her toward the lounge, sit down beside her on the purple velvet couch. "How are you doing?" I say.

She shrugs. "I'm not sorry he's dead."

I nod.

"It's just kind of weird, you know. Him dying like that."

You have no idea.

Shannon's eyes drift to a spot behind my head. I turn to see Jenny Cooper standing there, watching us with vacant eyes.

I jump to my feet, "Jenny!"

"Sorry for your loss," Jenny says to Shannon.

"Thank you," Shannon tells her.

Jenny smiles. "You're welcome."

"Did you kill him?" I ask her minutes later.

"What are you talking about?"

"I'm asking if you killed him," I repeat.

We're in Jenny's room, standing just inside the doorway. I've ushered her away from Shannon as quickly as I can, all but pushing her inside her apartment and closing the door behind me. I don't want to chance anyone overhearing our conversation.

"What makes you think I would do something like that?" Jenny asks, sounding impressively indignant.

"Because you told me that you kill people."

"Doesn't mean I killed Ralph McMillan."

"You were the one who found him."

"Yes, I found him. So?"

"What were you doing in his room?"

"How do I know? I have dementia. Remember?"

"Jenny . . ."

"Just how did I kill him, if you're such a smarty-pants?" she challenges. "Did I strangle him? Maybe I beat him to death. Or smothered him with a pillow." She waves her spindly arms in front of my face, arthritis-plagued fingers making a mockery of her words. "Or maybe, just maybe," she says, leaning toward me and lowering her voice to a whisper, "maybe I poisoned him . . ."

I feel my breath catch in my lungs. "Did you?"

A slow smile creeps into the corners of Jenny's lips. "Now where on earth would I get poison?"

The question hangs in the air between us like a stale odor.

A drugstore, I answer silently.

"What were you really doing in that drugstore?" I ask when I can find my voice.

"I was in a drugstore?"

"Everyone assumed you'd just wandered off. But maybe it was more deliberate than that. Maybe you knew exactly where you were going."

"And maybe you think too much," Jenny counters, pulling back in her seat. "Ever think of that?"

"You eavesdropped on my conversation with Shannon. You went missing soon after. They found you in a CVS. You used to be a pharmacist. You'd know all about poisons."

"Yes, I would. And you'd be surprised at just how lethal some over-the-counter products can be. Providing you know what to do with them." She laughs, clearly enjoying herself. "You think I have some sort of 'special recipe'?"

"Do you?"

"Did I ever tell you about my affair with Marlon Brando?" she asks, suddenly switching gears.

"What?"

"Before he got so fat. He was a very good lover. Very adventurous. He's dead now, of course. Maybe I killed him, too."

"Did you kill Ralph McMillan?"

"That's for me to know," she says with a wink. "And for you to find out."

CHAPTER NINETEEN

I arrive home just after four o'clock, slamming the car door as I exit, something I've taken to doing of late to alert Kleo and Mick of my presence. But I hear nothing as I approach the front door—no voices raised in anger, no TV blaring. *Nothing to worry about,* I assure myself, releasing a deep breath of sublimated anxiety as I unlock the front door. "Hello?" I call out. "Kleo, Mick, I'm home."

No answer.

"Hello?" I call again, stepping inside, half expecting to see Kleo in front of her computer at the dining room table, so caught up in working on her dissertation that she hasn't heard me come in.

But she isn't there.

Which is fine because it's really Mick I'm most anxious to see.

"Mick?" I call again, approaching his closed office door and knocking gently.

No answer.

"Mick?" I say again, gently opening the door and peeking my head inside.

I see him immediately. He's sitting at his desk in front of the window that looks onto the street, his back to me. The blinds are closed, so he hasn't seen me pull up, and he obviously has no idea I'm here, so wrapped up is he in what he's doing.

Which is staring at the large monitor of his desktop computer, watching a naked man slamming into a naked woman from behind, her huge breasts flopping back and forth with each violent thrust.

"Oh, my God!" I exclaim, the words shooting from my mouth before I have the chance to stop them.

Mick spins around in his chair. "Linda! Shit!" He jumps to his feet, quickly spinning back around to shut down his computer, almost knocking over his tall glass of beer in the process.

I watch the naked couple vanish abruptly as the screen goes dark. "I'm so sorry," I mutter, although, to tell the truth, I'm not sure exactly what I'm sorry about. I'm not the one watching porn and drinking beer in the middle of the afternoon when I'm supposed to be working.

"How long have you been standing there?" he asks.

"Not long," I say. *Long enough*, I think.

"Long enough," he says for me.

I nod. "I knocked . . ."

He shrugs, offers a sheepish smile. "I was just taking a break."

Another nod. Mine.

Another shrug. His.

"You ever watch porn? Or *did* you when you were younger?" he qualifies immediately, the idea of a woman my age enjoying this sort of thing clearly too much for his already flustered brain to handle.

And the truth is that he's right. Whereas what I just witnessed on his computer might have aroused me in my younger days, now it just looks painful.

"Not really your thing," he states before I can answer.

"Not really." I look around the small room, surprisingly empty of anything that resembles work. No books, no files, no papers stacked along the beige-carpeted floor.

"Yeah," he says. "Not Kleo's either."

"Speaking of whom," I say, relieved to be able to change the subject, "where is she?"

"Library. Where else?"

I turn to leave.

"Linda," he says, his voice stopping me.

"Hmm?"

"Is there something you wanted?"

Is there? "Oh. Oh, yes. Actually, I was hoping you could help me with something."

"What's that?"

"It's about Jenny Cooper . . ."

"The old lady who told you she kills people?"

"Yes. I've been to see her a few times . . ."

"I thought you promised Kleo you'd stay away from her," he says.

"Well, I didn't exactly promise."

"Not like you to keep secrets from your daughter."

"I just didn't want her to worry unnecessarily."

"Uh-huh." He nods, knowingly. "So, what about Jenny Cooper?"

"There have been a few developments." I fill him in on everything that's happened in the last few weeks.

"Okay, so let me see if I've got this straight," Mick begins. "She saw her father strangle her mother when she was a child, and then she grew up, became a pharmacist, started killing people, and now she's knocking off the residents of Legacy Place . . ."

"I know it sounds ridiculous."

What goes around, comes around.

"I think she might have started with her father."

"You think she murdered her father," he repeats dully.

"I think it's possible."

"And maybe you think too much?" I hear Jenny say.

"So, how can I help?" Mick makes no attempt to hide his budding grin.

"Well, I know her father's name and where they were from . . ."

"Which is . . . ?"

"Dan Prince from Morro Bay."

"You got anything else?"

"She had two brothers, Jake and Tommy, and she was named after her mother. Jenny said she was five when her father killed her mother, and she's ninety-two now, so I was hoping maybe we . . . well, *you* . . . could look up the death records in Morro Bay and see if there's anything, you know, that . . . I don't know . . . I'm being ridiculous . . ."

"What the hell," Mick says. "Can't hurt to try. Come on. We'll use Kleo's computer."

I'm about to ask why we can't just use his when I remember what's on it. "Is that a good idea?" I ask instead as he walks briskly past me into the short hall separating his office from the dining room. "I mean, she has her papers spread all over the table and . . ."

But Mick is already pulling up a chair and shoving Kleo's papers aside.

"Please be careful," I urge.

"Don't you worry," he assures me, about to activate Kleo's computer when we hear her car pull into the driveway behind mine. "Guess it'll have to wait till later," he says, with a wink.

I nod, start walking toward the front door.

"Linda," Mick calls after me.

I stop, turn back around.

"I'd really appreciate it if you didn't say anything to Kleo about . . . you know . . ."

I nod. *What good would telling Kleo do?* Besides, I've been keeping things from Kleo myself.

As if reading my mind, Mick says, "I'll keep your secret if you'll keep mine."

CHAPTER TWENTY

I wait almost a week before returning to Legacy Place.

I'm here to see Carol, my oldest and dearest friend, I tell myself.

I'm not here to see Jenny.

Mick wasn't able to find out anything substantial about her family. The records he'd managed to uncover showed only that her father had died of a heart attack some sixty-five years ago, and there was no record of her mother at all.

Which made sense if Jenny's father had indeed murdered his wife and disposed of her body only-God-knows-where.

"You want me to keep digging?" Mick asked.

"No," I told him. "I'm done playing detective."

I step off the elevator, half expecting to find Jenny waiting for me when the doors open.

But Jenny isn't waiting in front of the elevators, nor is she in the lounge or secreted behind some concrete pillar. I force a smile onto my face and proceed to Carol's room, hoping I won't discover Jenny poised over Carol's bedside.

I don't, and I'm more relieved than I care to admit.

Where the hell is Jenny this time?

I tell myself that she'll likely pop up by the time my visit with Carol is over.

She doesn't.

I walk past the nurses' station, not recognizing the dark-skinned young woman behind the desk, and head down the hall toward Jenny's room.

Her door is closed, so I knock, gently at first, and then louder. "Jenny? Jenny, are you awake?" I ask, pushing open the door.

The drapes are shut, and it takes my eyes a few seconds to adjust to the dark. "Jenny?" I say again, taking several tentative steps toward her bed.

Which is when I realize she's not in it.

Nor is she in the bathroom.

Has she taken off again?

I flip on the overhead light, spin slowly around, as if Jenny might be crouched in a corner, waiting to pounce.

She isn't.

My head is spinning. Where could she have gone? Another visit to the nearest CVS?

Who is she planning to kill this time?

I picture Jenny as she stepped off the elevator last week, Lance hovering. *"Don't let him touch me,"* I hear her plead, refusing to take her heavy jacket off despite the heat, wrapping it around her like a blanket as she settled into bed.

Before I have time to consider what I'm doing, I'm at her closet, rifling through the meager belongings hanging inside: a few dresses, two pairs of elastic-waist pants, half a dozen blouses, an old, ratty sweater, the heavy, olive-drab-colored jacket . . .

I pull the jacket toward me. It's shapeless and unremarkable, except for two very large pockets. Pockets big enough to hide . . . what exactly?

"You think I have a 'special recipe'?" I hear Jenny ask.

My hands push their way inside the pockets, return with nothing but a bunch of crumpled tissues. "Just what did you expect to find?" I ask myself out loud.

"What are you doing?" a voice suddenly demands from somewhere behind me.

Oh, God. I spin toward the door.

"I'm sorry, but who are you?" the nurse asks.

"Linda," I stammer. "Linda Davidson. I was visiting my friend Carol Kreiger, down the other hall?" I ask, as if I'm not sure. "And I thought I'd stop by to see Jenny. She's obviously not here . . ."

"Yeah, I'm sorry," the nurse says, her shoulders visibly relaxing. "There's been no word."

No word? "What do you mean?"

"There's been no word from the hospital."

"Jenny's in the hospital?"

"Yes. Apparently, she had some sort of attack last night and they had to call an ambulance."

"What hospital did they take her to?"

"Pretty sure it was Jupiter Medical Center over on South Dixie. That's where we send most patients."

"Was it a heart attack?"

"I really couldn't say."

"Is she . . . is she"—*dead?*—"okay?"

"Like I said, there's been no word. You can check with the hospital, if you'd like."

I nod, quickly brushing past her toward the elevators. *Jenny's in the hospital. She's had some sort of attack. Is this somehow my fault? I did everything but accuse her outright of having murdered Ralph McMillan!*

"Linda!"

I turn to see Lorne walking toward me.

"I was wondering when I'd run into you again." He leans in to kiss my cheek. "I was going to call, but I kept thinking I'd see you here. Unfortunately, our timetables haven't exactly meshed lately. Are you coming or going?"

I wish I knew, I think, my cheek still tingling with the touch of his lips on my skin. "Just leaving," I say.

"Oh, too bad. I was hoping we could grab a cup of coffee, maybe catch that movie we talked about . . ."

"I'm sorry. I can't today . . ."

"Tomorrow? Saturday? You name it. Whatever date works for you."

It's not a date.

Sounds like a date to me.

"Saturday afternoon might work," I hear myself say.

"Great. That's great. There's that new movie that Ben Affleck directed. It's supposed to be good. And it's just over at the plaza."

"Sounds good."

"I'll check the schedule. We can meet there. Or I can swing by and pick you up, if you'd prefer."

"No, that's okay. It's probably easier if I meet you there."

"Whatever works," he says again. "I'll text you the schedule."

"I don't really text," I tell him.

He laughs. "I'll phone. You have a cellphone, I assume."

"I have a cellphone." I give him the number and watch him enter it in his list of contacts.

"How was she today?"

It takes me a second to realize he's asking about Carol. "Pretty good," I lie.

"Yeah. Well . . . I'll just go and say hello. I'll phone you about Saturday."

I nod, watch him retreat down the hall.

It's not a date, I tell myself.

Mick's familiar retort echoes in my ear as I wait for the elevator. *Sounds like a date to me.*

The closest Jupiter Medical Center is located at 1210 South Old Dixie Highway. Leaving U.S. 1, I drive west on Indiantown Road to Alternate A1A, then south to Toney Penna Drive, where I turn right and keep going till I pass the railroad tracks, breathing a sigh of relief that I don't have to wait for a passing train. I take an immediate left onto South Old Dixie, and the gleaming white tower of the Jupiter Medical Center immediately springs into view.

I pull up in front of the main entrance, leave my key with the valet, and enter the lobby.

"I'm looking for Jenny Cooper," I tell the elderly volunteer at the information desk. "She was brought in late last night."

The woman types the name into her computer. "Room 311," she says.

"Room 311," I repeat as I walk briskly toward the elevators. If Jenny has a room, it means she's still alive. *Unless she died some-time this morning and they haven't had a chance to move her body,* I find myself thinking on the short ride to the third floor.

"*What goes around, comes around,*" I hear Jenny say.

"Room 311?" I ask a passing nurse.

"That way." She points down the corridor on my left. She's gone before I have a chance to inquire about Jenny's condition.

The door to room 311 is closed, but there's no sign advising me to keep out, so I knock gingerly before slowly opening the door.

Jenny is lying in the narrow hospital bed in the middle of the small private room, her left arm attached to a variety of tubes, her ghostly pallor the same shade as the white sheets surrounding her. Her mouth is open, her eyes closed. Were it not for the gentle rise and fall of her chest, I might think she was dead.

I breathe my own sigh of relief. To be honest, I'm not sure why I'm so relieved. I barely know this woman, and what I *do* know, if any of it is actually true, is unsavory, to say the least.

"Well, are you coming in, or are you just going to stand there?" Jenny demands, her eyes still closed.

I jump at the sound of her voice, the strength of its delivery.

"*Well?*" she asks again. "Either come in or get the hell out."

Get the hell out, a little voice echoes from somewhere deep in-side my solar plexus.

Instead, I grab the straight-backed wooden chair leaning against the wall, pull it up beside Jenny's bed, and sit the hell down.

CHAPTER TWENTY-ONE

Jenny opens her eyes, twists her head toward me. "Who are you?" she asks.

"It's me," I tell her. "Linda Davidson."

"Linda Davidson," she repeats. "Name doesn't ring a bell. Are you a doctor?"

"No."

"Then why are you here?"

"We're . . . friends," I offer.

"I don't have any friends."

"We met at Legacy Place. We've talked a few times."

"Really? What about?"

You told me that you saw your father strangle your mother and that you're basically a serial killer, I'm tempted to respond. Instead I say, "Nothing much. Just . . . stuff. You know."

"I don't know. That's why I'm asking. Who are you really? Are you with the CIA?"

"No."

"The FBI? The police?"

"No. No."

"Then what are you doing here?"

"What are *you* doing here?" I ask in return. Jenny may be delusional, but she's still as sharp as a tack. Again, I wonder if she's playing with me. The cat toying with the helpless bird, enjoying itself before going in for the kill.

"They thought I was having a heart attack." She laughs, although the sound is more a low gurgle. "Turns out it was just gas."

My turn to laugh. I know exactly what she's talking about. At a certain age, you start questioning every little twinge. *Is it a headache or a brain tumor? A muscle spasm or the first sign of ALS? Should I go to the hospital or the bathroom?*

I nod toward the various monitors to which she is connected. "A lot of equipment for just gas."

She motions toward the IV in her arm. "They said I was a touch dehydrated. But my heart's nice and strong, and my blood pressure's that of a child. They'll probably be releasing me later today."

"Glad to hear it."

"Why?"

"Why?" I parrot.

"Why are you glad?"

"I don't know," I admit, and she laughs again.

"You're an odd duck, aren't you, Linda Davidson?"

"I always thought I was pretty ordinary, to be honest."

"Oh, God. Don't do that. Honesty is such a bore."

"Is that why you make things up?" I ask.

She smiles, the smile reaching into her watery blue eyes. "Who says I make things up?"

"Do you?" I ask.

"Do *you*?" she echoes.

"No."

"You never lie?"

"I try not to."

"Liar, liar, pants on fire!" she taunts.

"I'm not lying."

"Really? I asked you what we talk about and you said, nothing much. That was a lie, wasn't it?"

I chuckle, raising my hands in a gesture of surrender. *What the*

hell? I think. *What is it they say? 'In for a penny, in for a pound'?*
"You told me that you kill people."

She leans forward, brings her index finger to her lips, casts a wary glance toward the closed door. "Shh. It's a secret."

"Is it true? Have you really . . . killed anyone?"

"What a question! Do I look like a killer?"

I shrug. "What do killers look like?"

"I used to be quite beautiful," she says.

I take a deep breath. "Did you kill Ralph McMillan?"

"Why are you so concerned with that miserable old man? The other people I killed were much more interesting."

Maybe so, I think. *But even if this is true, they died a long time ago, whereas Ralph McMillan died just last week. Which means you're still at it. Which means that none of the other residents, including my dear friend Carol, is safe.*

"Come on, Jenny. Stop playing games."

"I like games."

"I can see that."

"I used to love Monopoly and Snakes and Ladders." Jenny laughs. "That was my favorite. I used to love sliding down those snakes. Especially the big fat ones. What about you? I bet you were more of a Trivial Pursuit person, weren't you?"

"I was." *Am I really that transparent?*

"We're very different, you and I."

"Yes, we are." *Thank God.*

"Did you play Trivial Pursuit with your friend Carol?"

I struggle to keep calm at the sound of Carol's name on Jenny's lips. "You remember her name."

"Of course, I remember her name. Why wouldn't I?"

"You live in a memory care facility."

"So I do," she agrees, with a laugh. "Legacy Place. Where we met. And I told you that I have a secret, that I kill people."

"Yes."

"And you want to know about all the people I've killed," she says.

"Yes."

She sighs, the sigh sending visible tremors throughout her body. "Well, first there was my father. You kind of suspected that, didn't you?"

I nod, swallowing an unexpected surge of pride.

"He kind of had it coming, after he killed my mother. Wouldn't you say?"

"How did you kill him?"

"Poison. But you knew that, too."

"What kind of poison?"

She shakes her head. "I can't give away all my secrets, now, can I?"

"Did you poison Ralph McMillan?"

"Oh, pooh. Him again! I don't want to talk about him." She leans slowly back in her bed, until her head is resting securely on her pillow. "I'm very tired," she says, closing her eyes. "All this talk about murder has made me sleepy."

I nod, thinking about how I regularly fall asleep to *Dateline*.

I shudder. *Maybe Jenny and I aren't so different after all.*

CHAPTER TWENTY-TWO

Lorne is waiting for me in front of the movie theater.

I spot him standing by the glass entrance doors as I circle the crowded outdoor lot, looking for a parking space. It's almost four o'clock and the movie starts in twenty minutes. Lorne has already informed me that he made reservations at the Ke'e Grill for 6:45.

"The Ke'e Grill?" Mick said, eyebrows raised, when I told him and Kleo of our plans.

"It's not a date," I told him.

"Whatever you say," he said.

The knowing smirk on his face said otherwise, and made me want to smack him on the side of his head. Probably how Kleo feels much of the time.

I exit my car, watching Lorne walk briskly toward me, waving something above his head. "I got the tickets," he explains. "Row J. On the aisle."

"Perfect." I transfer the beige jacket resting in the crook of my right arm to the other arm, to get at my purse. "How much do I owe you?"

He shakes his head. "Please. My treat."

It's not a date.

"I insist," I say.

"And I won't hear of it."

"Lorne . . ."

"Tell you what, you can buy the tickets next time."

Next time?

He takes my elbow, leading me toward the theater before I have time to think of a suitable response. "You look lovely, by the way."

I glance at my baggy navy pants and white cotton blouse, the least date-like outfit I could put together, feeling a wayward blush spring to my cheeks. "Thank you. You, too," I offer without thinking.

"I look lovely?"

I laugh. *Was dating this awkward in our teens?*

Stop it! This is not a date!

"You look very . . . nice," I qualify, feeling the blush deepen, form two red circles in the middle of my cheeks. *Like a circus clown.*

"Nice?" he asks. "I think I prefer 'lovely.'"

"Handsome," I feel obliged to correct. I take note of his checkered shirt and crisp black trousers, the black sweater draped casually across his still-broad shoulders, its sleeves tied at the base of his neck. "How's that?"

He has the best posture, I recall Carol telling me soon after they met. *And the cleanest house,* she added incongruously. *We went back to his place after dinner, and I looked around, and everything was so neat and tidy. I thought, if he's as good in bed as he is at cleaning . . .*

And was he? I remember asking.

Even better. He does this thing . . . She giggles, raises her hand to illustrate. *He reaches over and gently tucks some hairs behind my ear. And then he slowly—oh, so slowly—lets his fingers trace a delicate line down my neck as he leans in for a kiss. I tell you, it's electric.*

And we laughed, like giddy schoolgirls.

I'm so sorry, Carol. I promise you this is not a date.

"Linda?" Lorne is saying.

"Sorry. What?"

"I said that was much better."

"What's much better?" I ask, hearing shades of Jenny Cooper in my voice.

" 'Handsome.' It beats 'nice' by a mile."

I smile, feeling the subtle pressure of his hand on my elbow as we walk toward the theater. I reach for the door, but he beats me to it, leaning across me to open it, then standing back so that I can walk through. "A gentleman always opens the door for a lady," he says.

I search my mind for a response, but by the time I come up with anything that won't sound embarrassingly lame, we're at the refreshment counter.

"Would you like something?" Lorne asks. "Popcorn? A drink?"

"Nothing, thank you."

"You're not on a diet, I hope."

"Me? No." I chuckle. "A little late for that."

"What do you mean? You look terrific."

"I look okay," I qualify. "For my age," I qualify further.

"For any age," he says. "And the word is 'terrific.' Not 'okay.' Sure you don't want anything?"

I feel another disconcerting blush spreading across my cheeks. "Positive. Don't want to ruin my dinner."

"Good thinking." His hand returns to my elbow to guide me toward the ticket taker.

"Theater Six," the young man directs, tearing the tickets in half.

We enter the dim theater and make our way up the steep steps to row J. *Were these steps always so steep?* I wonder, praying I don't trip and fall backward into his arms.

"It's freezing in here," I remark as I take my seat.

"They always have the air-conditioning on full blast," Lorne reminds me, helping me into my jacket. "Would you like my sweater over your legs?"

"No. I'll be fine. Thank you. You're probably going to need it yourself."

"I don't know about that," he says with a laugh. "I'm pretty hot-blooded."

Oh, dear, I think, as the theater darkens and twenty minutes of trailers and advertisements begin.

Luckily, the accompanying soundtrack is very loud, sparing us the need for further small talk. My mind, on the other hand, doesn't *stop* talking. *Is Lorne being flirtatious or merely polite? Is this a date or simply two friends commiserating? What would Carol think of our being together? Would she be horrified or happy?*

He has amazing stamina for a man his age, I remember her saying.

"Oh, dear," I mutter now.

"Sorry," Lorne says, leaning his head toward mine, so that we are almost touching. "Did you say something?"

"Did I?" I ask, Jenny's voice echoing in my ears. "Sorry."

"Why are you sorry?" she demands.

"Finally," Lorne says, his shoulder pressing against mine as he points toward the screen. "Movie's about to start."

I smile, pushing Jenny's voice aside and angling my body subtly away from Lorne's as the movie begins.

"So, what did you think?" Lorne asks as the young hostess—she looks barely out of her teens—leads us to our table.

We've driven over to the Ke'e Grill in separate cars and haven't had a chance to discuss the film, other than to agree we both enjoyed it.

"It was very exciting," I tell him, as we take our seats.

"You didn't find it too violent?"

I shake my head, glancing around the crowded, glass-walled restaurant, framed by outdoor palms and tiki lights. "I actually rather liked the violence," I admit.

He laughs. "You did?"

"You didn't?" I ask in return. It seems I've gotten used to speaking in questions, a holdover from time spent with Jenny Cooper.

"What is it that appealed to you about it?" he asks, as the waitress introduces herself and hands us our menus.

"I found it quite cathartic. The bad guys getting what was coming to them."

"Yeah," he agrees. "I see your point. Too bad it doesn't always work out that way in real life."

I smile, peruse the menu. *Tell that to Jenny Cooper,* I think.

CHAPTER TWENTY-THREE

Lorne orders the house salad and the swordfish; I select a Caesar salad and the filet mignon.

"How do you like that prepared?" the waitress asks.

"Rare to medium rare."

"A meat eater," Lorne remarks, as the waitress retreats. "And one who likes her meat bloody at that." He smiles. "I've known you for eight years and yet, you continue to surprise me, Linda Davidson."

Why is everyone suddenly referring to me by my full name? "It's just that we have so much fish at home," I explain, feeling a twinge of guilt that I am somehow betraying my daughter by not choosing the healthier option.

"A little red meat never killed anyone," Lorne says, as if reading my mind. "Are you sure you don't want a glass of red wine to wash it down?"

I shake my head. "I'm driving."

"As am I." He indicates the glass of Whispering Angel in front of him. "One glass?"

"I better not."

He nods, warm brown eyes narrowing. "Tell me, Linda, were you always such a good girl?"

I laugh to disguise both my budding discomfort and the tingling sensation that I'm unexpectedly experiencing in my body. "Is that a serious question?" I ask, when I realize he's waiting for an answer.

"It is. Absolutely."

"Then I guess the answer is yes."

"You've always played by the rules?"

"I've always tried to."

"Even when the rules are unfair?"

"Even then," I say, wondering if he is referring to his situation with Carol, if he could be hinting at a possible extramarital affair. *Am I reading way too much into what is, on its surface, a perfectly innocent question?* "Did you see Carol today?" I ask, in order to remind him of what connects us.

A slow frown overtakes the playful smile on his lips. His eyes darken. "I did."

"How was she?"

He shrugs, as if that is answer enough.

"It's hard," I acknowledge. "You two had such a special relationship."

"We did."

"I think it's wonderful that you visit her so often."

"What else have I got to do? I'm retired. I don't golf much anymore. I hate pickleball. Damn near broke my ankle the last time I played." He takes a long sip of his wine, looks toward the wall of windows at the palm fronds outside swaying with the breeze.

"It's hard," I say again. "But I feel in my heart that Carol knows you're there, that somewhere deep inside her, she knows who you are. She hasn't forgotten—"

"Look," he interrupts. "This is probably going to sound awful . . ."

"What?"

"Can we not talk about Carol? Just for a little while."

I open my mouth to speak, but no words emerge.

"Don't get me wrong. It's not that I don't still care about her," he says. "It's not that I don't feel terrible about what's happened to her, that I don't miss her, miss *us*. It's just that her condition is so all-consuming, and I'm trapped in this nightmare, this state of per-petual limbo that could go on for years. I can't get on with my life, I can't mourn her passing. Not that I wish her dead," he adds quickly, "although God help me, sometimes I guess I do, and I hate myself for feeling that way." He runs his hand through his hair. "My kids think I should move on. They say that Carol and I were only married for eight years, and she has five kids of her own who can look after her, that I shouldn't have to sacrifice whatever time I have left." He shakes his head. "I don't know. Is it so awful that I want to live my life? Does that make me such a terrible person?"

"You're not a terrible person."

"Tell that to your face. You look like you just met Jack the Rip-per."

"No. No. I'm sorry. Honestly, I don't think you're a terrible person."

"I bet you never had those thoughts about Bob," he states rather than asks.

I picture my late husband, first as he was before his diagnosis—a relatively youthful, spry, and dapper man with energy to burn—and then as the disease took hold, took over—a stooped, tired, and ultimately defeated shadow of his former self. I try pushing the latter image aside, but it lingers, refusing to disappear alto-gether. "Of course, I did."

"I don't believe you."

"It's true," I say. "It was so hard watching him suffer. I just wanted his pain to end." I swallow, take a deep breath before con-tinuing. "But there were also times when I felt as sorry for myself as I felt for him, when my tears were more about me than they were about what Bob was going through." I shake my head at the memory. This is the first time I've confessed this to anyone, the first time I've spoken these words out loud. I feel a wave of exhilara-tion, followed immediately by a larger wave of guilt. "So, not such a good girl after all," I say.

"I don't know about that. I, for one, think you're pretty ter-rific."

We fall silent.

I look around the large square room, trying not to read too much into Lorne's last remark. I see that every table is full, and the bar at the far end of the room is at least three people deep. I note at least three older women whose faces have become expression-less masks in their efforts to hold back the ravages of time. *What do these women see when they look in the mirror?* I wonder.

"Think you might ever get married again?" Lorne is asking.

"What?"

"I asked if you've ever thought you might get married again."

"Can't say that I have."

"What about sex?"

"Sex?"

"Sex?" I hear Jenny Cooper demand.

"Ever think about it?"

"I try not to," I say, although the truth is that I think about it more often than I'd like. Even more so since I saw the images on Mick's computer.

"I think about it a lot," he offers when I fail to ask. "I miss it."

I nod, say nothing. *Why am I more comfortable talking about death than I am about sex? And is it the thought of sex I'm un-comfortable with, or the thought of sex with Lorne?*

"You don't?" he asks.

"I'm seventy-six years old," I remind him, not for the first time.

"So what? I'm closing in on eighty. I still want to have sex. Maybe not as often as I used to," he says with a laugh. "But oc-casionally would be nice."

The waitress arrives with our salads.

Thank you, God, I say silently, digging into my Caesar salad as if I've never seen food before.

"How is it?" Lorne asks.

"Delicious. Yours?"

"Not bad," he says with a smile.

We finish our salads, watch as the waitress clears the plates from the table and returns with our main course.

"I've made you uncomfortable," Lorne remarks.

"No," I lie. "Not at all."

"Good," he says, his hand reaching across the table to cover mine. "Because I'd like to do this again."

CHAPTER TWENTY-FOUR

"We lived in this shitty little house in Morro Bay," Jenny is saying. "Morro Bay is on the coast of California, between Los Angeles and San Francisco, just north of San Luis Obispo. You've heard of San Luis Obispo, haven't you?"

"Isn't that where William Randolph Hearst had an estate?" I ask.

"Close enough. The Hearst Estate is actually in San Simeon, which is about forty miles north of San Luis Obispo."

I smile. *Interesting what facts the mind decides to keep and what it chooses to discard.*

"And what is William Randolph Hearst famous for?" she prods.

"He was a newspaper baron, I believe."

"You believe correctly. You get a gold star, Linda Davidson."

I feel my cheeks blush with pride. *Is this how my former students used to feel when I offered a tiny morsel of praise?*

"Why do you want to know about William Randolph Hearst?" Jenny asks.

"I don't."

"Then why did you bring him up?"

I start to protest, then stop. I am, in fact, the one who introduced his name. "You were telling me about your father," I remind her, trying to nudge her back into our initial conversation.

Jenny tucks some stray gray hairs behind her ear and frowns. "He was a horrible man. Awful. Awful. He strangled my mother. *To death!*" she adds, eyes opening wide, long, bony fingers smoothing the stained front of her loose-fitting gray blouse. "I saw the whole thing. Did I tell you that?"

"Yes. I can't imagine . . ."

"Who are you?" she asks suddenly. "Are you with the CIA?"

"No. I'm not with the CIA, the FBI, or the police," I recite, hoping to avoid going down this path again. We've already been through this several times since I arrived at Legacy Place some twenty minutes ago. "I'm Linda Davidson. Remember?"

"You came to see me in the hospital," she says, a flash of recognition lighting up her eyes.

"That's right."

"That was very nice of you. You're a nice person, Linda Davidson."

"You were telling me about your father," I say again. This is, after all, the reason I'm here, hoping to hear more, to figure out if Jenny Cooper could possibly be telling the truth. While I'm still highly doubtful that she's the cold-blooded killer she claims to be, I think that she might actually be telling the truth about her father.

"Oh, him." She makes a face, as if she's just smelled something bad. "He was mean. A meanie-poo, as my mother used to say." She laughs. "A poo-poo meanie," she adds in a weirdly childlike voice. "He used to beat my brothers with his big brown belt. My mommy tried to stop him, but then he'd beat her, too."

"Did he beat you?" I ask.

Her eyes cloud over with tears. "He said it was for my own good, so I wouldn't end up like Mommy. Do you know what Morro Bay is famous for?"

"I don't," I admit, hoping we aren't about to go off on another tangent. But this is how Jenny talks, I've come to understand. In fits and starts. Back and forth between sanity and madness. One foot in; one foot out.

Enter either at your peril.

"It's famous for Morro Rock, an ancient volcanic mound at the end of Morro Rock Bay, inside the Morro Bay State Park," she tells me, as if reading from some invisible guidebook. "Morro Bay is sometimes called the Gibraltar of the Pacific. Did you know that?"

"And that's where you grew up?"

"Yep." She starts rocking back and forth. "My father was a fisherman, so he was away a lot. We used to like it when he went away. Except he'd always come back. And he was usually drunk. Drunk as a skunk. Drunk as a skunk," Jenny sings out. "Do you know why they call it 'drunk as a skunk'?"

"I'm afraid I don't."

"I'll tell you why, and it's not because skunks drink," Jenny says with a laugh. "It's from this poem that was written in the late eighteen hundreds, goes something like 'To see a man come home so drunk, it makes her loathe him like a skunk.' Hah! That's a good one. 'Loathe him like a skunk.'"

I smile, trying to decide whether to stay and listen to more such gibberish or quit while I'm ahead. But my house is already crowded with two people working from home, and I don't want to disturb the delicate truce that seems to have taken root over the weekend. The truth is that I have nowhere else to be, and not much else to do.

In the past few weeks, I've finished cleaning out my closets and taking whatever was salvageable to Goodwill, made several unsuccessful trips to the Gardens Mall in hopes of finding something— *anything*—that looks even vaguely flattering, that doesn't make me look as if I'm trying too hard: to be current, to be hip, to be young. I've walked up and down the aisles at Barnes & Noble searching for a book that interests me, wandered through Target and Costco, hoping for something that might catch my eye, grab my attention. I've had my teeth cleaned and my eyes checked, and even made an appointment for my yearly checkup with our family doctor for sometime in June. I've made sure the prescriptions for my various medications—a statin to control my cholesterol, a pill to keep my blood pressure in check, yet another pill to maintain proper thyroid levels—are up-to-date. Just this morning, I did the grocery shopping for the entire week.

So now I have nothing to do and nowhere to be.

Story of my life, as Bob used to say.

It was different when Bob was alive. After we retired from teaching, we traveled—to New York, to England and France and Italy, to Toronto and Montreal—took several courses in both ancient history and current affairs through the Lifelong Learning program at Florida Atlantic University, went regularly to the theater, had frequent dinners with friends. Then Bob got sick, friends grew scarce, and my job—my life—became taking care of him.

And then he died.

And I was summarily let go from my job, left floating aimlessly through my life.

Then my best friend developed Alzheimer's and forgot who I was. Forgot who *she* was.

And who are we without our memories? I wonder now. Memories both shape and define us. We are nothing but empty shells without them.

And so, here I sit, talking to an old lady who saw her father strangle her mother when she was a child and subsequently murdered not only him but at least three other people.

Or not.

Maybe she's making the whole thing up, her imagination filling in for the memories that have deserted her.

Whatever the case may be, I have nowhere else to go and nothing else to do. I'm along for the ride, I decide, leaning back in my chair and smiling at her wizened old face. "Tell me about your father," I say.

CHAPTER TWENTY-FIVE

"He was a very handsome man, my daddy was. Even his name was handsome. Handsome name for a handsome man. He was very handsome, my daddy was. Did I tell you that?"

"Your father was a handsome man," I repeat, hoping to move the conversation along.

"Handsome man, ugly disposition. He was a drunk. Did you know that?"

"Drunk as a skunk," I offer.

"Hah! That's a good one. Where'd you hear that?"

"You just . . ." I stop, take a few seconds to gather my thoughts as Jenny stares at me expectantly. "What happened after you saw him kill your mother?" I ask.

"I told you. He took us to the diner."

"What about your mother's sister?"

"What about her?"

"You said that your mother had a sister she supposedly went to visit. She never called to speak to your mother? She never came by, wondered what happened to her?"

"What are you talking about?"

"You told me that your father said she'd gone to visit her sister . . ."

"I did not."

"I'm sorry," I say quickly. "I thought you said . . ."

"My mother was an only child. She didn't have any sisters."

"I'm sorry. Clearly, I misunderstood."

"Yes, you did." Jenny's lips form an exaggerated pout, as if she is holding back tears.

"What about your brothers?"

"What about them?"

"Are they still alive?"

"No. They died. I didn't kill them," she adds, unprompted.

I almost smile. "Tell me about killing your father."

She says nothing for several long seconds. I sit very still, not sure if she's heard me, has fallen asleep, or is simply ignoring me. I've just opened my mouth to voice my request again when she raises her index finger to her lips to quiet me.

"I left home when I was seventeen, right after my high school graduation," Jenny begins. "My brothers were long gone by that time. Good riddance, I say. They turned out just like Daddy. They both drank, did drugs. Tommy even spent time in jail. He died in a fight when he was in his twenties. Some drunk stabbed him. Not sure what happened to Jake, except that he's dead, too. But I didn't kill him."

"Where did you go when you left home?"

"Moved to Los Angeles. Went to UCLA."

"UCLA?"

"Don't look so surprised. I'm not stupid, you know."

"I know. I wasn't suggesting . . ."

"I was really good in school. Straight As."

I nod, say nothing.

"And I had this teacher—Mrs. Woolcott, her name was. She said I had a great head for math and sciences. And that I should apply to college. I told her we didn't have the money for that, and that even if we did, my daddy would never agree to it. But she told me that with my grades I could probably get a full scholarship, and she'd do whatever she could to help me. And she did."

"That's wonderful."

Jenny begins fussing with a tiny piece of lint clinging to the fabric of her chair. "I worked really hard, in school and out, bunch of odd jobs to support myself, and I took out a shitload of loans, had to, even with the scholarships, and eventually got my degree. Became a pharmacist. Went to work for this guy on Sunset Boulevard. I liked it there. He was a nice man."

"Did you kill him?"

"Hah!" She laughs. "You're so funny." The laugh becomes a snort. "You know what the best part of being a pharmacist is? Learning how easy it is to kill people with the right combination of drugs and without leaving a trace," she answers before I have a chance to ask. "You don't even need prescription medications. Actually, it's better without them."

I lean forward, realize that I'm holding my breath. "How old were you when you killed your father?"

She gives my question a moment's thought. "I'm not sure. Twenty-five, maybe twenty-six. Have you ever killed anyone?"

"What? No!"

"Ever thought about it?"

"Never."

"That's too bad. It can be quite cathartic," she states, matter-of-factly.

"Was killing your father cathartic?"

She lets out a veritable hoot of glee. "You bet your backside it was!" She begins playing with a button on the cuff of her sleeve. "I went home one Christmas. Found him in the kitchen, drunk as usual. Place was a mess. I offered to clean it up. Did a real nice job, too. Made him a wonderful dinner. Even brought my own special sauce. Watched him eat everything on his plate. Poured him a big glass of whiskey to wash it down. Then sat back and watched him writhe on the floor in agony for the rest of the night. Eventually, poor bastard choked on his own vomit." Jenny gives a final tug on her button, smiling as it pops to the floor.

Ralph McMillan choked on his own vomit.

I sink back in my chair, watching the joy radiating across Jenny's face, convinced she's telling the truth. *This frail old woman with whom I've been spending so much of my time, whose company I've grown to enjoy, even look forward to, is an unrepentant serial killer.* "You really poisoned him," I acknowledge, not sure which man I'm referring to.

"Shh. It's a secret. You can't tell anyone."

I nod. The woman is ninety-two years old and suffering from dementia. Even if I were to share her secret with the world, who would believe me?

"And the police never questioned you? They never thought his death was suspicious?" I ask, although I already know the answer.

"Hah." Jenny laughs. "You've been watching too much television, Linda Davidson. The police aren't interested in *solving* crimes. They just want to *close* them." She shakes her head. "They weren't going to let some nasty old drunk ruin their Christmas."

We lean back in our respective chairs. Neither one of us says another word.

CHAPTER TWENTY-SIX

"Hello, Grandma?"

It's almost noon, the day after my visit with Jenny, and I've spent most of the morning on the patio in my tiny backyard. Kleo has been hunched over the dining room table for hours, working on her dissertation, while Mick is in his office, his door firmly closed, supposedly hard at work. I'm trying not to imagine what he's doing. I'm also making a concerted effort not to recall the disturbing images I saw on his computer screen. Although what is it they say? Some things you just can't unsee.

So, here I sit, struggling to read a novel by a young man whom critics have dubbed the latest "most important voice of his generation." It's not the book's fault I'm struggling. It's that the "most important voice of his generation" is simply no match for the barrage of naked, faceless men I see slamming against the backsides of naked, faceless women, their acrobatics all but obliterating his impressive flow of words.

What's the matter with me?

After Bob died, I pretty much banished all thoughts of sex from my mind. At my age, I assumed it was likely a thing of the past. Nor could I imagine another man's hands caressing me, let alone penetrating me with the violence I witnessed on Mick's computer. And yet, I've been thinking of little else ever since.

So, I confess that it's something of a relief when the cordless phone I've taken outside with me rings, and I answer it before it can ring a second time. "Hello?"

"Hello, Grandma?" the voice says in return.

I smile. "Hayden, is that you?"

When my younger daughter, Vanessa, was sixteen, she announced that she intended to be married and have three children by the time she was twenty-five. Bob and I had exchanged worried glances. "Where did we go wrong?" I exclaimed.

Fortunately, things didn't go exactly as planned. Vanessa chose college over marriage to her high school sweetheart, and she graduated from Columbia with a master's degree in business. She eventually wed a successful hedge fund manager and enjoyed her own thriving career before deciding, almost a decade later, to have the first of the three children she'd always wanted. The oldest is now fourteen, the youngest ten. Two boys and a girl.

None of them named Hayden.

"Yes, Grandma. It's me," the voice continues. "How are you?"

"I'm fine, sweetheart," I answer, deciding to play along with the young man pretending to be my grandson. I know that such scammers are notorious in South Florida for preying on the elderly.

How does he know? I wonder. *Did he find my name online? Is there an asterisk beside my name that informs him of my senior status?* "How are *you*?" I ask.

"I'm okay," he says. "But . . ."

"What's the matter, darling? Has something happened? Your mother . . . ?"

"She's fine," he says quickly. "It's just that . . ."

"What is it, sweetheart? Tell me."

The sliding glass door to the patio opens. "Who is it?" Kleo mouths from the doorway, eyebrows raised in concern.

I shake my head. "Please, sweetheart. Tell Grandma what's wrong."

"Grandma?" Kleo whispers, knowing that my grandchildren have always called me Nana.

"It's just that . . . I've been in an accident."

"An accident? Oh, my God. Are you hurt?"

"Who *is* it?" Kleo whispers, alarm spreading across her pretty face.

"It's a scammer," I mouth.

"A scammer? What are you doing? Hang up!"

"Sweetheart?" I say instead, pressing the phone tighter to my ear.

"I'm okay," the young man rushes to assure me. "I was driving Mom's car, and I got this text, and I swear, I just looked down for a second, but next thing I knew, I slammed into the car in front of me."

"That's so horrible. You're sure you're okay?"

"I'm fine. But the other guy . . ."

"The other guy?" I prod.

"He wasn't so lucky. He went through his windshield."

"Oh, my God! Is he . . . dead?"

"Hang up!" Kleo says, louder this time, and I turn away, covering the receiver with the palm of my hand to block out the sound of her voice.

"No," the scammer continues, "but he's unconscious and they took him to the hospital. And . . ."

"And?"

"The police came and they arrested me."

"They arrested you? Oh, you poor baby."

"Mom, please," Kleo urges.

"So I called this friend of mine. His father's a lawyer. And he's offered to help me get bail."

"Oh, thank God."

"But here's the problem. I don't have any money, and I can't go to Mom and Dad because they'll be so mad, and I was hoping that maybe you . . ."

"Maybe I?"

"... could lend me the money? Just a few thousand dollars. I swear I'll pay you back."

"Of course you will. I know that. Tell me what I have to do."

"It's easy. You just go to the bank and do a wire transfer into this lawyer's account. Do you have a pencil to write his number down?"

"I'll go get one. Oh, and while I'm doing that," I say in my sweetest, most grandmotherly voice, "I need you to do something for me."

"Anything."

"I need you to go fuck yourself!" I promptly disconnect the call, smiling triumphantly at Kleo.

"Holy shit!" she says, her face ashen.

"I can't tell you how good that felt."

"Who *are* you?" she asks.

"What's going on out here?" Mick says, coming up behind his wife, munching on a fistful of peanuts.

"Mom just told a scammer to go fuck himself!"

Mick looks delighted. "She did? Good for her!"

"No. Not good for her! You don't know who these people are," she tells me.

"I know that they're a bunch of con artists trying to steal money from unsuspecting old people," I answer. "And I'm sick of it."

"You go, girl," says Mick.

"Please don't encourage her," Kleo says.

Mick shrugs. "I'm thirsty. Who wants a beer?"

The phone rings again.

"Don't answer it!" Kleo instructs.

"Don't be silly." I click on, bracing myself for a barrage of insults from the scammer I've just scammed.

"Linda, hi! I was hoping I'd catch you at home," the voice says.

"Lorne," I acknowledge, ignoring the wink I'm getting from Mick as Kleo leads him toward the kitchen. "Is everything okay? Carol . . . ?"

"Not having a great day," he acknowledges. "I was hoping

maybe you were free for dinner tonight. I could use a friendly face."

I'm not sure that's such a good idea, I think, although I'm not sure why. "Why not?" I hear myself say, refusing to think about it further. "Sounds nice."

CHAPTER TWENTY-SEVEN

We meet at Divino's, an Italian restaurant in a space that was once home to an International House of Pancakes. The restaurant is located in a tiny plaza just north of the intersection of U.S. 1 and PGA Boulevard, behind several other buildings, and not visible from either main street. Not exactly a tourist destination, and the restaurant would surely do better in a more visible, upscale location. But the food is terrific, and it's usually not too difficult to get a reservation, even on relatively short notice.

I squeeze my car into a space between two large SUVs, recognizing Lorne's late-model charcoal Porsche Panamera as I walk toward the restaurant's shrub-filled outdoor patio, expecting to see Lorne among the smattering of diners. But he isn't there, so I proceed into Divino's dark, air-conditioned interior.

"Linda! Over here!" a voice calls out immediately.

It takes a few seconds for me to spot him waving from a far corner. It's just past 6:00 P.M., so the restaurant doesn't have many diners yet, and most of those have chosen to sit outside, which isn't surprising. It's a beautiful, warm night, ideal for outdoor dining, and I can't help wondering why Lorne has chosen to sit inside.

Until I see him.

"My God, what happened to your face?" I exclaim, staring at the large bruise circling his left eye.

"Seems I ran into an errant right hook," he says, pulling out my chair for me.

"You were in a fight?"

"Not exactly." He returns to his seat, pointing to the glass of red wine in front of me. "I know you don't like to drink and drive, but I figured one glass would be all right, and if I remember correctly, Primitivo is your favorite red."

I nod. "Good memory." I recall the last time we shared a bottle of Primitivo, back when Bob was still alive and Carol was still Carol.

"She did this to you," I state more than ask, reaching for my glass. I take a long sip of the wine. Clearly, I'm going to need it.

"It wasn't her fault."

"What happened?"

He shakes his head. "You won't believe it."

"You'd be surprised by what I believe these days," I tell him, ignoring the quizzical look in his eyes and taking another sip of my wine.

"I went to see her this morning," he begins. "She wasn't in her room, so I went looking for her, eventually found her one floor down in some old guy's room, sitting next to him on the edge of his bed, giggling like a goddamn schoolgirl. She was staring at him, adoringly. He had his hand on her knee. Her blouse was unbuttoned."

"Oh, God."

"I won't lie. It was quite the shock."

"I can only imagine," I say, trying not to. Carol had never been much of a flirt, being far too direct to be a successful coquette. And she'd adored Lorne, would never have dreamed of looking at another man.

"I mean, they warn you about this sort of thing, people behaving inappropriately, forming romantic attachments with other residents, but . . ." Lorne shakes his head. "You just don't think . . ."

I motion toward his face. "So, what happened?"

"Well, first, I tried to ignore what I was seeing. I said something like 'Hey, Carol. How are you doing today? Why don't you come with me and leave this nice gentleman alone?' And she just smiled and didn't move, went back to gazing lovingly into his eyes. So I approached the bed, reached for her hand. But she pulled it away, gave me this really angry look. So, I tried again. A little more forcefully this time. And she started screaming at me to leave her alone, that I was a miserable son of a bitch, plus a bunch of other choice phrases . . ."

"None of which she means," I offer weakly. "You know that."

"Maybe not the old Carol. But this new one . . ." His voice disappears into the surrounding air. "They say that some people who develop Alzheimer's become the exact opposite of what they were like before," he says after several seconds. "If they were nasty and mean, they become sweet and nice; if they were sweet and nice, they become angry and mean. It's a bit like that movie *Invasion of the Body Snatchers*. You ever see it?"

"Can't say that I have."

"It's about these creatures from outer space who come to earth in the shape of giant pods and then gradually morph into the people around them, leaving their victims' bodies intact but robbing them of all human emotions." He shakes his head. "I guess a little bit of anger is preferable to no emotion at all."

I reach across the table to cover his hand with my own, in a gesture of sympathy and support. He quickly covers my hand with his free one, his touch sending unexpected, and unwanted, tingles up my arm.

"Is that when she hit you?" I ask, sliding my hand away from his and returning it to my glass. I take another sip of my wine. At this rate, I'll be drunk before we even order.

"I was reaching for her arm and she just spun around and clocked me. I went down like a ton of bricks. It's actually quite funny, when you think about it." He tries to laugh, but the laugh catches in his throat and dies.

The waiter approaches and announces the night's specials.

"You have to try the eggplant parmesan and the branzino," Lorne says. "They were Carol's favorites."

"Then that's what I'll have," I tell the waiter.

Lorne orders the antipasto and the lasagna, then lifts his glass, clicking it against mine in a toast. "To better days," he says.

"To better days," I agree.

We're leaving the restaurant when a gentleman at one of the outside tables stands up to block my path. "Excuse me," he says. "Mrs. Davidson?"

I stare at the balding, middle-aged man, whose noticeable paunch is pushing against the multiple palm trees of his Hawaiian shirt. "I'm sorry. Do I know you?"

"It's me," he announces, as if this is all the clarity I need. "Stan Tanner."

I smile, although neither his name nor his face is remotely familiar.

"Grade ten, English! I was the skinny kid in the back row, the one making farting noises."

"Oh, my God," I exclaim, watching the years fall from the man's face and his head fill with a shock of black curls. "I can't believe you recognized me. It has to be . . . what? Forty years?"

"You look exactly the same!"

"Well, that's not quite true."

"Your wife was the best teacher I ever had," he tells Lorne.

"Oh, no," I begin. "He's not . . ."

"She changed my life," Stan Tanner continues, ignoring my attempt to correct him. "Made me realize I could be more than the class clown, that I had real potential to make something of myself. It's thanks to your encouragement," he says, turning his attention back to me, "that I went on to college, became a lawyer, if you can believe it." He motions toward the other three people at his table. "This is my wife, Sarah. And our friends David and Wendy Barclay. This is Mr. and Mrs. Davidson," he says.

I'm about to inform him of his mistake when Lorne steps forward and offers his hand. "Pleasure to meet you," he says.

CHAPTER TWENTY-EIGHT

Twenty minutes later, I pull into the parking lot at Legacy Place.

It's just past eight o'clock, and I've been driving aimlessly around ever since I said good night to Lorne, needing to clear my head before going home. The startling events of the evening have combined to make me light-headed and disoriented.

What the hell is happening?

First, Lorne tells me that my best friend, the kind, loyal, and always gentle Carol, is not only openly cavorting with another man but has turned violent, her physical assault leaving him with a noticeable shiner. Then he lets a former student of mine believe that he is my husband. ("I just thought it was easier that way," he explained, as he walked me to my car.)

And then he kissed me.

Okay, so it was just a kiss on the cheek. But it lingered perhaps a beat too long, and I can still feel his breath brushing against the side of my lips as his arms moved to surround me in a goodbye hug.

I've been trying to convince myself that there was no romantic intent in that hug, that it was simply the embrace of two good friends saying good night, the way we used to when Bob and Carol were still in the picture, but I'm not so sure. And if I'm

being honest—and this is the part that is really making my head
spin—I'm not sure which scenario I prefer.

Friend or lover?

I've been a widow for two years. I thought that part of my
life was over. I'm not even sure things still work. My body has
changed. I can no longer predict how it will respond to once-
pleasurable stimuli. Still, I have to admit that it felt good to have
a man's arms around me, to have his lips brush gently against my
skin. To feel protected, to feel desired.

Do I really need the complication of a new romance at my age?
I think with my next breath. Especially with the husband of my
closest friend, even if she no longer remembers who he is, and has
apparently moved on? I remind myself that, despite the circumstances, Lorne is still a married man.

What will people think if they start seeing us together? How
open is Lorne prepared to be?

Of course, I could be reading too much into things. Lorne would
probably be flabbergasted to learn how his innocent actions have
been interpreted.

*Mis*interpreted.

Still . . .

Your wife was the best teacher I ever had, I hear Stan Tanner
tell Lorne. *She changed my life.*

Why didn't Lorne correct him?

For that matter, why didn't I?

And how can it be, I wonder as I sit behind the wheel of my car
in the now mostly empty parking lot of Legacy Place, that I could
have had such a profound effect on someone I can barely recall,
that I have almost no memory of a man whose life I apparently
changed?

And what in God's name am I doing here?

I stare at the white six-story facility in front of me, hearing the
roar of the ocean from the other side of the highway. Unless I'm
just imagining the sound. Unless I'm imagining everything.

Is this how it starts? I wonder, getting out of my car and walk-

ing toward the front entrance, the half-moon winking at me from
the side of the building. And is it preferable to lose one's health or
one's mind? Door number one or door number two? Which do
you choose?

I pull open the building's front door, happy that it isn't locked
for the night. Visitors are discouraged after nine o'clock in the
evening, when most of the residents are already asleep.

I make my way to Carol's room, intent on apologizing for time
spent with her husband, for the wild thoughts swirling through
my brain, hoping her shy smile will absolve me of the guilt I feel.
You deserve to be happy, I can almost hear her say as I push open
the door to her unit. *Take good care of him. Take good care of
each other.*

Instead, the voice I hear is harsh and accusatory. "What are you
doing here so late?"

It takes me a second to realize the voice is emanating not from
Carol's bed, but from somewhere behind me.

"Jenny!" I say, spinning around. She is standing in the middle
of the hallway, wearing a long pink flannelette nightgown, her
hair pushed almost violently away from her face, as if she's been
caught in a sudden windstorm. "You scared me."

"I saw you come in," she says. "I was in the lounge. You didn't
see me."

"No, I didn't."

"That's because I was hiding. Your friend's asleep," she adds in
the same breath, as if one thought naturally follows the other.

"Yes, she is."

"Good. Then you can come talk to me."

She turns and heads down the corridor toward her room, assuming I'm right behind, not bothering to check. "Is it breakfast
time?" she asks as we enter her apartment and settle into our respective chairs. "Have you brought me a raspberry croissant?"

"God, no!" I answer, wincing at the memory of the last time I
brought her raspberry croissants.

"What's your problem?" Jenny asks.

"What?"

"Your face went all funny, like you smelled a fart or something. I didn't fart. It wasn't me."

Grade ten, English! I hear Stan Tanner exclaim. *I was the skinny kid in the back row, the one making farting noises.*

"I had a funny thing happen to me tonight," I find myself telling Jenny. "I ran into a former student of mine."

"You ran into him? Did you kill him?"

"What? No! I didn't mean that I ran into him with my car . . . I just meant that I saw him."

"What's funny about that?"

"Apparently, I had a profound influence on his life, and I don't remember him from Adam."

"Who's Adam?"

"There's no Adam. It's just an expression."

"Silly expression."

"Tell me more about the people you killed," I hear myself say.

"Who says I killed anyone?"

"You did."

"Shh," she advises, trembling index finger rising to her lips. "It's a secret."

"I won't tell anyone," I say, another twinge of guilt poking at my side. I've already told Kleo and Mick. I wait for the usual follow-up questions—am I with the CIA, the FBI, the police?

Instead she says, "Who's Eudora Welty?"

"What?"

"Eudora Welty. Is she a real person?"

"She's a writer," I answer. "Or she *was*."

"She was real?"

"Yes. She won a Pulitzer Prize for fiction back in the seventies, I think it was. She's been dead for quite some time."

"How much time?"

"Twenty . . . thirty years. Why do you ask?"

"Don't know. Her name's been rattling around in my brain all day. Such a strange name. Don't you think? I thought she couldn't possibly be real, that I must have made her up. What kind of name is Eudora Welty?"

I shake my head. *Are we really having this conversation?*

"How did she die?"

"I have no idea."

"But you're certain she was real," Jenny says, wistfully.

"She was real," I concur, watching Jenny's eyes flutter and then close.

I wait a minute to see whether she'll reopen them. "I should go," I decide, pushing myself to my feet. "Let you get some sleep."

"Don't you want to know about the other people I killed?" she asks, eyes still closed.

I lower myself back into my chair. "I do," I say, watching a smile slowly stretch across the line of her thin lips. "Absolutely. I do."

CHAPTER TWENTY-NINE

"After I killed my father," Jenny begins, matter-of-factly, "I returned to Los Angeles. I was a pharmacist. I told you that, didn't I?"

"You did."

"And I was working in this big, fancy drugstore on Sunset Boulevard, just down the street from where I was living on Larrabee Street. Eleven-eleven Larrabee Street, apartment five. You ever been to Los Angeles?"

"Once," I tell her. "A long time ago."

"Did you visit the Sunset Strip?"

"I'm sure we did."

"Who's we?"

"My husband, Bob, and I. He died two years ago," I offer, before she can ask. "I didn't kill him," I add, and we both smile.

"The apartment building was one of those two-story numbers, built around a center swimming pool. Looked like one of those cheap motels. Nobody ever stayed there very long. You could rent by the month. Didn't have to sign a lease or anything. Los Angeles is a very transitory town—interesting word, 'transitory.' People were always moving in and out. Lots of aspiring actors and musicians. 'Aspiring.' Another interesting word. Don't you think?"

"Never really thought about it."

"It's hopeful. It's a hopeful word."

"Yes, I guess it is."

"'Transitory,' not so much."

"No," I agree, wondering where, if anywhere, we're going with this.

"Anyway, that's how I met my husband."

"I'm sorry. I must have missed something. *How* did you meet your husband?"

"I just told you."

"No, you didn't. You just said that L.A. is a very transitory town and that the apartment where you lived was full of aspiring actors and musicians."

"Interesting words," she says. "'Transitory' and 'aspiring.'"

"Did you marry one of those actors or musicians?" I ask, trying to get us back on track.

"God, no! What would I want with an unemployed actor or musician? The last thing I needed was some useless man like my daddy who couldn't rub two dimes together."

"I'm not sure I'm following."

"Well, pay attention, Linda Davidson!"

I nod, sufficiently chastised, deciding to remain silent. Interrupting Jenny's erratic chain of thought only seemed to move us farther off topic.

"Parker Rubini," she announces, with a firm nod of her head.

"Excuse me?"

"You're excused."

"I meant . . ."

She smiles. "Parker Rubini is the man I married." The smile turns into an unexpectedly raucous laugh. "Hah! What kind of name is Parker Rubini? Who the hell names a child Parker Rubini?"

"He didn't live in your building?"

"Who said that?"

"I thought you did."

"No," she says sternly. "I said there were lots of would-be actors and musicians in my building. I didn't say that's *all* there were."

"So, he *did* live in your building?"

"No."

Dear God.

"He lived with his mother in this big mansion in Bel Air. But he was friends with someone who lived in my building. This guitar player named—" The sentence comes to an abrupt stop. "Why do you want to know what his name is?"

"You were telling me about Parker Rubini," I venture, ignoring her question.

"You know who the hell names a child Parker Rubini?" she asks suddenly, eyes opening wide and filling with unmistakable fury. "Mrs. Francesca Rubini, that's who! May she rot in hell." The smile that follows is equal parts childlike and chilling.

"Okay, so let me see if I have this straight," I say. "Parker Rubini was friends with a guitar player who lived in your building . . ."

"Eleven-eleven Larrabee Street."

"And that's where you met."

"No."

Somebody help me, I plead silently.

You asked for this, comes the silent reply.

"Parker was out by the pool with his friend, the guitar player, and he got this terrible sunburn, and they came into the drugstore where I was working, needing some ointment. And he liked what he saw—I was quite beautiful in those days, if I say so myself—and he asked me out. And I figured, what the hell, so I said yes."

"And you got married?"

"Five months later! We eloped. I thought his mother would split a gut. She never thought I was good enough for her precious son."

"Why not? You were beautiful, smart, educated. You had a career . . ." *She didn't know you'd killed your father,* came the silent addendum.

"She was a widow and Parker was her only child. Her husband

had left her tons of money, and she probably assumed I was after Parker's. Wasn't true. I loved Parker. Or I *did,* in the beginning. But she had her heart set on him marrying a girl from a 'good' family, as she was always saying. And I sure wasn't that. Anyway, she never liked me. Did everything in her power to bust us apart."

"How long were you married?"

"Eleven miserable years."

"Surely they weren't all miserable?"

"How would you know?"

"I just assumed . . ."

"Never assume anything, Linda Davidson."

"Sorry."

"And stop apologizing. You apologize too much. I told you that."

"How old were you when you got married?" I ask.

"Not sure. Thirty. Maybe thirty-one." Jenny rubs her eyes and pulls at her hair. "I'm hungry. Is it breakfast time?"

"No. It's actually almost nine o'clock."

"So I missed breakfast?"

"At night."

"It's nine o'clock at night?"

"That's right."

"That's past my bedtime. I should be in bed. What are you doing here so late? You should leave."

I half rise from my seat. "Can you at least finish your story?" I ask, meekly.

"What story?"

"You were telling me about your husband."

"Which one?"

"Parker Rubini."

"What kind of name is Parker Rubini? You're making that up!"

"You said your husband's name was Parker Rubini."

"Huh," she says. "What else did I say?"

"That you were married for eleven years."

"Eleven-eleven Larrabee Street. *Correctamento!*"

"Did you kill Parker?" I whisper, hoping for one final moment of clarity before I leave.

"Yes, I did. I certainly did," she says, a mischievous grin over-taking her entire face. "But that was later. First . . . *first,* I killed his mother!"

CHAPTER THIRTY

"You killed his mother?" I repeat.

"Whose mother?" she asks.

Here we go again. "Parker Rubini's mother."

She looks confused. "Who names a child Parker Rubini?"

"Apparently, Francesca Rubini," I answer, my patience starting to wear thin.

Jenny laughs, loud and long. "Hah! You're right. You get a gold star, Linda Davidson!"

"You're playing with me," I acknowledge, the old doubts returning. "Is *anything* you've told me true?"

Another laugh. "How would I know? I'm demented. Remember?"

"Are you?"

"Are *you?*" she counters.

"I'm beginning to think so."

Yet another laugh, the loudest one yet. "I like you, Linda Davidson," she says. "You're funny."

"I like you, too, Jenny Cooper," I admit. "Did you really kill four people?"

"Which would make you like me more?" she asks, slyly. "If I did or I didn't?"

The question takes my breath away. I know what I *should* say—that of course, I'd like her more if she hadn't murdered four people. But the truth is I honestly don't know. Would I be sitting here talking to her if I felt she was just some pathetic old woman adrift in a sea of fantasies? If I weren't at least intrigued by the possibility that she could be the cold-blooded killer she claims to be?

Will I be disappointed to find out she's not?

"Tell me something interesting about yourself," she directs, unexpectedly. "Other than that you're fucking your best friend's husband. I already know that."

I jump to my feet. "I most certainly am not sleeping with my best friend's husband."

"Who said anything about sleeping?"

"Dear God." *What the hell am I doing here?* "I think you're right, that it's time for me to go."

"Oh, sit down. Don't be such a prude."

"I'm not *fucking* my best friend's husband," I say, adamantly.

"I killed four people," she counters.

I sit back down. "You win."

She laughs. "You have children, I assume," she says, as if our last few exchanges never happened.

"Two girls. You?"

"Me? No! I never wanted children," she says. "Tell me something interesting about your girls."

I shrug, deciding to play along. "Well, my daughter Kleo is a teacher, like her father and I were. She's taking some time off now to work on her PhD. She doesn't have any kids. Not that she didn't want any, but she didn't get married until she was almost forty, and by then, it was pretty much too late. Plus, her husband wasn't all that keen, so . . . My other daughter, Vanessa, she has three, two boys and a girl . . ."

"This is a very boring story," Jenny says, yawning widely.

"I'm boring you?"

"I told you to tell me something interesting."

Really, Linda. With everything that's going on in the world, is that the best you could come up with? I hear my mother say.

"We can't all kill people," I tell Jenny.

"Hah! That's more like it!"

"Why did you kill Parker's mother?" I ask.

"Because she was a witch. That's witch with a capital *B*."

"How was she a witch?"

"She was mean . . ."

A meanie-poo? A poo-poo meanie? I'm tempted to interject, but I remain silent, waiting for her to continue.

"She was living with us. Or technically, I guess, we were living with her, in that big old mansion of hers in Bel Air. So, she was always around, lurking in the shadows, digging into my background, asking questions about my mom and dad, my brothers, all that stuff I didn't want to talk about. She told Parker that she didn't trust me, that there was something 'off' about me. Threatened to hire a private detective to find out 'the truth,' as she liked to say, told Parker that he deserved someone better than me, that I was only after his money, and he should divorce me before I got pregnant and he'd have to pay me a shitload of alimony and child support. It didn't work—in those days, I pretty much had Parker wrapped around my little finger. A good blow job goes a long way," she says, giving me a knowing wink.

"Oh, God," I mutter.

"There you go, getting all prudish again! Were you always such a prude, Linda Davidson?"

Were you always such a good girl? I hear Lorne ask.

"Can we go back to talking about how you murdered your mother-in-law?" *Could those words really have come out of my mouth?*

"She said she was going to change her will, if that's what it took for Parker to come to his senses," Jenny continues without further prompting, "leave everything to charity. Said she'd make sure I never saw a cent. And all this time, I was busting my backside trying to be a good wife, a good daughter-in-law. I was determined to kill the old bat with kindness. And then finally, I just said, 'Fuck kindness, I'm gonna kill her for real.' So I did."

"How?" I ask, the only word I can manage to push out of my mouth.

"Poison. Same way I killed my father. Same way I killed them all."

I nod. "Your special recipe."

"With a few modifications, of course. I had to be more careful where Francesca Rubini was concerned. Couldn't afford to have her writhing around all night on the floor in pain, much as I would have enjoyed that. I had to make it look like just another run-of-the-mill, old-fashioned heart attack." She shrugs. "And I did. Easy-peasy."

"Easy-peasy," I repeat.

"Easy-peasy, pudding and pie."

"And nobody suspected . . . ?"

"Nope. Francesca talked tough, but poor thing had a history of heart issues. Arrhythmia or something like that. Killing her turned out to be a piece of cake."

Piece of cake and pudding and pie.

"When was this?"

"When was what?"

"When did you kill her?"

"Let's see. Think it was just after my fifth wedding anniversary. Not sure. What difference does it make? The wicked witch is dead and gone. You ever think about dying?"

I take a deep breath, try to stop my head from spinning. "Hard not to at my age."

"Does it scare you?"

"Not really."

"Guess you're not worried about going to hell," Jenny says.

"Are you?"

"Looking forward to it, actually."

I'm chuckling as I push myself to my feet. *I wouldn't have expected anything less.* "I should go, let you get some sleep."

She smiles. "Sweet dreams, Linda Davidson."

CHAPTER THIRTY-ONE

In my dream, I'm lounging by the side of a large outdoor swimming pool, munching on a large raspberry croissant. A young man approaches. He's wearing a tuxedo and carrying a tray full of exotic-looking beverages. "Pick one," he directs.

I remove a tall glass from the tray, take a long sip. "Oh," I say. "It's just beer."

But the young man is already gone, replaced by some children playing at the side of the pool, one yelling, "Marco!" Another answering, "Polo!"

"I used to play that game," Jenny Cooper announces from the lounge chair beside me. "I love games. Don't you?"

I take another sip of my beer.

"How is it?" Jenny asks.

"Delicious."

"It's my special recipe," Jenny says.

The glass slips from my hand and shatters on the concrete.

"Oh, my God!" I cry. "You've poisoned me."

"What did you expect, Linda Davidson?"

"I thought we were friends."

"Have you never heard the story of the scorpion and the frog?" she demands, laughing. "Silly woman! Don't you know? It's my nature!"

Which is when I bolt up in my bed, my body covered in sweat. "Holy crap," I mutter, waiting for my heart to stop racing before making my way to the bathroom to splash cold water on my face. "Holy crap," I say again, returning to my bed.

I glance at the clock on my bedside table. "That can't be right." I reach for my watch, check the numbers on its face. "That's impossible. It can't be almost ten o'clock!"

"In the morning?" I can almost hear Jenny demand.

I throw on a robe and open my bedroom door.

"Well, look who's up!" Mick exclaims from the living room sofa. He's picking at the bowl of peanuts on the coffee table in front of him and glancing through the most recent issue of *People* magazine. "I take it your date last night went well."

"It went," I tell him, "and it wasn't a date."

"You didn't get home till after ten. Kleo and I were already in bed."

I glance toward the dining room. "Where *is* Kleo?"

"Where she usually is when she's not at the dining room table. Library. Where were *you* that you didn't get home till after ten o'clock?"

"I stopped at Legacy Place after dinner."

"To see Jenny Cooper," Mick states, laying the magazine down on the coffee table and eyeing me expectantly.

"Yes."

"And?"

"She told me she poisoned her mother-in-law."

He laughs, grabs another handful of peanuts. "This story just keeps getting better and better. Did she say why?"

"Apparently, her mother-in-law was a witch with a capital *B*."

"You want me to see if I can dig up anything?"

"You think you can?"

He shrugs. "What's her name?"

"Francesca Rubini."

"What kind of name is that?"

Really? I provide him with the few details I have, suggesting the years for him to concentrate on, based on the vague information

Jenny has given me. "And Parker Rubini. Might as well check him out."

"Parker is . . . ?"

"Jenny's first husband. She killed him, too."

"Of course she did. Any idea what year that was?"

"Well, Jenny said she was married for eleven years . . ."

"Eleven-eleven Larrabee Street!" I hear Jenny interject.

". . . and that she killed her mother-in-law just after her fifth anniversary, which means that he would have died six years later . . ."

"Correctamento!" Jenny cries.

"Anyway . . . see what you can dig up. If it's not too much trouble." I glance toward the coffee table. *I can see how busy you are,* I think, but don't say.

"Let's give it a shot." Mick makes a beeline for Kleo's computer.

"Wait," I say, hurrying after him. "Why can't we use *your* computer?"

"Because I'm right in the middle of some pretty important stuff . . ."

What stuff is that? I think, remembering the last images I saw on his computer screen. Instead I say, "Kleo's work is important, too."

"Of course, it is." He sits down in front of Kleo's computer and types in her password. "Don't worry. I'm not going anywhere near her precious dissertation."

I'm about to protest when the phone in the kitchen rings. "Excuse me," I tell him as Kleo's screen lights up. I walk into the kitchen, lift the phone from its charger. "Hello?"

"Mom, hi! How's it going?"

"Good, sweetie. How are things in Connecticut?"

"All good here," Vanessa says. "I mean, the weather's been pretty crummy. Winter's still hanging around, refusing to leave, even though it's almost May, for God's sake."

"The kids are good? School going okay?" I probe. It's not like Vanessa to call without a reason. *Please let everything be okay.*

"Everything's fine," she assures me, as if I've voiced this thought out loud. "I just wanted to give you a heads-up."

"About what?"

"Turns out I have to be in Florida next Wednesday on business. There's this conference in Miami that my bosses want me to attend, and I thought maybe you guys could drive down and meet me for dinner Friday night before I head home."

"Sounds wonderful."

"Great. Look, I have a meeting in five minutes, so I have to go. But I'll text Kleo the details, and see you next week."

"Sounds wonderful," I repeat, but the line is already dead.

I return to the dining room to find Mick at the computer, shaking his head. "Problems?" I ask.

"Stupid thing froze on me. I'll have to force quit, tackle it later."

"Is that a problem? Could it endanger Kleo's work?"

"Nah, it'll be fine," he says, dismissing my concerns as he presses the appropriate keys and the screen goes instantly dark. He swivels back toward me, his smile a perfect blend of indulgence and condescension, the kind of smile you give a small child who asks "Why?" too many times. "Anyone ever tell you that you worry too much?"

CHAPTER THIRTY-TWO

I'm back at Legacy Place later that afternoon.

Kleo is still at the library and I have no desire to be home with Mick. For a man who's supposedly working hard to get his new business off the ground, he takes an alarming number of breaks. More than once I walked into the living room to find him stretched out on the sofa, cellphone in one hand, beer in the other. "On hold with a potential client," he whispered as I walked by the first time, but I suspect he was really playing videogames. The last time I walked by, he'd all but given up the pretense and was sleeping soundly and snoring loudly, another empty beer bottle resting on the coffee table beside him.

It was all I could do to keep from hurling it at his head.

Which was when I decided it was probably a good idea for me to be elsewhere.

So here I am, walking down the familiar hall to Carol's room.

"Hello, Ada," the old man calls as I walk past his room.

"How are you doing today?" I call back. I don't expect a response, so I'm not disappointed when I don't get one.

The door to Carol's room is open and I walk inside, expecting to find her standing in her usual place by the east window. But she isn't there. Nor is she in bed or the bathroom.

"Do you know where Carol is?" I ask, approaching the nurses' station. "She isn't in her room."

Selena looks up and down the hall before staring off into space, careful to avoid looking directly at me. When she speaks, her lips barely move. "You might try one floor down, room 307."

"What's in room 307?"

"Not what. Who. James Usher."

"James Usher?"

"She's been spending a fair bit of time with him lately."

I think of what Lorne told me about finding Carol with another man, her blouse unbuttoned. "Do you think that's wise, allowing the patients to roam free?" I ask.

"This isn't a hospital and we don't call them patients," comes Selena's gentle rebuke. "We refer to them as residents. And what I think doesn't really matter. As long as they aren't creating a disturbance, they're free to come and go as they please. They're not supposed to leave the premises without supervision, of course, for their own protection. But they're perfectly free to socialize with whomever they like."

I nod, turning toward the elevators.

"You might want to knock first," Selena advises.

I decide to take the stairs, holding tight to the railing as I descend. I don't want to risk a fall, which I'm told could be catastrophic at my age. The last thing I need is to break a hip.

The third floor is an exact replica of the fourth, and I proceed down the appropriate corridor to apartment 307. The door is closed and I decide to take Selena's advice and knock.

No one answers.

I knock again, louder and harder. "Carol?" I call, my lips brushing against the door. "Carol? Hello? Is anybody there?"

Still no answer. If Carol and James Usher are indeed together—and there's no certainty that they are—they might have gone for a stroll around the premises. Or maybe they're enjoying a movie in the main-floor theater. More likely, they've decided to go for an early dinner in the communal dining room on the second floor.

My mind is racing through all the preferable alternatives I can conjure up when I hear a sharp cry, followed by a low moan and a muffled scream.

"Carol!" I shout, fearing that James Usher is hurting her. I push open the door. "Carol!"

It takes a few seconds for my eyes to adjust to the dark. The curtains are shut tight, and only a sliver of light peeks through. Unfortunately, it is more than enough light for me to make out the two naked figures I discover on the bed, entangled in each other's arms. As with the glimpse of porn I caught on Mick's computer, I recognize that this is a sight I'll likely take with me to my grave.

"Who are you?" the man I assume to be James Usher demands, pushing himself up on his knobby knees, knees that are straddling the woman giggling beneath him. If either of them is at all embarrassed at being discovered in such a compromising position, neither shows it.

"Linda?" Carol asks, eyes peering through the darkness to connect with mine.

"Oh, my God! You know me?"

"Of course, I know you. How are you? Have you met . . . ?" She looks toward the man on top of her, offers nothing further.

The man on top of her looks equally puzzled.

This isn't happening.

"You should get dressed," I tell Carol when I'm able to find my voice. "Let me take you back to your room."

"I don't want to go back to my room."

"I think maybe you should."

"I'm sorry, dear," she says sweetly. "Do I know you?"

I shake my head, understanding that her moment of clarity has passed. "You're my best friend in the world," I tell her, softly.

She smiles. "How nice."

"Carol . . ."

"I don't want to go back to my room. You can't make me."

"No, I can't. But . . ."

"You should go now," James Usher says.

I nod, recognizing there's nothing more I can do. And hell, who am I to deny my best friend a few fleeting moments of pleasure? When was the last time a man's touch made me groan and cry out, let alone scream?

Is it possible I'm a little jealous?

I back slowly out of the room, closing the door behind me, then I race down the remaining two flights of stairs, not bothering to use the handrail, not really caring whether I fall. *Did what I just witnessed actually happen? Is anything about my life real anymore?*

I push open the door to exit the building, gulping at the outside air as if it were water.

"Linda!"

Oh, God.

"Were you just in with Carol?" Lorne asks, approaching from the parking lot.

I nod, afraid to say anything lest my voice betray me.

"How's she doing?"

"Hard to say," I lie. "She's been sleeping pretty much the whole day. I tell you what," I continue in the same breath, "since she's sleeping, why don't we grab a bite to eat and you can visit her later?" *Hopefully she'll be out of James Usher's bed by then.*

Lorne checks his watch. "Well, it's a little early . . . but sure, why not? It's a date."

"It wasn't a date," I tell Kleo and Mick.

"You called us at a quarter to five to tell us you wouldn't be home for dinner, and it's after seven now," Mick remarks.

"What can I say? He's a slow eater."

"Lucky you," Mick says, his leer stretching into a lascivious grin.

"For God's sake, Mick. This is my *mother*!" Kleo says from her seat in front of her computer. "Shit!"

"Okay, sorry. Don't go getting all upset . . ."

"No, it's not that."

"What then?"

"I'm missing a bunch of my research," Kleo says, frantically searching through the various files on her computer.

"What are you talking about?" Mick asks, moving quickly to her side.

"What I've been working on for the past few weeks, I can't find it."

"It's got to be there somewhere."

"I'm looking. I can't find it. You haven't touched anything, have you?"

"Of course not," Mick says. "What are you accusing me of?"

"I'm not accusing you of anything. I just asked . . ."

"Why would I touch your computer?"

"Well, we *did* use it to check out those names, remember?" I interject.

"You did *what*?" Kleo asks.

"I didn't go anywhere near your precious research," Mick insists.

"What are you talking about?" Kleo says. "What names were you checking out? Would someone please tell me what's going on."

"I'll leave that to your *mother*," Mick says, shooting me an angry look as he walks to the front door, opens it, and in what is now becoming too frequent an occurrence, slams it shut behind him.

CHAPTER THIRTY-THREE

"What just happened?" I ask.

"You tell me," Kleo says. "What's this about checking out names on my computer?"

I take a deep breath, then tell her everything: my visits with Jenny Cooper, Jenny's series of alarming confessions, my asking Mick for help to determine the veracity of her outlandish claims—

"So, wait," Kleo interrupts, pushing thoughts of her missing files temporarily aside. "All those times you were supposedly visiting Carol, you were spending with this lunatic?"

"I *was* visiting Carol," I tell my daughter, trying not to picture my best friend in bed with a man whose name she couldn't recall. "And Jenny's not a lunatic. She's just a lonely old woman who I'm pretty sure was sexually abused by her father when she was a child . . ."

"What? *What?*"

"Not that she told me that. I think she may have blocked it."

"She remembers killing four people but she blocks out being sexually abused?"

I shrug. "I could be wrong, of course. But there was something in the way she reacted when she thought Lance was going to touch her . . ."

"Who the hell is Lance?"

"He's one of the orderlies. After Jenny disappeared . . ."

"Wait. Jenny disappeared?"

"She went to a drugstore after she overheard me talking to Shannon . . ."

"Shannon?"

"Shannon's grandfather is . . . *was* . . . in the apartment across from Carol's. Apparently, he molested Shannon when she was a child, and I think Jenny overheard our conversation and—what is it they say now?—it *triggered* her, and now he's dead, and I think Jenny might have poisoned him . . ."

"Stop! Please, Mom! Are you listening to yourself?"

"I'm not sure I understand why you're so upset."

"You don't understand? Mom, this is getting way out of hand. You're not a psychiatrist or a social worker. You are not equipped to deal with people like this." Kleo throws her hands in the air. "Is there anything else I should know?"

I shake my head, deciding not to tell her about discovering Carol in bed with James Usher. My daughter has clearly had about as much as she can take for one night. "I'm so sorry about your missing files. Mick assured me that he wasn't disturbing anything." I don't tell her about the computer freezing and Mick having to force quit. While I feel guilty about keeping this from her, I'm not sure it has anything to do with the fact that her files are missing, and telling her will only make things worse between her and Mick.

"I just don't understand why he didn't use his own computer," Kleo says, sinking back into her chair at the dining room table and resuming her search.

"Can I do anything to help?"

"I think you've done enough."

"I'm so sorry."

"No, *I'm* sorry," she apologizes quickly. "This isn't your fault. Mick had no business . . . Oh, shit!"

I hold my breath. "What?"

"I found them."

"You found your missing files?"

"I must have put them in with these other files by mistake. Shit!"

"What?"

"I pretty much accused Mick of sabotage."

"No, you didn't. You just asked him if he'd touched anything. And he *had*!" I remind her.

The look on her face tells me I've said enough.

"I should go to my room," I tell her, "let you get back to work."

"Mom," she calls after me.

I stop, turn back around.

"You didn't tell me about your date."

I shrug. "It wasn't a date."

"Okay. It wasn't a date. I just want you to know that I have no trouble with your . . . with your *seeing* anyone. I mean," she continues before I can interrupt, "I know how much you loved Dad, and I know how hard these last few years have been for you, and you're still relatively young, you have your own life to live, and I just want you to be happy, you deserve to be happy, so if you want to start *seeing* anyone . . ."

"Sweetheart . . ."

"It's okay with me. Honestly."

"Thank you, darling. I appreciate that. But it's really not an issue."

"You're sure? No one would judge you if you and Lorne got together."

"Maybe not," I tell her. "But Carol is still my best friend, no matter what the circumstances"—*even if she's carrying on with another man,* I add silently—"and Lorne is still her husband"—*even if she doesn't know who he is anymore.* "And we need to leave it at that." *At least for the time being,* I think but decide not to say. "Anyway, I'll let you get back to work, and I'll go climb into bed, turn on the TV, and see if I can rustle up an old episode of *Dateline.*"

"Mom?" she calls before I reach my bedroom door.

"Yes, sweetheart?"

"The next time you're looking for information about Jenny Cooper, I'm happy to help out."

"Thank you, darling. But you're right about this getting way out of hand. There won't be a next time."

CHAPTER THIRTY-FOUR

"She was *where*?" Vanessa asks, finishing the last of her pistachio ice cream and dropping her spoon to the table.

"In a CVS, a mile or so down the road."

"What was she doing in a drugstore, for heaven's sake?"

"Who knows?" I answer. "Jenny used to be a pharmacist, so maybe she forgot she wasn't one anymore." *Or she went there to pick up the ingredients she needed to poison Ralph McMillan.*

I stare across the table at my two beautiful daughters, thinking that while they are unmistakably sisters—the same oval-shaped face, the identical big hazel eyes and bow-shaped lips—they couldn't be less alike. Vanessa is all effortless sophistication in her cream-colored linen pantsuit, dangling gold hoop earrings, and rush of long, brown hair, whereas Kleo looks decidedly uncomfortable in the white cotton shirtwaist she hasn't worn since she stopped teaching.

"What a bizarre story," Vanessa says.

We're sitting at an outside table at Makoto, a crowded upscale Japanese restaurant, on the third floor of the Bal Harbour Shops, a high-end outdoor shopping mall located in North Miami. The mall is anchored by Neiman Marcus and Saks Fifth Avenue and boasts one hundred stores, most of them designer, in a spectacular garden setting.

Miami is like nowhere else in Florida, the population an intriguing mix of Hispanic, Black, and white, with a sprinkling of Russian émigrés tossed in for good measure. Visiting this city for me is like traveling to another planet, one inhabited by skinny young men in even skinnier, shiny suits, and overly, but meticulously, made-up young women with big hair, bigger lips, and surgically enhanced bosoms and butts.

When did a big ass become something to be desired? I find myself wondering, my eyes following one such woman as she struts past our table in four-inch open-toed stilettos.

"I don't like that word," I hear Jenny chastise. *"You should say 'backside.'"*

I turn my attention back to my daughters, trying to focus. Kleo and I made the hour-and-a-half-plus drive down from Jupiter to see Vanessa before she catches the last flight home to Connecticut. Mick begged off, ostensibly to give mother and daughters some much-needed time together to catch up, claiming that he'd only be in the way. I suspect it has more to do with the continuing tension between him and Kleo, but either way, he got no argument from us.

We've spent most of the dinner listening to Vanessa talk about the demands of her job, the important people she's meeting, her latest bonus, her successful husband, and her beautiful children. "So, what about you?" she asked Kleo toward the end of the meal, as if suddenly aware her sister might have something interesting to contribute. "Tell me what you're up to these days."

"The usual," Kleo responded. "Still working on my dissertation."

"God, are you ever going to be finished with that thing? Seems like you've been working on it forever."

"Feels that way sometimes."

"What are you going to do with a PhD anyway? Does it mean you get more money when you go back to work?"

"I hadn't really thought about that."

"No? Well, maybe you should." Vanessa laughed. "Unless you're planning on living with Mom forever, that is."

I watched a sudden flash of pain streak through Kleo's eyes. Which was when I decided to tell Vanessa about Jenny Cooper, hoping it would prove enough of a distraction to alleviate the sting of her offhand remark.

Vanessa signals to the waiter for the check. "Well, you'll have to let me know how it all turns out."

I reach for my oversize leather handbag.

"Don't you dare," Vanessa says. "This is my treat."

"This was a very expensive meal," I argue. "Let me at least pay for half."

"No chance." Vanessa hands her charge card to the waiter before I can object further.

"Well, thank you," I say.

"Thank you," Kleo echoes as Vanessa signs the receipt.

"We have one more stop to make and then I really have to run," Vanessa informs us. "Follow me."

Kleo and I do as directed, both of us understanding that there is no point arguing. Vanessa is a woman used to getting her way. I have always marveled at her confidence, wishing she could transfer even a small part of it to her sister.

"What are we doing here?" I ask, as we reached the entrance to Louis Vuitton.

"We are buying you a new purse." Vanessa flings open the door and walks inside the brightly lit shop.

"I don't need a new purse."

"Are you kidding me? That thing you're lugging around is a disgrace to handbags everywhere."

"What are you talking about? It's a perfectly nice bag."

"You're getting a new purse and that's the end of the discussion. Excuse me," she calls to one of the salesladies. "Can I see that bag over there?" She points to a medium-size brown-and-tan bag with the familiar Louis Vuitton logo running up and down its sides. "Yes, that one." She removes the bag from the saleslady's hand, arranges it over my shoulder. "There. Look at that. Looks great. Don't you think?" she asks in Kleo's general direction.

"Looks great," Kleo agrees.

"Then it's settled. She'll take it," Vanessa says, removing the purse from my shoulder.

I catch a glimpse of the price tag as she hands the bag to the saleslady to be wrapped, along with her credit card.

"Vanessa, no! It's way too expensive . . ."

"Happy Mother's Day!" she interrupts. "I know it's not for another week or so, but I'm here now, and I won't be then. So, wear it in the best of health and enjoy."

What else can I say but "Thank you."

"My pleasure." Vanessa signs the chit, drops her credit card inside her own designer bag, and glances at her phone. "Okay. Looks like my Uber is downstairs, so I'm going to have to leave you guys to wait for them to finish with the wrapping. It was so great seeing you." She grabs us each in a quick embrace before disappearing into the continuing parade of well-heeled passersby.

"She's right, you know," Kleo says. "What am I doing wasting my time on this stupid PhD, when I should be out there making money? Who cares about the rise of a bunch of self-conscious women in modern American literature?"

"Well, I, for one, can't wait to read all about them," I tell her.

"You have to say that," she says. "You're my mother."

The saleslady approaches with my new purse. It is buried under a sea of tissue paper inside a large white paper bag with the designer's name in big, bold black letters printed across both sides. "What a generous daughter you have," she says, handing it to me by its string handles. "You must be very proud."

"I'm proud of both my daughters," I say.

The saleslady's smile freezes on her face. "Yes, well, have a lovely evening, and enjoy your new bag."

"You didn't have to say that," Kleo says as we walk toward the elevators.

"Why wouldn't I say it? It's the truth."

We stop in front of the elevator for the parking garage. Kleo bursts into tears.

"Oh, sweetheart. Please don't cry."

"You know that probably all you'll be getting from me this Mother's Day is a bunch of fresh-cut flowers from Publix."

"I love fresh-cut flowers from Publix."

The elevator doors open.

"You going in?" a man behind us asks when neither Kleo nor I move.

"Oh, yes. Sorry about that."

"No worries," he says.

Maybe not for you, I think.

"I love *you,*" Kleo whispers as we step inside.

"I love you more."

"Impossible," we say together as the doors close.

CHAPTER THIRTY-FIVE

"Is that a new purse?" Jenny demands, pointing an almost accusatory finger at the bag Vanessa bought me.

We're in the small sitting area of her apartment. Despite my promises to Kleo about curtailing my visits, despite my own resolve, I can't seem to stay away. *Is this what drug addiction is like?* I find myself wondering. *Has Jenny become my drug of choice?*

I sigh. "Yes, it is."

"Designer," she says. "Expensive, I bet."

"Yes."

"Where'd you get it?"

"My daughter bought it for me. For Mother's Day."

"I don't have a mother," Jenny says, wistfully. "Do you?"

"Not anymore, no."

"Me neither. My father killed her."

"Did you kill Ralph McMillan?" Despite Jenny's recent confessions, she has yet to admit to murdering Ralph McMillan.

"I don't much care for the name 'Ralph,' do you?"

"Did you kill him?"

"Are you with the police? Are you wearing a wire?"

"No, of course not."

"Take off your blouse," she directs.

"What?"

"Take off your blouse."

"I'm not taking off my blouse."

"I'm not saying another word until you do."

"This is ridiculous."

Jenny leans back in her chair, says nothing.

"For God's sake, I'm *not* wearing a wire."

"I saw this TV show once. The FBI pressured this poor woman to wear a wire in her bra, right between her you-know-whats."

Oh, God. "Okay, listen. I'll make you a deal."

"Let's Make a Deal!" she shouts. *"Linda Davidson, come on down!"*

"How about I just unbutton my blouse and you can see that there's no wire?"

Jenny gives my proposition a moment's thought. "Okay. That might work."

My hands move to the front of my pale pink linen shirt, my fingers struggling with the small, delicate white buttons. I undo the top three and hold the blouse open, revealing the age-spotted skin above the flesh-colored bra beneath. "Satisfied?" I ask, motioning toward the space between my breasts. "No wire. Not even any *under*wire!"

"No underwire in your underwear," Jenny recites, laughing. "You know who used to love bras with underwire? Parker Rubini, that's who."

"Your first husband," I acknowledge, wondering where this sudden shift in the conversation is about to lead.

"May he rest in pieces," she says, the laugh morphing into a witch's cackle.

I get a sudden picture of Jenny with an ax, leaning over the body of her dead husband. "Are you saying that you cut him up?"

"Are you crazy?"

"You said, may he rest in pieces . . ."

"It's just an expression, Linda Davidson. Jeez. What's wrong with you?"

I have no answer for that, so I remain silent.

"Parker was always trying to get me to wear those damn bras with underwires that squish your boobies together and make them pop out. He loved that sort of stuff. Well, why wouldn't he? He didn't have to wear them." She cups her hands over her breasts, pushes them together. "Pop!" she squeals, letting them go. "He kept buying me these cheesy-looking thingies, with the nipples cut out, and lacy, crotchless panties. You ever wear crotchless panties, Linda?"

"Can't say that I have."

"Yeah, well, Parker got a real kick out of those. And he was always after me to play dress-up in bed. You ever play dress-up in bed with your husband?"

"I'd really rather not get into that."

"So, you did," she says.

"Sometimes," I admit, recognizing that to do otherwise would be a waste of time. "When I was a lot younger."

"And I bet you looked pretty good, didn't you?"

"Not bad."

"There you go," she chastises. "Putting yourself down again. I bet you looked a whole lot better than *not bad*. I bet you looked *pretty damn good,* and I want you to say it!"

"Jenny . . ."

"Linda . . ."

"I looked pretty damn good," I say. *What the hell? Why not?*

"Again," she directs. "Louder this time."

"*I looked pretty damn good!*" I all but shout.

"That's more like it." She slaps at her knees. "And for being such a good sport, I want you to sit back and relax while I tell you all about how I killed good old Parker Rubini."

CHAPTER THIRTY-SIX

I sit back, but I hardly relax.

"I think I enjoyed killing him most of all," Jenny says, as I struggle to appear unfazed and nonjudgmental.

"Why is that?"

"I think it was the look on his face when he realized what was happening." Jenny's smile all but lights up the room. "He didn't think I had it in me." Her smile grows even wider, stretching the deep wrinkles around her mouth toward the bottom of each ear. "He was wrong."

"Why did you kill him?"

"I didn't say I'd tell you *why* I killed him," Jenny says. "I said I'd tell you *how*."

"I'm assuming you poisoned him."

"Never assume, Linda Davidson."

"You didn't poison him?"

"No, I poisoned him all right."

Here we go again.

"But then I pushed him down the stairs."

"You pushed him down the stairs?"

"Is there an echo in here?"

"You poisoned him, and then you pushed him down the stairs?"

"That's correct. Not sure what actually killed him, the poison or the fall."

"Why did you push him down the stairs?"

"Because he was standing right in front of them, and it seemed the prudent thing to do. I like the sound of that word, don't you? *Prudent*," she repeats. "Pru-*dent*."

"I'm not sure I follow," I tell her.

"You're a bit slow, aren't you, Linda Davidson?"

I laugh. "I guess I am."

"That's all right. I'm a very patient woman. Look how long I waited to kill that miserable son of a you-know-what."

"How long you waited?"

"Almost six years after I killed his mother!"

"What took you so long?" I hear myself ask, not quite believing the words coming out of my mouth.

"Not sure. Just seemed like the prudent thing to do." She giggles. "There's that word again."

"How do you mean?"

"Well, his dying couldn't come too quick after his mother's passing. Two deaths in too short a time might arouse unnecessary curiosity, cast unwanted suspicions. I may be demented," she says proudly, "but I'm not crazy."

I laugh again, something I realize I do often in her presence. *What kind of person does this make me?*

"Where were we?" she asks.

"You just pushed your husband down a flight of stairs." *Did I really just say that?*

"Ah, yes. There's something so satisfying about actual physical contact, that feeling when you reach out and just . . . *push*. You don't get that with poison."

"But why do both?"

"I had to. Parker left me no choice."

"How's that?"

"It was night, around ten o'clock. We were in the bedroom, getting ready for bed. He wanted me to dress up, you know, like I told you. I suggested we have a drink first, to get me in the mood and all, and he thought that was a good idea. He was always up for a drink, old Parker was. Just like my daddy. So, I went downstairs and mixed us some cocktails, added a little something special to his, brought the drinks upstairs, watched him drink his down. Then I went into the closet, pretended I was changing into one of those crotchless little numbers he was so fond of, assumed that by the time I came out, he'd be moaning on the floor. The throes of death and all. But when I came back into the bedroom, he was just sitting there on the bed, this dumb, quizzical look in his eyes. And he said, 'What did you do to me, you . . .'" Jenny lowers her voice to a whisper. "He used a really bad word, the one that starts with a *c*. You know the one?"

I nod.

"And then he lunged at me." Jenny's eyes grow wide, as if watching the scene play out in front of her. "I ran into the hall, but the bugger was right behind me, although he could hardly put one foot in front of the other without tripping all over himself. And you know, the stairs were right there . . . so I . . . I pushed him. And you should have seen the look on his face. It was just the best feeling in the world, I tell you, watching him go down those stairs."

"And then what?"

"Then I called an ambulance, told them my husband had taken a few sleeping pills before bed and fallen down the stairs, and I needed help right away. And they came, got there pretty quick, as I remember. And that was that. Goodbye to Parker Rubini. What is it they say? *Good riddance to bad rubbish!*"

"And the police never questioned you . . . ?"

"Oh, they questioned me. They kind of had to. But the cause of death was pretty obvious. Parker's neck was broken. There was no reason to check for anything else. I already told them he'd taken a few sleeping pills. And I was so distraught and everything, could hardly get any words out, I was crying so hard. I deserved an Oscar for that performance, I tell you."

"I'm sure you were very impressive."

She smiles at the perceived compliment. "Do you ever wonder about how you'll die, Linda?"

I wait to hear my last name, but it doesn't come. It feels strange now, hearing one without the other. "I try not to think about it too much," I admit.

"But you do . . . think about it."

"Of course. I'm seventy-six."

She laughs. "Hah! Wait till you get to be *my* age. How would you like to die?" She leans forward in her chair, as if eager for my reply.

"I would prefer not to be murdered," I say, pointedly.

Jenny's turn to laugh. "Hah! I would never kill you, Linda Davidson. You're my best friend."

"Good to know," I tell her, trying to disguise the shocking degree of pride I feel.

"Cancer or heart attack?" she probes.

"That's some choice."

"Fast or slow? A long, lingering illness or being hit by a bus?"

"Wow! This just keeps getting better." I shrug. "Somewhere in the middle, maybe. I mean, I don't want to suffer or be in pain, but I don't want to be here one minute—"

"And gone the next?" Jenny says, finishing the sentence for me.

"I guess I'd like a little bit of notice, time to get my house in order, say my goodbyes."

"Are you afraid?"

"Of dying? No, not really. It's more that I just can't imagine being . . . gone."

"You can't imagine the world continuing on without you," she states.

"More like I wonder what that feels like, to not be here anymore."

"You remember that afternoon back on December nineteenth, 1712?" she asks.

"How could I possibly remember that?"

"Exactly. That's what it feels like," she exclaims, triumphantly.
I laugh, long and loud.

"What are you thinking about right now?" she asks.

"That you might be the sanest person I know," I tell her honestly.

She takes several seconds to absorb this, then brings an index finger to her lips. "Shh," she says. "It's a secret."

CHAPTER THIRTY-SEVEN

"So, are you going to tell me *why* you killed him?" I ask, after a pause of several minutes.

"Why I killed *who*?"

Why I killed *whom*, I emend silently, shaking my head. *Once an English teacher, always an English teacher.* "Parker Rubini or Ralph McMillan," I say. "Take your pick."

"Hah! You're trying to trick me."

"I doubt that's possible."

"Who says I killed Ralph McMillan?"

"Did you?"

"He wasn't a very nice man."

"No, he wasn't."

"He molested that lovely young girl."

"Yes, he did."

"He deserved to die."

"Probably. Did you kill him?"

"Maybe I did. Maybe I didn't," she says, her voice a singsong. "What's the difference?"

The difference, I think but don't say, *is that these other murders happened—if they happened at all—in the distant past, but Ralph McMillan died less than a month ago, which means that you're still killing people, that there could be others, that no one here is safe, and that if I sit back, do nothing, wait for more people to die, then I'm an accomplice.*

"Do you want to hear about why I killed Parker Rubini or not?" Jenny demands.

"I assumed it was because of the sex." I decide not to ask any more questions about Ralph McMillan. At least for the time being.

"What about the sex?"

"That he made you do things you didn't want to do."

"Yes," she confirms. "I guess that was part of the reason I killed him."

"What was the other part?"

"What difference does it make?" She shrugs. "Oh, okay. It's simple, really. What's the expression? 'Follow the money'? There you have it. Easy-peasy. I killed Parker for the money. Same reason I killed his mother. I had to get rid of her first, of course, so Parker would inherit. Which he did. Lots and lots of money. Which the idiot then proceeded to throw down the toilet with his drinking and his gambling. The moron once bet two hundred thousand dollars on the coin toss at the Super Bowl, if you can believe it. The rate he was going, we would have been broke in no time. I couldn't let that happen, now, could I? So I killed him. Simple as that."

"I don't think anything about you is simple, Jenny."

"What are you saying? That you don't believe me?"

"Let's just say I believe it's more complicated than you're letting on."

"Then suppose *you* tell *me* why I killed him," she directs. "Go on, little Miss Marple," she says when I hesitate. "Tell me."

I give what I'm about to say a moment of serious thought. I know it would be *prudent,* as Jenny would say, to keep my opinions to myself. I'm not a psychiatrist after all, as Kleo reminded me, and whether Jenny is a deranged killer or merely deranged, I'm clearly in way over my head. "I think you killed Parker for the same reason you married him," I offer anyway.

"And what reason is that, pray tell?"

I ignore the defensiveness creeping into her voice. "Because he reminded you of your father."

Jenny sits back in her chair. "I hated my father. Why would I want to marry anyone even remotely like him?"

"They say that we go with what's familiar."

"Oh, they do, do they?" she says. "Just who are *they*?"

"Psychiatrists, therapists, people who understand this sort of thing."

"None of which you are," she notes.

"No."

"You're just a retired schoolteacher with too much time on her hands."

"True enough."

"Encouraging the babblings of a senile old woman for her own amusement. You're pathetic. You know that?"

"I'm sorry. I obviously shouldn't have said anything."

"Parker wasn't anything like my father. He was weak; my father was strong. Tell me how they were in any way alike."

I shake my head. "I've already said too much."

"Maybe. But you can't stop now. Tell me."

"Well, you said they were both handsome," I begin, "that they both drank, that they were abusive . . ."

"Who said Parker was abusive?"

"He made you do things—sexually—that you didn't like, that you didn't want to do."

Jenny starts rocking back and forth. Her eyes glaze over, roll back in her head. For an instant, I'm afraid she might be having a seizure. When she finally speaks, her voice is so low that I have to lean forward to hear her. "He said that it was my fault for being so seductive, that he was only responding to the signals I gave out . . ."

I know instantly that she's talking about her father now, and not Parker. I hold my breath, say nothing.

"He said that he was only doing those things because he knew I liked it, that it was my fault . . ."

"It wasn't your fault," I tell the little girl inside her.

"I overheard you talking to that girl in the lounge. I heard what she told you about her grandfather . . . The man deserved to die."

"So you killed him."

We sit for a few moments in silence so heavy, you can almost touch it.

"Jenny," I say, reaching over to clasp her hands, which are ice cold. "I think we need to tell Selena."

Jenny's eyes fill with alarm. "We can't do that. She'll call the police."

"This is too big a secret to keep locked up inside you," I tell her. "I think you want to tell people the truth, that you've been wanting to confess for a long time, that that's part of the reason you told *me* the things you did. I don't think you want to kill anyone else."

Jenny suddenly jumps to her feet and lunges for the door, bounding into the hall before I grasp what is happening. "Everybody!" I hear her yell. "Everybody! Out of your rooms! I have a confession to make."

I run into the hall to find Selena advancing warily toward Jenny as Lance approaches from the other corridor. Several residents peek out from their doorways. I watch Lorne emerge from Carol's room.

"I killed him!" Jenny shouts. "I killed Ralph McMillan!"

"Okay, Jenny," Selena cautions. "You have to calm down. You're upsetting the other residents. You didn't kill anyone."

"I did. I shot him right between the eyes!"

What?

"Ralph McMillan died from choking on his own vomit," Selena informs Jenny quietly, as Lance moves closer.

"That's disgusting!" Jenny says.

"You didn't have anything to do with his death," Selena says.

Lance surrounds Jenny with his arms. She offers no resistance as he leads her back toward her room.

She winks at me as they walk by.

CHAPTER THIRTY-EIGHT

"I don't know what the hell I was thinking," I say, sitting beside Lorne in the visitors' lounge, trying to make sense of what just happened. "She's right—I'm just a retired schoolteacher with too much time on my hands. Worse—I've been taking advantage of a senile old woman for my own amusement. What's the matter with me?"

"There's absolutely nothing the matter with you," Lorne says, covering my hands with his, much as I did with Jenny earlier. "You're a kind, generous woman who was just trying to provide comfort and company to a lonely old woman who's clearly not operating with a full deck."

Doesn't mean she isn't telling the truth, I hear my son-in-law say.

"What if she's not so crazy?" I ask Lorne.

"What do you mean?"

In my mind's eye, I see Lance leading Jenny down the hall toward her room. I watch her wink as she walks by. "What if she played me? What if she's playing all of us?"

"I'm not following," Lorne says.

"Okay, this is going to sound really off the wall, so bear with me."

Lorne gives my hand a reassuring squeeze.

I tell him about all the time I've been spending with Jenny, including her murderous confessions and my suspicions regarding Ralph McMillan's death.

"Except that she claimed she *shot* Ralph McMillan," he reminds me, "and Ralph McMillan wasn't shot."

"Exactly."

"Still not following," Lorne says.

"Okay, so this is the part that gets really bizarre . . ."

"As opposed to everything else you've just told me," he interjects.

"I think that Jenny poisoned Ralph McMillan, the same way she poisoned the others, and when she thought I might go to the police with my suspicions, she decided to confess. Except she told everyone she *shot* him, which was clearly not what happened, and which made her sound as crazy as everyone already assumes she is."

"Or maybe she's just crazy," Lorne says.

"*I may be demented,*" I hear Jenny say, "*but I'm not crazy!*"

"Listen," Lorne says. "You may be right. It's unlikely, but hell, anything's possible. Maybe she did all the things she claims she did. Maybe she even poisoned poor Ralph McMillan. But nobody's going to believe her. Nobody's going to believe *you*. And even if they did, what's the point? There's no way this ever goes to trial. Who's going to prosecute a ninety-two-year-old woman with dementia? And even if they did, even if she were to be found guilty, what are they going to do? Lock the old bat away? She's already locked away, for all intents and purposes."

"But what if she kills someone else?"

"You really think that's a possibility?"

"I don't know." I shake my head. "I don't know anything anymore."

"Look," Lorne says after a silence of several seconds. "It sounds to me like you could use a few days away from all this. I know I could."

I'm not sure what to say, so I say nothing. Something I should have done with Jenny.

"When was the last time you were in Key West?" he asks.

"Oh, God. Years ago. Probably when the girls were little."

"Yeah, it's been a long time for me, too. I was thinking it might be nice to drive down for a few days. Kevin is flying in from New York to see his mother this weekend, so I was thinking that it might be a good time to go."

"Sounds nice."

"So, how about it?"

"How about what?" I ask, although the pounding in my heart tells me that I already know what.

"Would you be interested in joining me? I'd do all the driving," he adds, as if this would be my main concern.

"You're asking me to go away with you for the weekend?"

"I know this lovely little hotel on the beach. We'd have separate rooms, of course," he explains quickly. "Look, I just thought we could both use the break."

"It does sound lovely."

"So . . . that's a yes?"

"I don't know . . ."

"I tell you what. Why don't you think about it overnight and let me know tomorrow?"

I nod.

"Great," he says. "I really think it would do us both a world of good."

"Of course, I'm going to say no," I tell Kleo and Mick at dinner that night.

We're sitting in the den off the living room, plates on our laps, finishing the last of the pizzas we ordered for dinner, watching the nightly news on TV.

"Why would you say no?" Mick asks, pouring himself a second beer.

"I remind you that the man in question is the husband of Mom's oldest friend," Kleo says, taking the words out of my mouth.

"And I remind *you* that your mom's oldest friend has no qualms about fucking another man."

"That's different. She doesn't know what she's doing."

"She's still doing it," Mick says. "Besides, a little adultery never hurt anyone."

"Seriously?"

"Okay, okay," I interrupt, sensing a shift in tone and hoping to stave off a budding argument. "Nobody's committing adultery here. We'd be staying in separate rooms."

"Yeah? Who's paying for these rooms?"

"Obviously, I would insist on paying my own way."

"Obvious to who?" Mick asks.

Obvious to whom, I correct silently.

"Obvious to whom," Kleo corrects out loud.

"What?" Mick says.

"It's 'obvious to *whom.*' 'Whom' is object of the preposition 'to.'"

"Object of the . . . What the fuck? You're seriously correcting my grammar? Who the fuck do you think you are?"

"Okay," I say. "Let's all just calm down."

"Don't tell me to calm down!" Mick says.

"Don't talk to my mother in that tone!"

"Don't tell me what to fucking do!"

"Can we please just take a deep breath . . ."

"Stay out of this, Linda! This isn't your fight."

"No, but it *is* my house! I have a right to be comfortable in it," I remind him, my outburst surprising me almost as much as it does them.

"Fine. You're absolutely right. It's your fucking house!" Mick throws what's left of the pizza in his hands to his plate. It misses and falls to the floor, leaving a large splatter of tomato sauce on the ivory carpet.

"Great. Just great," Kleo says. "You gonna clean this mess up?"

"Clean it up yourself," Mick says, storming from the room. "You created it."

The front door opens and slams shut. Neither Kleo nor I move.

"I'm so sorry," she whispers.

"Me, too."

"I shouldn't have corrected his grammar."

"And he shouldn't overreact like that. He was way out of line."

We stare at the glob of tomato sauce at our feet.

"Maybe it's not such a bad idea," she says moments later, as she soaks up the sauce with a wet towel, "you getting away from all this for a few days."

I smile. "I was just thinking the same thing."

CHAPTER THIRTY-NINE

Lorne picks me up at nine o'clock Friday morning.

I'm standing at the window as he pulls his car into the driveway, wondering idly if any of the neighbors are watching, and what they might be thinking. Not that I'm particularly friendly with any of them or am overly concerned with their opinions. Bob was of the firm belief that it was never a good idea to get too chummy with the neighbors, so while we were never less than cordial, we weren't exactly exchanging recipes or offering up our services as emergency babysitters. I regret that now. One can never have too many friends.

"Looks like your gentleman caller has arrived," Kleo says, coming up behind me. "Looking very dapper, I might add."

"Dapper" is, in fact, the perfect word for how Lorne looks. He's wearing a pale yellow short-sleeved shirt and neat khaki pants, and looks at least a decade younger than his years. I glance down at my navy slacks and navy-and-white checkered shirt, wondering if he'll feel the same when he sees *me*. Part of me feels a sudden surge of excitement; the other part of me feels immediately guilty.

"You look great," Kleo assures me, as the doorbell rings. "You want me to get that?"

"Please." I take a deep breath, still not convinced I'm doing the right thing by going away this weekend.

It's not just Lorne who's concerning me. To tell the truth, he's not even my main concern. It's Kleo I'm worried about.

There's still a great deal of tension in the house, and I'm torn between giving my daughter and her husband the space they need to work out their problems and being around to support Kleo in whatever way I can, torn between refusing to take sides and acting as a buffer should one be required, torn between letting things play out without any interference from me and being around to make sure they don't escalate out of control.

Kleo waited a long time to get married, and I know how desperately she wants this marriage to work, how disappointed in herself she will feel if it doesn't.

Unlike her younger sister, Kleo is modest by nature, one of those women who has always underplayed both her looks and her accomplishments. Mick, on the other hand, is one of those men whose exaggerated opinion of his worth has always exceeded his abilities, a man whose easy charm and good looks surpass his good nature and disguise his innate laziness, a man whose first impression is always the best impression he will ever make.

Mick has been absent for much of the last three days. He didn't come home at all on Monday night—something he's never done before—which of course led to another fight when he did return, which led to his storming out and disappearing for most of Tuesday, which led to another fight, which resulted in his staying out till after midnight and coming home "drunk as a skunk," as Jenny would say, which led to more fights, more slamming doors, more bitter accusations and recriminations. The nights he's been home, he's been sleeping on the couch in his office. Judging by Kleo's swollen eyes and pallid complexion, I doubt she's slept at all.

I know I haven't.

So much for being comfortable in my own house.

I feel so helpless. It kills me to watch my daughter being so unhappy. And while she's not entirely blameless, I know the effort she's put into making this marriage work. Since they moved in with me, I've been a witness to it, firsthand.

Maybe I've seen too much.

Maybe it's time for them to move out.

Or maybe I'm overreacting. Couples fight, after all. And I've had nothing this week to distract me from the ongoing family drama, having chosen to distance myself from Jenny Cooper.

Whether or not she killed Ralph McMillan, whether or not she killed *anyone,* isn't what's been keeping me away. In fact, it's almost beside the point. The point being that while Jenny may be out of her mind, she's right about one thing, and that's that I've been using her as an amusing way to fill my time. My very own *Dateline,* I acknowledge silently. I know I'll miss her stories of murder and revenge. I'll miss our sly bantering, the playful back-and-forth of our exchanges.

I'll miss *her.*

At any rate, I haven't been back to Legacy Place all week. Partly because I don't want to see Jenny, but mostly because I haven't been able to bring myself to face Carol, knowing I'll be spending the weekend in Key West with her husband.

Even if we'll be staying in separate rooms.

Even if there's nothing between us but a shared grief.

Or is it because I find myself hoping that Mick has been right about him all along?

"Hello, Mr. Kreiger," I hear Kleo say as she opens the front door. "It's nice to see you again."

"It's been a while," Lorne agrees. "And please, call me Lorne."

"Lorne," I say, approaching with my overnight bag.

"You all ready to go?"

I smile. *As ready as I'll ever be.*

"Here. Let me take that." He grabs the handle of my small bag and wheels it outside, loads it into the backseat of his car.

"Are you sure you're going to be all right?" I ask my daughter, taking her in my arms. *How thin she feels. How fragile.*

"I'm positive," she tells me.

"I don't have to go."

"I'm a big girl. I can handle Mick."

"I know you can. It's just that—"

"Mom," she interrupts. "I don't want you to worry. I want you to go and have a good time. You deserve it. I'll be fine here. What do you always tell me? *Things have a way of working out?* And they will. Yes, this was a particularly bad fight, but we'll figure things out. It won't happen again. You'll see. By the time you get back, Mick and I will have talked things through and everything will be back on track."

Are you sure that's what you want? I have to bite my tongue to keep from asking out loud.

"How long a drive is it?" she asks Lorne as he holds open the passenger door of his Porsche.

"Five and a half hours, give or take," Lorne says as I slide into the front seat. "Every hour out of Miami absolutely worth it. One of the most scenic drives in the world. Nothing beats the Seven Mile Bridge for pure, unadulterated beauty."

I picture the narrow sliver of thin concrete in the middle of the Atlantic Ocean that connects the Keys to the mainland, the word "unadulterated" slamming against my brain.

"Drive carefully," Kleo instructs Lorne. "Call me when you get there."

"Will do," I say.

"Love you," she calls as Lorne backs out of the driveway onto the street.

I catch sight of Mick watching from his office window, see Kleo waving from the doorway. "Love you more," I whisper.

CHAPTER FORTY

Key West is a U.S. island city, the most glamorous of the Florida Keys, located at the southernmost tip of the state, and known for its lively nightlife, magnificent beaches, historic sites, and colorful, conch-style houses.

We arrive at our boutique hotel on Smathers Beach approximately six hours after leaving Jupiter, having made several pit stops along the way to use the washrooms and grab a bite of lunch.

"Finally!" Lorne says, exiting the car and handing his keys to the waiting valet. "We made it!"

Another valet rushes to open my door, and I step gingerly onto the pavement, gently unwinding my body and trying to straighten my back without making too obvious the effort this takes. While the drive from Miami to Key West is as beautiful as advertised, the drive to Miami from Jupiter is a traffic-filled exercise in frustration, and my aging bones aren't used to sitting for so long in a car, even one as luxurious as Lorne's. There isn't a part of me that isn't sore, from my neck to my toes. I glance at Lorne and marvel at how spry and unaffected he seems.

"How are you doing?" he asks, as the valet disappears with his car.

"A little stiff," I admit.

"'A little stiff' cries out for a good stiff drink." Lorne smiles, looking toward the glorious spray of pink and purple bougainvillea surrounding the entrance to the hotel. "What do you think so far?"

"It's beautiful."

"Yeah, it's a real gem. Small, first-class, luxurious without being overly ostentatious, plus all the amenities one could ask for."

"You've obviously stayed here before."

"Actually, this is my first time," he says, as yet another valet holds the heavy glass door open for us and we enter the flower-filled, dark-wood-and-white-marble lobby. "My second wife, Ruth, and I used to stay at a bigger hotel about a half mile down the beach. We'd come every anniversary."

"How long were you two married?"

"Almost twenty-five years. She died shortly before I met Carol." His eyes sweep the lobby. "But I always wanted to stay here. It just looked so, I don't know, *special*. Nice to see it's exactly the way I remember it. Palm trees are a little taller," he observes of the large potted trees stretching toward the high ceiling that are scattered throughout the lobby.

We approach the long black marble reception counter. "Dr. Lorne Kreiger," he tells the handsome young man behind it whose name tag identifies him as Vic. Vic is wearing a flowered, short-sleeved shirt and a wide smile that showcases a mouthful of alarmingly big white teeth. "Two nights, two rooms."

"One for Linda Davidson," I clarify.

"Linda Davidson, come on down!" I hear Jenny shout.

I swing around, as if she might be hiding behind one of the potted palms.

"Everything okay?" Lorne asks.

"Sorry," I say with a laugh. "Thought I heard something."

"Linda Davidson," Vic repeats. "I'm afraid I'm not seeing anything here for that name . . ."

"That's because both rooms are under my name," Lorne explains to both Vic and me. "It was easier that way," he says casually, as he said that night at Divino's when we encountered my former student.

Clearly a man who prefers things easy. "I insist on paying my share," I whisper, watching Lorne extend his credit card across the counter to Vic.

"Don't be silly. This is my treat. I'm the one who invited *you*."

"Be that as it may . . ."

"Be that as it may," I hear Jenny sneer. *"What does* that *mean?"* I sneak another peek over my shoulder.

"Okay. Whatever you say," Lorne says. "We'll settle up later. Let's just leave it for now."

I nod, not wishing to argue. I've had my fill of arguments.

"I have two adjoining suites on the main floor overlooking the ocean, king-size beds, breakfast included," Vic says, still smiling.

I've always marveled at how anyone can talk and smile at the same time, I'm thinking as Vic hands several key cards to Lorne. This thought keeps me from perseverating on the mention of adjoining suites.

"Down that hall, all the way to the end," Vic instructs. "The valet will bring your bags to your rooms momentarily. Enjoy your stay."

"Thank you. I'm sure we will."

"I hope you don't mind the adjoining rooms," Lorne says, as we proceed down the long hall, carpeted in green-and-silver swirls. "It was just easier that way."

A young couple in matching blue bathing suits are exiting their room as we near the end of the corridor. They're literally all over each other, their arms and legs so intertwined it appears as if they share one body. "Sorry. Newlyweds," the young man explains, extricating himself from his giggling bride's embrace, a sheepish grin on his clean-shaven face.

Is he even old enough to shave? I find myself wondering.

Followed by *Was I ever that young?*

I watch them disappear down the hall, their bodies lean and taut, backsides high, firm, and round.

Backsides? I scream silently. *Backsides?*

There's no way I'm putting on a bathing suit, I decide in that moment. No way I'm putting my wrinkled flesh and sagging buttocks on display. I almost laugh. I remind myself that nobody's looking.

I used to believe that even as various body parts gave in to gravity, they somehow retained their shape.

But then, I used to believe a lot of things: in Santa Claus and the tooth fairy; in the power of positive thinking; that love would conquer all; that things have a way of working out, as Kleo reminded me earlier.

I don't know what I believe anymore.

I don't know what I want.

I don't know who I am.

Everything is changing, disappearing, dying. No amount of exercise or expensive creams and lotions can halt the body's inevitable decline. I might think of myself as being somewhere between forty-five and fifty-five, but the rest of the world knows the truth. They see me for who I am. Increasingly, I see myself for who I am *not*: not a wife, not a teacher, not worth their notice.

"Here we are," Lorne announces, rescuing me from my thoughts.

The door swings open to reveal a beautifully appointed suite with sliding floor-to-ceiling glass doors that lead to a covered patio overlooking the ocean. A Chagall-inspired mural of exotic birds and plants floating through an azure sky fills the wall behind the king-size bed, on top of which rests a matching down-filled duvet.

"What do you think?" Lorne asks.

"It's amazing." I follow him to the door that connects the two suites, sneaking a peek into the pink-and-white marble en suite bathroom as I walk past. *These rooms must cost a fortune,* I think as Lorne unlocks the door to reveal the second, virtually identical room.

"Take your pick," he directs.

"This one's good." I plop down on the edge of the bed. Seconds later, a valet arrives with our luggage.

Lorne wheels the two overnight bags inside, placing them side by side in front of the door. He makes no move to take his bag into the other room. Instead, he moves toward me, about to sit down on the bed beside me.

I quickly push myself to my feet, my knees cracking in protest. "How about that stiff drink you promised me?"

CHAPTER FORTY-ONE

We're sitting at the outside bar beside the large octagonal infinity pool that overlooks the ocean. About half the blue-and-white-striped deck chairs around the pool are occupied. The honeymooners we encountered earlier are making out at the pool's far end, oblivious to the middle-aged man doing laps around them.

A bare wisp of breeze buzzes around my head, like a tiny insect. It echoes the tiny buzz *inside* my head. I'm on my second piña colada, which is two more piña coladas than I normally imbibe.

I've never been much of a drinker. Spending a night throwing up in the bathroom of my college dormitory after a frat party, my then-boyfriend holding back my hair, pretty much cured me of the taste for exotic beverages. True, I enjoy the occasional glass of wine, but that's about it. I haven't had one of these rum-fueled concoctions in years. I'd forgotten how good they taste, how potent they can be.

"I've forgotten how good these taste," I say out loud.

Lorne smiles, swallows the last of his gin and tonic. "Never cared much for coconut," he says.

"No, Carol never liked it either," I hear myself say.

Did he just wince at the mention of her name?

"So, what do you think you'd like to do tomorrow?" he asks.

"I imagine that as a former English teacher, you'd be interested in seeing Hemingway's house."

"That would be great." I vaguely recall having visited the island's most famous tourist attraction when I was here years ago, but I don't remember much about it. I wonder if that's how Carol feels about most of her life.

"As for the rest of today," Lorne says, "I thought we could just relax, maybe have a little nap before dinner . . ."

Shit! Is he suggesting we take one together? "I've never really been one for naps," I tell him, although the truth is that I love naps and would dearly love to take one now. "But please. Feel free to go lie down. You must be exhausted. You did all the driving."

He waves away my concerns with a flick of his hand. "I'll be fine." He signals the bartender for another gin and tonic.

I look toward the honeymooners, her legs wrapped around his waist, his hands tangled in her long, wet hair, their lips seemingly glued together. I feel a stab of envy at their passionate abandon.

"Remember when we used to carry on like that?" Lorne says, as if privy to my thoughts.

"Bob was never one for public displays of affection," I tell him. "It was all I could do to get him to hold hands when we were out."

"That's too bad," he says, extending one hand across the top of the bar to pat mine.

I immediately wrap my hand around my drink and lift the glass to my lips before our flesh can make contact, trying desperately to think of something to say. We've already discussed the medical practice he retired from approximately a decade ago, my career in teaching, politics both local and national, art, the theater, our favorite movies and TV shows, the general state of the world, during our six-hour drive. I'm not sure there's much left to say. "Tell me about your first two marriages," I hear myself direct.

He laughs. "What would you like to know?"

"Whatever you'd like to tell me."

I listen as he recites the basic facts, but the truth is that I already know most of what he's telling me from the things Carol has previously shared: that he married his high school sweetheart, Karen, right after graduation and that she worked to put him through med school, that the marriage produced three children and lasted more than thirty years before she was struck by a car and killed; that he met his second wife, Ruth, a year later and married her soon after; that they were married almost twenty-five years before she succumbed to cancer; that he met and married Carol eight months after that.

The man has been married virtually his entire adult life, I realize. Clearly, this is a man not comfortable with being alone. He needs a woman by his side. *Any* woman, I understand with a start. I'm nothing special. I'm simply the most convenient.

"Something the matter?" Lorne asks.

"No. Sorry. Just felt a little dizzy for a second there." I lower my drink to the bar. "That's enough of that, I think."

"Sure you're all right?"

"Fine. But I think maybe I *will* go lie down for a bit before dinner. You stay here. Enjoy the sun."

"Nonsense. I'll come with you."

He's on his feet before I can stop him, taking my elbow and leading me back into the main lobby.

"Wait here," he says as we near the concierge desk. "I'll go make reservations for dinner."

The concierge is on the phone, so Lorne signals me to hold on. I take him literally, reaching for the top of a nearby chair to steady myself. My head is spinning. *What happens when we reach our rooms?* I'm asking myself. *What do I do if he makes a pass?*

Makes a pass, I repeat silently. *Makes a pass?*

Do people even use this expression anymore?

"You *take* a pass," I say out loud, giggling as I sneak a look around to make sure no one has overheard me.

Which is when I see a man and woman walking purposefully toward the concierge desk. The man is about Lorne's age, the hair at his temples an unnatural shade of red, the woman probably my age, her streaked blond hair several shades lighter than my own. "Lorne Kreiger?" the man calls out.

Lorne swivels toward him.

"I thought it was you! Alan Frysinger," he says, extending his hand. "God, how long has it been?"

"At least five years," Lorne says, shaking the man's hand. He looks quickly in my direction, his eyes urging me to stay put.

No need, I think. I couldn't move if I tried.

"You remember my wife, Gina."

"Of course. Nice to see you again."

"We heard about Carol," Gina says. "How's she doing?"

"Not great. She's in a memory care facility."

"So sorry to hear that."

"Her son Kevin is visiting from New York this weekend," Lorne continues, "so I thought I'd give them some space, come down here for a few days, try to relax."

"I'm sure you could use the break," Gina says.

"We're just off to the main drag to do some shopping, but please join us for dinner," Alan says.

"Oh, no. Thank you, but no!"

"I insist," Alan says. "You don't have other plans, do you?"

"Well, no," Lorne demurs. "But I . . ."

"No buts. Seven o'clock? I understand the food here is the best on the island."

"I really don't want to intrude . . ."

"Intrude?" Alan asks with a laugh. "We've been married almost fifty years. You'd be doing us a favor. Please change the reservation for Dr. Alan Frysinger from two people to three at seven o'clock," he directs the concierge before turning back to Lorne. "See you at seven. No arguments."

"No arguments," Lorne agrees.

CHAPTER FORTY-TWO

Unlike our chatter-filled drive from Jupiter to Key West, the drive from Key West back to Jupiter two days later is largely silent. Country music fills the car and permeates the heavy, blank space between us—songs of love and heartbreak, of trucks and dirt roads, of drinking and more drinking. Lorne concentrates on the driving; I concentrate on the scenery. Our exchanges are brief, to the point, matters of necessity more than matters of interest. *Do you need to use the restroom? Are you hungry? Would you like to stop and stretch your legs?*

What more is there to say, after all?

I watch the weekend play out in my mind's eye, a series of jagged images streaking across the ocean waves like bolts of lightning as we drive.

"I'm so sorry," I hear Lorne say, as he walks toward me, his eyes darting furtively about the hotel lobby to make sure the Frysingers are out of sight. "I take it you heard everything?"

I see myself nod.

"I panicked. I didn't know what to do, what to say."

"I understand."

"The man literally left me no choice. I didn't want him to think . . ."

"Really. I get it. Who is he anyway?"

"Just someone I knew professionally. Carol and I had dinner with him and his wife a few times. Look. I'm really so, so sorry. I didn't know how to explain being here with you without making it look . . ."

Like you've gone away for the weekend with a woman who is not your wife? Your wife who is in a memory care facility suffering from Alzheimer's? A woman who happens to be your wife's oldest and dearest friend?

"I know. I understand," I repeat, trying to shake away the nagging guilt I've been keeping at arm's length. "So, what do we do now?"

He shakes his head, leads me down the long hallway. "Look," he says, as we reach my door. "Maybe it's for the best. It's been a long day, and I know you're tired. This way, you can relax, order room service, and maybe we can have a drink on the patio when I get back. I promise I won't be late."

I nod, marveling at how easily Lorne has made it seem as if he's doing this as much for my benefit as for his own.

We enter my room, stand awkwardly beside our overnight bags. He reaches for my arm.

"You should probably go change for dinner." I take a step back, feel my leg brush up against the side of the bed.

"I'm really so sorry," Lorne apologizes again.

I watch him wheel his overnight bag toward the adjoining room.

"Till later," he says.

I smile and shut the door after him.

"He actually left you alone to go out to dinner with these people?" I hear Kleo shriek when I phone to tell her what happened. "I don't believe it."

"What don't you believe?" Mick asks from somewhere in the background.

Kleo relays the details of what I've just told her, and I hear Mick hoot.

"I told you that scumbag was no good," he says. "When are you girls going to start listening to me?"

They laugh, and I feel an immediate rush of gratitude. If they're laughing, they're not fighting. So, maybe this trip wasn't all for naught. My being out of the house, even for a short time, has given my daughter and her husband the freedom they needed to forgive each other and get on with life. *Maybe*, I'm thinking as I look over the menu for room service, *this story will have a happy ending after all.*

I hear Lorne return to his room at just after nine o'clock.

Minutes later, there's a soft tapping on the door between our suites. "Linda?" he calls.

Immediately, my body stiffens.

I'm lying on top of the duvet, wrapped in the luxuriously thick white terry-cloth bathrobe the hotel provides, watching the opening minutes of *Dateline*—a prominent member of an upscale community is suspected of murdering his wife and son—and I've spent the last few hours anticipating this moment, trying to decide what I should do when Lorne returned. Should I feign sleep or let him in? If I let him in, then what?

My head is a steaming cauldron of mixed emotions. Part of me understands—is even grateful for—what's happened. The other part of me is angry. Angry at being shunted aside, put on hold, expected to wait patiently in the shadows, like the proverbial other woman.

At my age, I'm not about to be anyone's secret.

"I've got a secret," I hear Jenny say.

"Go away, Jenny," I admonish, reaching for the remote control and turning off the TV.

"Linda?" Lorne calls again, louder this time.

"Come in," I call back, climbing out of bed and securing my

robe tight around me. Underneath the robe is the pale pink silk nightgown that I purchased yesterday, just in case . . .

In case of what? a voice asks. But this time, the voice isn't Jenny's. It's Carol's.

"Go away, Carol," I whisper.

"Door's not locked," I tell Lorne.

I watch the door open and Lorne cross the threshold, a glass of champagne in each hand. "Well, don't you look all nice and cozy," he says.

"How was your evening?"

"Boring as hell. Couldn't wait to leave." He holds out a glass for me to take. "I missed you."

My breath becomes shallow. "Why don't we take these out on the patio?" I manage to say.

I feel his breath on the back of my neck as I slide open the patio door.

The sound of the ocean fills the night air. We quickly occupy the two lounge chairs, spend a few minutes quietly absorbing the star-filled sky, inhaling the scent of the surrounding bougainvillea, sipping our champagne.

"So, what'd you have for dinner?" I ask when the silence begins drifting toward oppressive.

"Lobster," he answers. "You?"

"Same. It was delicious."

"Yes," he agrees.

"How long will the Frysingers be here?"

"They leave tomorrow morning, thank God. So, we're good to go."

Good to go where? I wonder.

Just where is this going?

We continue sipping our champagne, spend several minutes in aimless chatter before lapsing into another silence. Our glasses empty. The silence remains.

"It's been a long day," I say finally. "We should probably get some sleep." The word "we" slams against my brain. *We.* Not *you.* Not *I.* I've left the door open, I realize, pushing myself out of the chaise longue with as much delicacy as I can muster, bubbles of champagne floating around my eyes, clouding my vision, slowing my steps.

Lorne locks the patio door behind us as we reenter the bedroom. He takes the now-empty glass from my hand and puts it on the dresser, then turns back toward me. I open my mouth to say something—what, I'm not sure—but his lips are already covering mine, and I feel the gentle flick of his tongue against my teeth.

What would Carol think? I find myself wondering, as we sink toward the bed, Carol hovering nearby, watching as Lorne's hand moves to the nape of my neck, his fingers dancing gently across the creases of my flesh to tuck a few wayward hairs behind my ear.

He does this thing, I suddenly hear Carol say. *He reaches over and gently tucks some hairs behind my ear. And then he slowly—oh, so slowly—lets his fingers trace a delicate line down my neck . . . I tell you, it's electric.*

Except that the rush of electricity I'm expecting to feel isn't there. In fact, what I'm feeling is more irritation than excitement. I realize in that moment that, while I genuinely like Lorne, I'm just not attracted to him in that way. Am I being silly? Is it foolish to be hoping for real romantic sparks at my age? "Stop!" I hear myself say.

"What's wrong?"

I jump to my feet. "I can't do this."

"It's all right . . ."

"It's not all right," I counter. "Carol is my best friend."

"Carol would be the first person to understand, the first person to say 'Go for it!'"

"Maybe," I agree. "But . . ." *What if it's not just Carol? What if I don't want to go for it? What if I realize that, while I may eventually be open to a romantic relationship, it won't be with you?* "I'm sorry. I just can't."

Lorne remains seated on the end of the bed for perhaps another minute, then he slowly pushes himself to his feet. "You're sure about this?"

"I am."

"So, what happens now?" he asks when he reaches the adjoining door to his room.

"I hope we can still be friends," I offer.

He nods, then opens the door, closing it after him.

I return to my bed, burrowing under the comforter and flipping on the TV, returning to the last few minutes of *Dateline*. Let Lorne believe that my rejection of him was based purely on my feelings for Carol, I decide.

It's easier that way.

CHAPTER FORTY-THREE

"Where the hell have you been?" Jenny demands as I step off the elevator onto the fourth floor of Legacy Place. She's dressed in her pajamas, despite the fact that it's two in the afternoon. I wonder if she's been standing here the whole time I've been gone.

"Jenny," Selena warns from her desk. "What did we talk about? Be nice."

"I'm always nice," Jenny shoots back. "Where have you been?"

"It was a busy week," I lie.

"Busy with what? Busy fucking your boyfriend?"

"Jenny . . ." Selena says.

"He's here now, you know. Visiting his wife. Does your best friend know you're fucking her husband?"

"Jenny!" Selena rises from her chair, one hand on her phone.

"I am *not* fucking her husband," I tell Selena. "Sorry for the language."

"Sorry, sorry, sorry, sorry." Jenny pushes her hair away from her face, moving a giant bobby pin from the side of one ear to the other.

"No apologies or explanations needed," Selena says.

"Linda!" a voice calls from down the hall.

"Speak of the devil!" Jenny shouts.

I turn to see Lorne walking toward me. We haven't spoken since Key West. I'm relieved to realize that it's nice to see him.

"What do *you* want?" Jenny demands.

"Jenny . . ." Selena cautions. "Am I going to have to call Lance?"

Jenny's response is to stick out her tongue. "I'll be in my room," she tells me, "when you're finished with this loser." She dismisses Lorne with a flick of her wrist, then shuffles down the corridor to her room. "Don't keep me waiting too long, Linda Davidson," she hollers when she reaches her door. "I have much to tell you."

"As lovely as always," Lorne notes, waiting until Jenny has disappeared into her apartment before continuing. "I'm glad you're here," he says. "I was going to call you."

"Has something happened?"

"Carol's son Eric and his wife drove up yesterday from Miami," he begins without further preamble, "and we had a group chat on Zoom with her other sons, and it was decided that, in light of everything that's been going on, the situation with James Usher and everything, it's probably best if we move Carol to another facility."

"What?"

"Eric's wife has already found a place in Miami, not far from where they live, that has a vacancy. He's confident that we can move her in by the end of the month."

"Do you really think that moving her is a good idea?"

"Trust me, it wasn't a decision any of us took lightly, but yes, I think it's the right one." He lowers his voice. "Look. I know that this will be difficult for you, that it won't be as convenient for you to visit her as often as you've been doing, if at all . . ."

"What are you talking about? Of course, I'll visit."

"I'm just saying that I'd understand—we all would—if you choose to make a clean break."

"A clean break," I repeat. "Is that what you'll be doing?"

Lorne's cheeks redden, as if he's been slapped. "This isn't easy for me either, you know."

A rush of air escapes my lungs. My eyes fill with tears. "I'm sorry. That was uncalled for. You'll let me know the details?"

"Of course."

"Is she awake?" I ask. "Can I see her?"

"Of course," he says again.

We walk side by side down the long hall. The door to the room once occupied by Ralph McMillan is open, and I catch sight of an elderly woman standing in the middle of her small sitting area, a painfully familiar blank look on her face.

We enter Carol's apartment to find her standing at the window. She's wearing an ill-fitting flower-print dress that I recall she never liked, and her lipstick has been haphazardly applied, so that it misses much of her bottom lip. "Carol, hi," I say in greeting.

She doesn't bother turning around.

"It's Linda, honey," Lorne says.

She nods. "Where's James? I want to see James."

I watch Lorne wince. "He's pretty much the only person she seems to want anything to do with these days."

"I'm so sorry."

"Carol, honey. Why don't you come sit with us for a few minutes?" Lorne sits down on the sofa, pats the seat beside him.

Carol remains at the window. "Where's James? I want to see James."

"You can see him later," Lorne snaps. "Sorry," he apologizes immediately. "It's just hard," he whispers, although there's really no need. I understand his frustration, and Carol isn't listening.

"No apologies or explanations necessary," I tell him, much as Selena told me earlier. I sink into one of the salmon-colored chairs, turn my attention back to Carol. "Lorne tells me that Kevin flew in from New York last week to see you, and that Eric and his wife drove up from Miami yesterday."

Carol's head turns in my direction, but there's no sign of recognition in her eyes, no indication that she sees me at all.

We hold our positions for several seconds of uncomfortable silence.

"Linda!" a voice suddenly catapults down the hallway. "Linda Davidson! Where are you? Aren't you done yet?"

Shit.

Lorne lowers his head into his hands.

"Linda! Linda Davidson!"

"Go see your friend," he instructs. "Whatever she has to say has got to be better than this."

"Linda Davidson!" Jenny calls from just outside the room.

I push myself to my feet. "You'll be in touch?"

"As soon as I have all the pertinent information."

I step toward Carol, wanting to take her in my arms, hoping my touch will trigger memories I need to believe are still lurking just below the surface.

She shudders as I approach and recoils from my embrace.

I step back, drop my arms to my sides. "Take care," I whisper as Jenny appears in the doorway, hands on her hips.

"I'm sorry," Selena says from somewhere behind her. "I tried to stop her."

"That's okay."

"Coming?" Jenny asks.

I lift my hands in the air in a gesture of surrender. "I'm all yours."

CHAPTER FORTY-FOUR

"You were a long time," Jenny says, as I usher her back down the hall toward her apartment.

"Sorry about that."

"That's okay. The important thing is that you're here now. I missed you, Linda Davidson."

"I missed you, too," I admit, entering her apartment and closing the door behind us. "Kill anyone while I was gone?"

Jenny lets out a resounding whoop. "Hah! You're so funny!" She guides me toward the sofa, sits down so close beside me that I can smell the mint toothpaste on her breath. "And the answer is no, if you must know. Not since you-know-who."

"Ralph McMillan?"

"Don't know who you mean," Jenny says, tucking some hairs behind my right ear. "You look so pretty. Did you do something different with your hair?"

Round and round we go, I think. *And where she stops, nobody knows.*

"Actually, yes," I tell her, as flattered as I am surprised. She's the first person who's noticed the change. "I had it done at this place in Key West," I say, "and they thought it would look nice if I parted my hair from left to right instead of from right to left, the way I've always done, and I think I like it, so . . ."

"This is a really boring story," Jenny says.

I laugh, realizing just how much I've missed her company, her complete lack of a filter. "You're right."

"Not to hurt your feelings, but you *do* go on. A simple yes or no is all that was required."

"I'll keep that in mind."

"When were you in Key West?"

"The weekend before last."

"With your friend's husband, the one you're . . ."

"Don't say it."

"*Not* fucking! Can I say *that*?"

"Can I stop you?"

"Hah! You're so funny. How is she?"

"Not great. Her family is moving her to Miami, so I won't be able to visit her as much."

"More time for me!" Jenny claps her hands in delight, before her face suddenly darkens. "You'll still come see me after she's gone, won't you?"

Will I? Part of me views Carol's impending departure as an opportunity to stop this nonsense with Jenny once and for all; the other part of me doesn't want it to end. At least until I've heard the whole story, and determined how much of it is true.

Can any of it be true?

"Please," Jenny urges. "You have to come. There's still so much I have to tell you."

Who—whom—am I kidding? "Of course, I'll visit," I concede.

"Yay!" Jenny shouts. "You're a good egg, Linda Davidson."

"I'm not so sure about that."

"I am," Jenny states. "What sign are you?"

"What?"

"What's your astrological sign? No, wait! Don't tell me. Let me guess. I know, I know, I know. You're a Pisces!"

I laugh. "You're right." *Of course she's right.*

"Guess what sign I am."

"I have no idea."

"Come on. Take a guess."

"I really don't put a lot of stock in all that."

"I didn't ask you that. I asked you to guess what sign I am."

I sigh. "I don't know. Leo?"

"No. Guess again."

"Taurus?"

"God, no. You're really bad at this, aren't you? I'll give you a hint. I have a birthday coming up next month."

I try to recall the astrological sign for June. "Gemini?"

"Right you are, Linda Davidson! The twins. Split personality, that's me. A study in contradictions. See how easy that was? Now, what'd you want to tell me?"

"You said that *you* had a lot to tell *me*," I correct.

She stares up at the ceiling, as if the things she wants to tell me are scrawled across its surface. "Did I tell you that I killed my brother?"

What? "You told me that you *didn't* kill your brother," I remind her.

"Which one?"

"Either."

She laughs. "Well, that was a lie. A real doozy. A whopper! A Big Mac!"

"You lied?"

"Don't look so shocked, Linda Davidson," she says. "People lie all the time."

"Are you lying now?"

"About what?"

"Did you kill your brother?"

"Jake," she says. "I killed Jake. I didn't have to kill Tommy. Some other guy took care of him, saved me the time and trouble."

"Why would you kill Jake?"

"Because he was just like Daddy. I told you that."

"He molested you?"

"I didn't say that. Who said that?"

"You said he was just like your father."

"Yes, he was. So was Tommy. But I didn't kill him. Some other guy took care of him, saved me the time and trouble." She starts rocking back and forth.

"When did you kill Jake?"

Jenny gives my question a moment's thought. "Not really sure. I know it was sometime after I killed Daddy because I was back home trying to sell the house, and Jake turned up, thinking he was just gonna take over everything, and he got good and drunk and burst into my bedroom, like he used to when we were younger, and he was saying things like 'You think you're too good for your big brother, do you, 'cause you're some big-shot pharmacist now?'" She shakes her head. "So, he didn't leave me a whole lot of choice, did he?"

"You poisoned him?"

Another shake of her head. "No. I didn't have time for that. I was leaving the next day, going back to Los Angeles. So I just waited till he was fast asleep, and then I stabbed him *right through the heart.*"

Holy crap! "And then what?"

"He died."

"I meant, what did *you* do then?"

"Oh. I wrapped his body in a sheet and put him in the back of my car and ditched him in the middle of nowhere, figured that by the time anybody found him, I'd be long gone." She shrugs. "And I was. Easy-peasy."

"Nobody ever questioned you?"

"Nobody gave a rat's backside! I mean, Jake wasn't exactly a model citizen. He was always in and out of trouble, here one day, gone the next. No real friends, other than a bunch of drunks and lowlifes just like him. Nobody even knew he was missing until some hiker stumbled across his body a few weeks later, and by that time, the animals had pretty much had their way with him." She laughs. "Had their way," she repeats. "That's such a funny phrase. Anyway, I got a letter when I was back in L.A., notifying me of his death. That was the end of that." She smiles, gives a little shrug.

"So, he was the fourth person you killed," I say.

"I guess."

"Which means that you didn't kill your second husband."

"I didn't kill him?"

"Did you?"

"Pretty sure I did."

"But you told me there were four."

"Four what?"

"You said you killed four people."

"Hmm," she says, mulling this over. "I may have lied."

"You may have lied?"

"People lie, Linda Davidson. I told you that!"

"So . . . there may have been more?"

Jenny nods. "There may have been more."

CHAPTER FORTY-FIVE

"How many more?" I ask.

"I don't know," Jenny says. "It's not like I kept a journal or anything."

"Ballpark," I say.

"Shea Stadium," she answers.

"What? No. I didn't mean to name a ballpark."

"Then why'd you say it?"

"It's just an expression."

"I don't get it."

"It means, give me an approximate number."

"You say 'ballpark' and I'm supposed to know that means to give you an approximate number? That doesn't make any sense."

"I think it has to do with statistics. Baseball is famous for its statistics."

"What does how many people I killed have to do with baseball?"

"It doesn't."

"Then why did you say it?"

"Believe me, I'm sorry I did."

"Don't be sorry, Linda Davidson. You apologize way too much. I told you that."

"Many times."

She smiles. "Wrigley Field, Fenway Park, Yankee Stadium. Your turn."

"Dodger Stadium," I offer, deciding to play along. To do otherwise will only waste time and increase my frustration. Although if I'm being honest, I'm more amused than frustrated. "Oriole Park at Camden Yards."

"Oriole Park at Camden what?"

"Camden Yards, in Baltimore. Home of the Baltimore Orioles."

"Never heard of Camden Yards. Are you sure? How do you know that?"

"My husband was a baseball fan," I tell her. "We used to watch a lot of games together, especially after he got sick."

"Was your husband a nice man?"

"He was."

"Did he ever cheat on you?"

"No."

"You're sure of that?"

"Very."

"Hmm."

"Was your second husband a nice man?" I ask.

"David Huston was a scoundrel," Jenny pronounces. "He was definitely *not* a nice man. He cheated on me the whole time we were married."

"How long was that?"

"Three years."

"How old were you when you married him?"

"I don't know. Forty . . . fifty. It's a long time ago. I'm ninety-two, remember? Going to be ninety-three next month. We're talking almost half a century."

"It's a long time," I agree.

"You can kill a lot of people in fifty years."

"Did you?"

"My share," she says.

"What does that mean?"

"It's just an expression. Something people say." Jenny smiles. "Will you buy me a cake for my birthday, Linda Davidson?"

"If you'd like," I answer. "What kind of cake?"

"I'd like a white cake from Publix. They make the best birthday cakes in the whole world! Just like the cakes you used to get when you were a kid, the kind my mother used to get for me, until, you know . . . my daddy killed her. Do you know the kind of cakes I mean?"

"I know exactly. My mother used to get them for me, too, and I bought them for my girls . . ."

"You're going on again."

"Oh. Sorry."

"I want a two-layer vanilla cake with white icing and lemon filling between the layers," Jenny continues. "And lots of soft pink flowers along the top edges. Not the hard ones made of solid sugar that you can't eat. The soft ones made of icing. And I want it to say, *Happy Birthday, Jenny!* in big red letters. Can you get me one like that?"

"If you promise not to throw it at me," I say, recalling the raspberry croissant that she threw at my head.

"Why would I do that?" she asks.

"Tell me about David Huston," I direct.

"He was not a nice man. He cheated on me the whole time we were married."

"Why did you marry him?"

"Why does anyone marry anyone? Why did you marry *your* husband?"

"Because I loved him."

"Love," she scoffs. *"Feh!"*

"Feh? What kind of word is that?"

"A good one. Don't you think? It's one of those words that means exactly how it sounds. You understand what I'm saying?"

"I actually do," I admit. *Feh,* I repeat silently, the word bouncing around my brain. "So, why did you marry him, if you didn't love him?"

"I don't know. He was good-looking, rich, not very bright. I always found that combination very attractive."

I laugh.

"What's funny?"

"That you find stupid appealing."

"Why is that funny? Men are always marrying women who are as dumb as they are beautiful. Nothing like an unlined face staring up at you adoringly, as if every idiotic thing that comes out of your mouth is manna from heaven. Why are you looking at me like that?"

I shake my head. "Just trying to decide how crazy you really are."

CHAPTER FORTY-SIX

"Well, of course, she's crazy," Kleo exclaims when I tell her about my latest conversation with Jenny. It's seven o'clock that evening, and we're sitting at the kitchen table, having finished our dinner of chicken and rice. Mick is out for the evening, trying to woo a prospective new client. "I remind you that the woman has dementia, the literal translation of which is 'out of one's mind.'"

"I know. It's just that there are times she sounds so . . . sane."

"Sane people don't claim to have killed . . . how many people?"

"Apparently, the number's up for grabs."

"Lovely." Kleo studies me for several long seconds. "You're not going to keep seeing her, are you? After they move Carol to Miami, I mean."

"I kind of promised her that I would."

"Why on earth would you do that?"

"To be honest, I like her."

"You *like* her?"

"She's funny."

"She's nuts!"

"Not all the time."

"No. Only when she's killing people. Mom! You can't be serious about this. If Jenny is telling the truth, she murders everyone who gets close to her."

"Not everyone."

"Her father, her brothers . . ."

"Only one brother . . ." I correct.

"Two husbands . . ."

"That hasn't been definitely established."

"The old guy on her floor . . ."

"Again, we don't know that for sure. According to Selena, he choked on his own vomit."

"Because she poisoned him."

"Or she didn't."

"Either way you're putting yourself in danger if you keep seeing her."

"Danger? No. That's ridiculous. Feh!"

"*Feh?* What kind of word is 'feh'?"

"It's one of those words that means exactly how it sounds," I explain.

"That doesn't make any sense."

"Oh. I thought it did. At any rate, it's her birthday next month, and I promised I'd buy her a cake . . ."

Kleo's eyes fill with worry. Seconds later, the worry morphs into resolution. "Okay," she says. "Obviously, I can't stop you from seeing her. But the next time you visit her, I'm going with you."

"What? Why?"

"Because I want to meet the woman who has such a strong hold over my mother."

I open my mouth to argue, but no words emerge. What can I say after all? My daughter is right. Jenny has an undeniable hold on me, one I'm strangely reluctant to release.

"Did you do something different with your hair?" Kleo asks, suddenly.

I laugh. "They did it like this when I was in Key—" I stop, re-membering Jenny's admonition. "Just thought I'd try parting it the other way."

"Looks nice."

"Thank you, darling."

Kleo pushes herself out of her chair. "Now, if you don't mind, I'm going to go finish this research I was working on before Mick gets home."

"Of course, darling. I'll clean up in here."

Kleo disappears to the dining room while I load the dishes into the dishwasher. I'm wiping off the table when she sticks her head back into the room. "Mom, you didn't, by any chance, move anything on the dining room table, did you?"

"No. I didn't touch anything. Why?"

"I can't find the article I was reading. I'm sure I left it right next to my computer."

"Maybe it's under something."

"I've checked everywhere. It's nowhere."

"Well, it can't have disappeared into thin air." I follow her into the dining area. "Tell me exactly what I'm looking for."

"It's an old issue of *The Atlantic*."

"When was the last time you saw it?"

"I was reading it before I started making dinner. I put it down right here." She bangs on the table. "Where the hell is it?"

"Is it possible you took it into the bathroom?" I start rifling through the stacks of research papers on the table.

"I don't think so, but I guess anything's possible. I'll go look."

I glance toward the closed door to Mick's office, a knot growing in the pit of my stomach. The last time there was an issue with Kleo's work was after Mick played around with her computer. Is it possible that he had something to do with the magazine's disappearance?

I open the door and step inside, taking a quick look around. Mick's office is neat, way too neat for someone claiming to be up to his eyeballs in work. There is literally nothing on his desk but a lamp and his computer—no paper, no pens, no books. Nothing on the small green leather sofa against the west wall.

Nobody is that neat, I think, moving to his desk and opening the top and middle drawers, finding nothing of interest in either.

I'm pulling open the bottom drawer when Kleo appears in the doorway.

"What are you doing?" she asks, sneaking a peek over her shoulder, as if she suspects Mick might be lurking.

"I thought you might have wandered in here to talk to Mick, and inadvertently put the magazine down," I say, wondering if the lie sounds as obvious to her as it does to me.

"You thought I *inadvertently* put the magazine I was reading in the bottom drawer of Mick's desk," she repeats, her voice underlining how ridiculous this explanation sounds.

I shrug. *What can I say?*

"And did I? Leave the magazine in the bottom drawer of his desk?" She steps around me, reaches into the drawer, and extricates the contents. "Shit!"

"You found it?"

"Not exactly." She hands me three magazines, each glossy cover depicting nude women in various stages of bondage. "These are disgusting," Kleo says, leafing through the top one: women bound and gagged, in dog collars and chains, being tortured with whips and dildos. "What the hell would he be doing with these?"

A whoosh of air escapes my lungs as I recall the porn I witnessed on Mick's computer. I have no answers for her.

Kleo returns the magazines to their former hiding place and ushers me quickly back into the hall, closing the door behind her.

"Has Mick ever . . . ?" I begin, unable to finish the question, the idea that anyone would ever abuse my daughter in such a way filling me with an almost murderous combination of fear and rage.

"Has he ever . . . ?" Kleo repeats. "Oh, God, Mom. No! I swear. Never. Shit!" She looks helplessly around the hallway. "What am I supposed to do? I can't even ask him about this without him realizing I was snooping through his things."

"Well, technically, *I* was the one snooping."

"Yes, that's so much better." Kleo drops to her knees on the floor and buries her head in her lap. "Oh, my God," she says, as she lifts her head. "There's my magazine."

"What? Where?"

"There. Under the dining room table, near the wall."

"How did it get all the way over there?"

"I must have dropped it," Kleo says, crawling on her hands and knees across the hall to the far end of the dining room table and retrieving the magazine from the floor.

Which doesn't explain how it got all the way over there. Someone would have to have deliberately placed it there, I think, knowing that "someone" could only be Mick.

But why would Mick want to deliberately sabotage Kleo's dissertation?

Does he want her to go back to her job, so that she can start bringing home a paycheck again, thereby taking some of the pressure off him? Or is it more insidious than that? Is he jealous—of the time she's spending on it, time it takes away from him? Does he not want her to succeed?

I decide to keep these thoughts to myself. I've already done enough damage for one night.

"Whew," Kleo exclaims, tightly grasping the ancient issue of *The Atlantic* as she clambers to her feet. "That's a load off."

We stand facing each other for several seconds in a silence as thick as a dense fog. In my mind's eye, I'm picturing pages of naked women, blindfolded and gagged, hands tied behind their backs, their bodies twisted into tortuous positions and bound by ropes. I can tell by the expression on Kleo's face that she's seeing the same thing.

"I should get started on this article," she says.

"Of course. I'll leave you to it."

"Mom," she calls as I turn to go. "Please don't think badly of Mick because of what we found. He was probably just curious. You know how men are."

I nod, but say nothing.

I'm wondering what Jenny would say.

CHAPTER FORTY-SEVEN

"Jenny, I'd like you to meet my daughter Kleo," I say, introducing the two women. "Kleo, this is Jenny."

"Nice to meet you, Jenny," Kleo says.

"Nice to meet *you*," Jenny replies.

So far, so good.

Kleo has been after me all week to let her accompany me to Legacy Place, and I finally ran out of excuses and gave in. Besides, things have been even tenser than usual at home. Mick failed to secure that client he'd been courting and has been sullen, uncommunicative, and snippy all week. He leaves the house for hours at a time without explanation and comes home reeking of beer. If questioned, he locks himself in his office, refusing to come out till dinner, then plops himself down in front of the TV in the den until it's time to go to bed. Any attempt at conversation is met with either sarcasm or stony silence.

"It's just really hard for him right now," Kleo says, trying to make excuses for her husband's behavior. "Things will get better as soon as his business picks up. If he could just land that one big client . . ."

I'm not sure if she's trying to convince me or herself.

At any rate, it's starting to take a physical toll on her. She's lost weight, her porcelain skin is paler than usual, her energy level noticeably down. Work on her dissertation has all but come to a standstill. I decided that, if nothing else, a visit with Jenny might prove a welcome diversion, something to take her mind off her husband's increasingly unpredictable and unpleasant behavior.

So now, here sit the three of us in the fourth-floor visitors' lounge at Legacy Place: Kleo in white capris and a blue T-shirt that flatter her figure, I in a shapeless rose-colored shift that does its best to conceal mine, and Jenny in what can only be described as a mesmerizing collection of mismatched colors, checks and stripes, none of which complement the flowered, ankle-length socks on her shoeless feet. Her gray hair hangs limp around her face, held more or less in place by a rhinestone-covered navy velvet headband.

She is, truly, a sight for sore eyes.

"How do you know Linda Davidson?" Jenny asks my daughter only seconds after their initial introduction.

Kleo steals a wary glance in my direction. "She's my mother."

"You never told me you had children," Jenny says, a hint of accusation in her voice.

"Yes, I did. I have two daughters. I told you that."

"No, you didn't."

"I thought I did. I'm sorry."

"What are you apologizing for?" Jenny asks. "Your mother is always apologizing. Is she like that at home?"

Kleo manages a slight smile. "She probably apologizes more than she should."

"No question about it," Jenny says. "Who are you?" she asks with her next breath. "How do you know Linda Davidson?"

"I'm Linda's daughter Kleo. How long have you lived here, Jenny?"

"I'm ninety-two," Jenny replies.

"I meant, how long have you lived in Legacy Place?"

"I'll be ninety-three next month. Which makes me a Gemini. What sign are you?"

"Just go with it," I whisper.

"I'm an Aquarius," Kleo says quickly.

"I'm a Gemini."

Kleo nods. "The twins."

"What twins?"

Kleo looks toward me, her eyes appealing for help.

"That's quite the outfit you have on today," I tell Jenny.

Jenny looks down at her red-and-white-striped cotton top and yellow-and-black-checkered pants, the zipper of which is coming undone. "Do you like it?"

"I do. It actually reminds me of an outfit that Kleo put together when she was little. She used to insist on dressing herself, and one day she went to school with this flowered top and striped pants and red rubber boots . . ."

"This is a really boring story," Jenny says.

"Oh, my God," Kleo says, stifling a laugh.

"What are you laughing about?" Jenny asks her.

"Sorry. I . . ."

"Who are you anyway?"

"I'm Kleo, Linda's daughter."

"Are you with the CIA?"

"The CIA?"

"She's not with the CIA," I interject.

"Did Linda tell you I kill people? Is that why you're here? She wasn't supposed to tell anyone."

"She didn't," Kleo lies.

"It's a secret," Jenny says.

"I won't tell anyone."

"John Kennedy."

"What?"

"I killed John Kennedy."

"You killed John Kennedy?" Kleo repeats.

"Shh. Everyone thinks it was Lee Harvey Oswald. Who is this person?" she asks me. "Why is she here?"

"She's my daughter."

"She's very beautiful. Doesn't look anything like you."

"No," I admit, watching Kleo cover her face with her hand to hide the grin spreading across her cheeks. "She takes after her father."

"I killed my father," Jenny says.

"Holy shit!" Kleo says.

"Shit, fuck, fart," comes Jenny's quick retort.

"And on that happy note, I really should get going." Kleo rises to her feet. "It was very interesting meeting you, Jenny."

"Interesting meeting *you*," Jenny parrots.

"I'll walk you to the elevator," I say.

"You're coming right back, aren't you, Linda Davidson?"

"I'm coming right back," I assure her.

"So?" I ask my daughter as we reach the elevator. "What do you think?"

"Truthfully, I'm not sure *what* to think. The woman is obviously out of her ever-loving mind, but I guess she's harmless enough."

The elevator arrives.

"You headed home?" I ask as she steps inside.

"Not yet. I have a doctor's appointment." Kleo leans forward, presses the button for the main floor.

This is the first I'm hearing about a doctor's appointment. "Is everything all right?"

"I'm sure everything's fine. Nothing to worry about." Kleo waves as the doors close. "See you later, Linda Davidson."

I smile, hearing footsteps coming up behind me.

"Who was that?" Jenny asks, resting her chin heavily on my shoulder.

"That was my daughter Kleo," I say, swiveling toward her.

"Strange name, Kleo. Not sure I like it."

I take Jenny's elbow, guide her back toward her room. "She was named after my husband's grandmother, who was originally from Greece, and . . ."

"Is this a long story?"

I laugh. "You have a better one?"

"Why, yes, Linda Davidson," she says. "I believe I do."

CHAPTER FORTY-EIGHT

"I met David Huston soon after I moved to Florida," Jenny begins once we're comfortably ensconced in the sitting room of her apartment.

"What year was that?"

"What difference does it make?"

"It helps me get a clearer picture," I try to explain.

"Clearer pictures aren't always the best thing," she states. "Have you ever had cataract surgery?"

I shake my head. My latest eye exam revealed the existence of budding cataracts. No need to do anything about them yet, the doctor has advised. But likely in the next year or two.

Assuming I'm still around.

"Worst thing I ever did," Jenny continues. "I was about your age, starting to have problems seeing things, even with my glasses. So, I go to the doctor. She says I need cataract surgery. I say, 'Okay.' No big deal. Next thing you know, it's like things go instantly from black-and-white to Technicolor. I'm seeing colors sharper and brighter than I have in years." She snorts. "I'm also seeing every speck of dust on the floor, every crack in the walls, every damn wrinkle on people's faces, every damn line on *my* face. That was the worst. I used to be quite beautiful, you know."

"I'm sure you were."

"Not after I had that surgery, I wasn't. You get my point?"

"Clearer pictures aren't always the best thing," I say, repeating her earlier pronouncement.

"Damn right." She removes her hairband, drops it to her lap, vigorously scratching her scalp until her hair is shooting out in all directions, as if she's standing on an electric current. "Your daughter's quite beautiful. What did you say her name is?"

"Kleo."

"Not sure I care for that name."

"You were telling me about David Huston," I prompt.

"What did I tell you?"

"That you met him soon after you moved to Florida."

"Right. It was March of 1980," she volunteers. "I remember because . . . I don't remember," she admits after a long pause.

"You met him in March of 1980 . . ."

"No, I moved to Florida in March 1980," she corrects. "I met David in June."

"How'd you meet?"

Jenny starts picking at the rhinestones on her headband. "He came into the pharmacy where I was working. I'd only been working there a few weeks. He came in to fill a prescription for his diabetes. David was diabetic."

"Was that here in Jupiter?"

"What difference does that make?"

"Just curious."

"Still trying to get a clearer picture?" she asks, with a grin.

"I guess."

"It wasn't Jupiter. It was Sarasota. You ever been to Sarasota?"

"Yes. It's beautiful, all those white, sandy beaches."

"I used to be beautiful," Jenny says.

"Why'd you leave Los Angeles?"

Jenny shrugs. "It was time to move on. Too much water under the bridge."

Too much water? Or too many bodies? "What made you choose Sarasota?"

"I didn't move there right away. I lived in a bunch of other places first. Austin, Denver, Atlanta. Went on a holiday to Sarasota. Liked what I saw. All those white, sandy beaches," she says, repeating my words.

"How long did you live there?"

"Around four years, I guess. I left after David died."

"He died or you killed him?"

"Same difference."

"Is it?"

"I still lived in Sarasota the same length of time, no matter how he died," she tells me.

I have to laugh. "True enough."

"Is Kleo married?" she asks.

"Yes."

"Happily?"

"Sometimes," I answer, honestly. "When did you marry David?"

Her eyes narrow as her lips purse. "Nine months after we met. I didn't have to get married. I wasn't pregnant. I was forty-five years old, for God's sake," she says. "The nine months was just a coincidence."

"Why did you marry David if you didn't love him?"

"Who says I didn't love him?"

"So, you *did* love him?"

"Are you crazy? Of course, I didn't love him."

"Then why did you marry him?"

"Same reason I married Parker Rubini. He was handsome, rich, and dumb as a plank. Plus, he had diabetes, so I was kind of hoping he wouldn't be around all that long."

"You were married for three years," I say.

"Three years. That's right. Cheated on me the whole damn time. And then he died."

"Was it the diabetes that killed him?"

"That's what it says on his death certificate."

"What do *you* say?"

She laughs. "His diabetes might have had a little help."

"Did you kill him because he was cheating on you?"

"I never said I killed him! Although infidelity is as good a reason to kill someone as any, wouldn't you say? Men aren't supposed to cheat on their wives."

"And you've never felt any remorse?" I hear myself ask.

"Well, I certainly regret having had that cataract surgery, I can tell you that."

"But not for killing your father and your brother? And Parker and Francesca Rubini. And David Huston . . ."

". . . and Ralph McMillan."

"So, you *did* kill Ralph McMillan."

"Don't forget John Kennedy," she advises, as a rhinestone from her headband pops off and falls to the floor. "Hah! Everyone thinks it was Lee Harvey Oswald," she says, triumphantly.

"And the others?" I ask, ignoring her interruption, trying to decide if her reference to JFK is a delusion or a deliberate deception.

"Who says there were others?"

"You did," I remind her.

"So I did, Linda Davidson," she says as another rhinestone pops off her headband and drops to the floor. "So I did."

CHAPTER FORTY-NINE

"So," Kleo says when I get home later that afternoon. She's standing in front of the stovetop, stirring a pot of spaghetti sauce she's making for dinner. "Who else did she kill? Marilyn Monroe? Elvis? Tupac?"

"Who?"

"He was a rapper. It doesn't matter. She didn't kill him any more than she killed Kennedy. Face it, Mom. She's just a lonely old woman suffering from dementia."

"You don't think she killed anyone?"

"Do *you*?" Kleo asks, sounding more than a bit like Jenny. "*Seriously?*"

"Seriously, I don't know what to think."

"Who else did she tell you she killed?" Kleo asks again.

"She said she'd tell me next time."

"Of course she did. What better way to keep you coming back?"

"Well, if it's a ploy, it's working. I admit it, I'm hooked. Does that make me an awful person?"

The door to Mick's office opens and he ambles into the kitchen. "Who's an awful person?"

"Mom thinks she is because she wants to hear more of Jenny's stories."

"She's right. You're an awful person," he tells me with a smile. "Any more names you want me to check out?"

"John Kennedy," Kleo informs him. "Everyone thinks it was Lee Harvey Oswald who killed him, but apparently it was Jenny Cooper."

"Why aren't I surprised?" Mick says. He leans toward the stovetop. "That smells absolutely delicious. Save me some."

"What do you mean, save you some?" Kleo asks. "Where are you going?"

"Meeting," Mick says.

"Now? Dinner will be ready in twenty minutes."

"I'll eat when I get back."

"When will that be?"

"Depends."

"On what?"

"On how the meeting goes."

"Who are you meeting?"

"Prospective client. And I think you mean, *whom* am I meeting, don't you?"

"I don't understand," Kleo says, ignoring the sarcasm. "Why didn't you tell me about this meeting before?"

"Because it just came up." He kisses her forehead. "Gotta run." He touches my arm as he walks past. "Wish me luck."

"Always," I say.

Seconds later, we hear the front door open and close.

"Excuse me," I say to the young man stocking shelves at Publix. "But I'm looking for the bakery."

"To the left of the front door when you come in," he directs. "You can't miss it."

I return to the front entrance, but the bakery is nowhere to be seen. "Excuse me," I say to one of the checkout girls. "What have you done with the bakery?"

"What do you want from me?" she asks.

"*What do you want from me?*"

"I'm picking up a birthday cake for a friend."

"Vanilla cake, lemon filling, pink flowers, *Happy Birthday* in bright red letters?"

"Yes, that's the one."

"That will be one hundred dollars."

"A hundred dollars? Are you insane?"

"*Are you insane?*"

"Do you want the cake or don't you?" She opens the cake box, lets me peek inside.

"It's not right," I say.

"*It's not right!*"

"It says *Happy Birthday, Joanie,*" I tell her. "It's supposed to say *Happy Birthday, Jenny!*"

"Are you crazy?" the checkout girl asks, her voice deepening, becoming noticeably more masculine. "You're ridiculous, you know that!"

"Would you lower your voice! You'll wake up my mother!"

Which is when I realize that Kleo and Mick are in the middle of another argument, that their fight has landed just outside my bedroom door, and that their voices have infiltrated my dream.

I sit up in bed, my heart racing, trying to decide what, if anything, I can, or should, do.

"You're the one making a big deal out of nothing," Mick is saying.

"You don't tell me you're going out until you're leaving, then you don't come home till almost midnight. What am I supposed to think?"

"Think whatever the hell you want. It was a business meeting. I had no idea it would go on as long as it did or that it would include dinner."

"Which is another thing—all these charges for expensive dinners piling up on our credit card . . ."

"What am I supposed to do, Kleo? Make my pitch and then hand the client the check? That's not how things work. Or have you been locked up in that ivory tower of yours for so long, working on that stupid dissertation that nobody in the real world is ever going to read or give two shits about, that you've forgotten how things really operate? Hasn't anybody ever told you that sometimes you have to spend money to make money?"

"Thank you for that resounding vote of confidence," Kleo says, her voice all but disappearing into a flood of tears.

"Oh, so you can accuse me of all sorts of things, tell me how to run my business, tell me I'm inconsiderate and rude for not phoning to tell you I'd be late, but if I say one word about your precious dissertation, *I'm* the bad guy?"

"Would you please just lower your voice."

"I'll lower my voice when you shut the fuck up!"

"Mick, please. You'll wake up my mother . . ."

"Right. God forbid we do anything to upset Mommie Dearest."

"That's not fair. My mother has never been anything but wonderful to you."

"How? By reminding me that this is *her* house, not ours?"

"It *is* her house."

"Yeah? Well, I'm sick of always having to be on my best behavior, of having to tiptoe around here, around *her.*"

"I don't understand how this argument is suddenly about my mother. She's not staying out till midnight, coming home reeking of beer. She's not the one spending hundreds of dollars on dinners she can't afford."

"No. She's the one spending hours every day talking to some crazy old woman who claims she kills people. You think that's normal?"

"What are you saying?"

Mick lowers his voice, although I can still hear every word. "I'm saying that maybe—just maybe—she's losing it a little, that it might be time for her to consider moving into an assisted living community, not a memory care facility or anything like that, just somewhere where there are people her own age she can socialize with. That way we'd have some privacy . . ."

"You want to kick my mother out of her own house?"

"That's not what I'm saying."

"Really? Because it sounds exactly like that's what you're saying."

"Okay, well. Think what you will. I've said my piece. I'll sleep in my office. You can go to hell."

"Already there," Kleo and I whisper together.

CHAPTER FIFTY

I'm still shaking when I wake up the next morning.

In truth, I don't think I got more than a few hours' sleep all night. Mick still hadn't come home by the time Kleo and I went to bed, and it was almost midnight before I heard his key turn in the lock and the real trouble began.

When my girls first started dating, I could never fall asleep until I heard them come home and knew they were safe. It's been the same way since Kleo and Mick moved in.

"Why can't he at least call?" Kleo asked me around nine o'clock last night. And then again, an hour later. "Is that too much to ask?"

I understood that the questions were rhetorical and that my daughter wasn't expecting an answer, which would have been "Of course, he should call. It's the least he can do." So I bit my tongue and said nothing. Not that there was any need for words. Kleo could see the answer in my eyes.

The problem is that Mick is a man who's gotten used to doing the least he can. His natural good looks and practiced charm have made it possible for him to get away with this kind of behavior for far too long. But the charm is wearing thin. It's starting to throw unflattering shadows across his once-handsome face.

Irresponsibility is a young man's game. It's tolerated and, to a degree, even expected. It grows less tolerable with age. By fifty, it's closing in on unforgivable.

Kleo tried phoning Mick, but his line went directly to voice-mail. Ultimately, she gave up, put the leftovers she'd saved for him in the fridge, and went to bed. I doubt she slept. I know I didn't.

I think I must have dozed off shortly after he came home, but it wasn't long before their fighting woke me up again, busting its way rudely into my already unpleasant dream.

I marvel now at Mick's ability to sidestep his own failings, to twist the argument in his favor, so that he emerged the aggrieved party, and I somehow ended up the villain, as if his never-before-stated fear of having to tiptoe around me makes me responsible for his bad behavior, or that my relationship with Jenny Cooper signals I might be losing my faculties, that it might be time for me, that it would, in fact, be in my best interest, to move out of my own home into an assisted living community where I could enjoy the company of people my own age.

I shake my head at both his audacity and his self-absorption as I relive their argument again and again, recognizing how little control I have over what is happening under my own roof.

But I think what upsets me most of all is Mick's obvious lack of respect for everything Kleo has accomplished and everything she's trying to achieve, his disdain for all her hard work, his reference to "that stupid dissertation that nobody in the real world is ever going to read or give two shits about."

His unkind words echo in my brain as I load my breakfast dishes into the dishwasher. Neither Kleo nor Mick has emerged from their respective rooms, and I'm still not sure what to say to them when they do. Do I confront them with what I overheard or pretend to be oblivious, act as if I slept through the whole thing, despite the fact that it was happening just outside my door? How do I do what is best for my daughter? Do I even *know* what is best for my daughter?

Not to mention, what's best for me.

Kleo may have chosen this marriage, but I did not.

At my age, I don't want to be walking around on eggshells in my own home. Nor can I afford too many sleepless nights or days filled with gut-wrenching anxiety, my heart racing out of my chest, my blood pressure scaling dangerous new heights. I would never have put up with this kind of behavior from Bob. That it is happening to my child is even worse because there's only so much I can do.

Fortunately, I don't have to do anything right now. Lorne called me yesterday to tell me that they would be moving Carol to her new residence in Miami sometime this morning, and if I wanted to say goodbye, I should get to Legacy Place early. So, I return to my bedroom, make my bed, and put on the yellow sundress that Carol once admired. I apply a tinted moisturizer, blush, and I hope enough concealer to disguise my lack of sleep and hide whatever worry remains etched into the lines around my eyes and mouth. I leave a note for Kleo, telling her where I've gone, so she won't worry. Maybe Mick will see the note and realize how little effort it takes to be considerate.

"Who am I kidding?" I mutter as I leave the house, quietly closing the door behind me.

Carol is sitting on the bed in her apartment when I arrive. She is neatly dressed in a pair of gray slacks and a light-blue blouse, a pair of beige flats on her feet. Her hair has been freshly washed and hangs in unflattering waves around her face, a face that used to be both full and full of life but is now angular and devoid of expression. Still, there is a palpable sadness in her eyes. I see her and my heart breaks, for all that was and for everything I know will never be again.

Lorne is puttering around, making sure all Carol's personal items have been packed, that nothing is being overlooked or left behind. He smiles when I walk in. "Carol, honey. Look who's here."

"Linda," she says, breaking into a smile. "It's so good to see you."

"Oh, my God!" I utter, as Lorne freezes where he stands. "You know who I am!"

"Of course I know who you are," she says. "How are you?"

"I'm well." The growing lump in my throat prevents me from saying more.

"You look so pretty," she tells me. "I've always liked that dress on you."

I wipe an errant tear from my cheek, nod a silent thank-you.

"Why are you crying? Is something wrong?"

"Just that I'm going to miss you so much."

"Why would you miss me?"

I look toward Lorne.

"Because you're moving to Miami to be closer to Eric," he tells her. "Remember? I explained everything to you this morning."

"Are you coming with us?" she asks me.

"No. No, I'm so sorry. I can't. But I'll come visit you as often as I can. Would you like that?"

"That would be lovely." Carol shifts from side to side, as if trying to see behind my back. "Is Bob here? Did he come with you?"

My heart sinks. I tell myself that I can't expect her to recall that Bob's been dead for two years, that it's more than enough that she remembers me, that I can't expect miracles. Yet all it took was the mention of my name on her lips to have me hoping for exactly that.

"Is Bob here?" she asks again, when I fail to answer.

I steal another glance at Lorne, but he says nothing, clearly as shaken by what's happening as I am.

"No, he couldn't make it," I tell her, deciding that it will serve no useful purpose to say anything else.

"Tell him I'm sorry I missed him," Carol says.

"I will." I move forward, take her in my arms, feel her arms wrap around my body in a tight embrace.

We hold this position until I feel Lorne's gentle pat on my shoulder. "We should get going," he says. "The limo will be here any minute."

"I love you," I tell Carol, as we pull apart.

"I love you, too."

I watch Lorne lead my oldest and dearest friend from the room. "Love you more," I whisper.

CHAPTER FIFTY-ONE

After Carol leaves, I collapse on the edge of her bed and let the tears flow. I make a silent promise to visit her in Miami once a week, although even as the pledge is forming, I recognize it as wishful thinking. I hate driving on I-95. No one signals; everyone tailgates; people chat away on their phones or, worse, text; a simple fender-bender up ahead can leave you sitting in your car for hours, waiting for the lanes to clear; serious accidents are frequent occurrences. I amend my promise to visiting once a month. Maybe I can convince Kleo to accompany me from time to time.

Thoughts of my daughter cause the tears to come faster. By the time I realize that someone is standing in the doorway, I'm sobbing so hard that my body is all but convulsing. I look up, see Jenny walking toward me. I prepare myself for a barrage of questions and accusations: *Why are you sitting here crying when you could be visiting with me? What's the matter with you, Linda Davidson?*

Instead, Jenny plops down beside me and surrounds me with her arms. She says nothing, simply holds me as I lean into her chest, crying into the flannel of her nightgown.

We remain in this position until the staff arrive to clean the unit.

Jenny leads me from the room, guiding me slowly down the corridor to her apartment. We enter her bedroom and resume our former positions. I've stopped crying, but I have no desire to leave the comfort of her arms. It's been a long time since anyone has held me with such tenderness. I'd forgotten how good it feels.

Seventy years disappear in a flash, and I cling to her like a child to its mother, breaking away only when I feel her stir. She smiles, patting my cheeks dry with the tips of her long, bony fingers. "Feeling better now?" she asks.

"Much. Thank you."

"Good." She stands up. "Let's go into the garden, and I'll tell you all about how I killed Ralph McMillan."

The garden is a large rectangular oasis of colorful flowers and majestic palms running parallel to the ocean, whose roar we can hear but not see. A high fence prevents anyone from entering and the residents from leaving. There are wide chairs and wooden benches scattered at strategic intervals throughout the lush space, small groupings arranged for privacy, larger ones for when privacy is no longer a concern.

There are only a few people in the garden, likely because of today's stultifying humidity. Jenny selects one of the smaller groupings, two chairs with white cushions facing each other. She's still wearing her flannel nightgown but seems oblivious to the heat. I, on the other hand, am perspiring heavily, despite my yellow sundress being sleeveless.

"You have good arms," Jenny tells me. "Not too wrinkly. You lift weights?"

"I used to. Haven't in some time."

"Don't much care for that dress, though."

I smile. "Yes, I remember that you don't like yellow."

"Who said I don't like yellow?"

"You did. When we first met."

"Still don't like it," Jenny says.

"You were going to tell me about Ralph McMillan," I venture after a moment's silence.

"What about him?"

Despite the fact that there are only a few residents in the garden and none within hearing distance, I lower my voice to a whisper. "How you killed him."

"I killed Ralph McMillan?" she asks, her voice uncomfortably loud.

I continue to whisper, hoping she'll take the hint. "You said you did."

"Oh, yes. I remember," Jenny says. "He was an awful man. He deserved to die."

"How did you do it?" I ask.

She shrugs. "I have a special recipe."

"You poisoned him with the items you stole from the drugstore," I state.

"Who says I stole anything from the drugstore?"

"Didn't you?"

"He deserved to die," she says, as if that answers the question.

"But how did you manage it?" I ask, genuinely curious about how a senile old woman could commit cold-blooded murder in full view of the staff of Legacy Place.

And get away with it.

She shrugs again. This time the shrug involves her whole body. "It was morning. Breakfast was over. The shift was changing, so nobody was paying too close attention. I took him a biscuit and a glass of orange juice, said the nurses brought them to me by mistake, that it was meant for him." Jenny smiles. "I watched him eat the biscuit and drink the juice in one long gulp. Wasn't long before he started gagging, waving those skinny arms of his in the air like he was choking. Next thing I know, he's on the floor, eyes rolling back in his head, pieces of biscuit all over his mouth. I took the glass back to my apartment and rinsed it out, then went back to his room and pretended to find him. Easy-peasy."

"Easy-peasy, pudding and pie," I hear myself say.

"Who said anything about pudding or pie?" Jenny demands.

"Sorry. It's just . . . Sorry."

"Why were you crying before?" she asks, suddenly shifting the focus of the conversation to me.

"I was sad because my friend is moving to Miami," I tell her, "and I won't be able to see her as often."

"That's not why you were sad," Jenny startles me by saying.

"It wasn't?"

"Tell me the real reason you were sad."

What the hell? I think. "It's my daughter Kleo. She and her husband are having problems."

"What kind of problems?"

"Just . . . problems."

"*Feh.*" Jenny lifts her eyes toward the ceiling. "What's that saying? 'Men, can't live with 'em, can't shoot 'em.'" She laughs. "Of course, you don't have to shoot them. There are simpler ways."

I can't help but chuckle. "Easy-peasy."

She chuckles along with me. "Easy-peasy, pudding and pie."

CHAPTER FIFTY-TWO

I don't go home.

Instead, I drive. I need time to clear my head before I confront Kleo and Mick, time to decide what I plan to do or say, if anything. What happened with Jenny has unsettled me. Not so much her latest confession—I still vacillate between believing she's a cold-blooded killer and thinking she's just a sad old lady with a wild imagination—but the compassion I felt in her arms when she was comforting me, how safe I felt, how protected.

How strange, I can't help thinking, to feel more protected by a possible serial killer than I ever felt by my own mother.

A psychiatrist might theorize that, in a strange way, Jenny has been something of a mother substitute for me, although you might assume that at age seventy-six I would no longer require mothering.

But I don't think it's something you ever outgrow.

What's that expression—hope springs eternal?

I no longer believe that wisdom comes with age. Just the fact that I know more things doesn't make me wiser. Just the fact that I have no choice but to accept the outcome of choices already made won't guarantee me peace of mind.

Old fears—*Will my face break out before the prom? Will I get my period on my wedding night? Will I be a good lover?*—have been replaced by new ones—*Is that numbness in my legs a sign of ALS? Does having to voice a thought the second I think it or lose it altogether signal I'm about to suffer the same fate as Carol? Will I die in my sleep? What have I accomplished with my life? What have I got to show for all these years? What do I want to do with the time I have left?*

"Fuck if I know," I say to my reflection in the rearview mirror.

I was never terribly ambitious. I wanted to be a good teacher, a good wife, a good mother. I wanted to be happy. I wanted my children to be happy.

They say you're only as happy as your unhappiest child.

I know Kleo isn't happy.

What I don't know is what, if anything, I can do about it.

I find myself driving along North Highway A1A until I reach Lighthouse Cove, the site of two miniature golf courses, a Burger Shack, and a three-scoop ice cream parlor. The last time I was here was when Vanessa and her family visited at Christmas. What the hell, I decide, turning in to the parking lot and getting out of the car. A round of miniature golf, followed by a burger and three scoops of ice cream, might be just what the doctor ordered.

It isn't.

My putting is terrible and the heat unbearable. The burger sits heavy in my stomach and the three scoops of ice cream can't compete with the blazing sun. The ice cream quickly dissolves, dripping down the cone I'm holding and seeping through my fingers onto the front of my yellow sundress, where it mixes with the perspiration already staining the pale cotton. My hair is now a massive frizz ball, the ends of which hug my sweat-soaked, sunburned cheeks, giving me the look of a deranged clown.

A toddler at a nearby table takes one look at me and bursts into tears.

I interpret this as a sign that it's time for me to leave. I throw what's left of the soggy cone in my hand into the closest trash can and head for the parking lot.

Fifteen minutes later, I pull into my driveway. I climb out of the car, slamming the door to alert Kleo and Mick to my presence.

Home sweet home.

"My God, what happened to you!" Kleo exclaims from her seat in front of her computer when I walk through the front door. "You look like you've been through a carwash."

"I went miniature golfing." I plop down on the living room sofa and grab a handful of peanuts from the bowl on the coffee table.

"In this heat? Are you out of your mind?"

"I think I might be."

"What would possess you to go miniature golfing?"

"It seemed like a good idea at the time?" I venture, looking around. "Mick in his office?"

Kleo shrugs. "He went out about an hour ago."

"Can we talk about what happened last night?" I hear myself ask.

"Shit. You heard?"

I nod.

"I'm so sorry, Mom."

"Maybe you and Mick should consider counseling," I offer, the safest thing I can think of to say. "I'm happy to pay for it."

"He'd never agree to it. And you already do way too much."

Which is when the phone rings.

"I'll get it," I say, pushing myself off the sofa and heading for the kitchen. I answer it in the middle of its third ring. "Hello? Hello?" I say again when no one answers. I sigh. In another second, a recorded voice will undoubtedly inform me that there have been a number of suspicious charges on my Visa card or that my nonexistent subscription to eBay will be cut off if I don't pay the required fee, or that another one of my young grandchildren has been in an accident and will go to jail if I don't transfer money into some phony lawyer's account. I'm in no mood for this nonsense. "Oh, fuck off!" I shout, slamming down the receiver and heading back into the main part of the house.

"Another scam?" Kleo asks.

I'm about to answer when the phone rings again.

"Just don't answer it," Kleo advises as I stomp back to the kitchen.

"Hello?" I shout into the receiver.

"Am I speaking to Kleo Asher?" the female voice asks tentatively, as if bracing for another outburst.

"No. That's my daughter. May I ask who's calling?"

"It's Dr. Shiff's office," the woman says as my daughter approaches.

"Did you just call here?" I ask the woman.

"I did."

"I'm so sorry," I apologize. "I thought it was . . . Here's Kleo." I quickly hand my daughter the phone.

"This is Kleo. Yes, sorry about that. She thought it was a scam."

I watch my daughter's face cloud first with worry, then with anger, as she listens to what the woman is saying.

"Yes, thank you. I'll go pick it up now." Kleo returns the phone to its charger. "That bastard!"

"What is it? What's the matter?"

"Can I borrow your car? I have to go pick up a prescription for antibiotics."

"What for? What's wrong?"

Kleo takes a long, deep breath before responding. "It seems I have chlamydia."

CHAPTER FIFTY-THREE

After Kleo leaves, I use my phone to look up chlamydia. I learn that it's a common sexually transmitted disease that can affect both men and women but can be potentially much more serious in women. It's transmitted through vaginal, anal, or oral sex with someone who has it.

Which means that Mick has it and has passed it on to Kleo.

Which means that Mick has been cheating on my daughter, and it doesn't take a genius to figure out that all his late nights with prospective clients have been nothing of the sort, that the hundreds of dollars' worth of charges he's racked up on their credit card are not because he's been trying to woo a potential client but rather to impress another woman. Maybe even several, one of whom has given him chlamydia.

Which he has now given to my daughter.

"You bastard!" I say, using Kleo's word. It fails to satisfy. "You miserable motherfucker! I hope you rot in hell," I embellish, which feels much better.

Minutes later, I hear a car pull into the driveway and know that it's Mick. I have no idea what to say to him. I know what I'd *like* to say to him, but until I know how Kleo intends to handle things, I also know that it's not my place to say anything.

Which isn't going to be easy.

I decide the best course of action is to retreat to my bedroom until Kleo comes home. Unfortunately, Mick breezes through the front door before I'm halfway there.

"Hey, Linda," he says, his voice a smile. "How's my favorite mother-in-law?"

The mother-in-law you think is losing it? The mother-in-law you want to put in a home? "Fine," I mutter, refusing to look at him.

"You don't sound fine."

I shrug. *Keep walking.*

"What's going on? I'm getting some strange vibes. Something wrong?"

"Just a lot on my mind."

"Why do I think that includes me?"

I shrug again. *Because you're a self-centered prick?*

"You want to talk about it?" he asks.

"Not really."

"Suit yourself." He looks around. "Kleo not home?"

"She had to go out."

"At the library, no doubt."

"Probably working on that stupid dissertation that nobody in the real world is going to read or give two shits about," I say before I can stop myself.

The silence that follows is so thick you can choke on it.

"So that's what this is about," Mick says. "You heard us last night."

"Kind of hard not to."

"Yeah, sorry about that. We sometimes forget there's someone else in the house."

My house. "As I recall, Kleo tried to remind you of that fact several times."

"Yeah, well . . . Look. I know she's your daughter and that you're always going to take her side, and I get that, I really do—"

"That's very generous of you," I interrupt.

". . . but she isn't exactly blameless in all this."

"Really?" I ask. "How is she to blame for last night? Is she the one who stayed out until almost midnight without so much as a phone call?" *Okay. Enough.*

"No, I admit that's on me. But she could be a little more understanding. That's all I'm saying."

"You think she could be more understanding," I repeat. *Stop now. Stop before this goes any further.* "Understanding of what, exactly?"

"That it takes a lot of time and effort to start a new business, that I'm working my ass off trying to get clients, and that means meetings, some of them at night, some that come up unexpectedly, some that go on longer than planned, that mean the occasional expensive dinner that puts a strain on our bank account. And yes, I could have called, I *should* have called, you're both right about that, and I'm sorry, I really am, but sometimes things just get away from you, and Kleo needs to understand that . . ."

Oh, you're good. You're very good. "What else should she understand?"

"What do you mean?"

"Should she understand about the porn you've been watching on your computer when you're supposedly working your ass off? And speaking of *backsides*," I continue, purposefully substituting Jenny's word, "should she be more understanding of the bondage magazines you keep hidden in your desk drawer?"

"Whoa! Hold on a minute. You've been snooping through my things?"

"What else should she be more understanding of?" I shout. "That you're a lying piece of shit? That you've been having an affair? That you've given her chlamydia?"

Okay. Now you've really done it! No going back now.

"*Chlamydia?* What the hell are you talking about?"

"I'm talking about the fact that you gave my daughter a sexually transmitted disease!"

"I don't have chlamydia."

"Oh, you have it all right. You're probably asymptomatic, which apparently is not unusual with men."

"So now, what . . . you're an expert on STDs?"

"I am. I read all about them on my goddamn phone! I'm actually expecting a report from my watch at any moment."

Mick stares at me as if I've taken total leave of my senses. "You're crazy. You know that? Jenny Cooper has nothing on you, lady."

"I'll take that as a compliment."

"Yeah, well, you do that. But tell me, if you know so goddamn much, how do you know it wasn't Kleo who gave the STD to *me*?"

Okay, you asked for it! "Because I know my daughter, you miserable son of a bitch. I know she'd never cheat on you. I also know how hard she actually *has* been working, not to mention I know where she's been each and every night she's been living here." I take a deep breath. "And I know you."

"Oh, you do, do you?"

"Trust me. You're not that complicated."

Mick moves menacingly toward me, his right hand forming a fist at his side.

"What? You're going to hit me?"

The front door opens.

"What the hell is going on here?" Kleo asks, her eyes darting between her husband and me.

"Ask your mother," Mick tells her, pushing his way past her out the door. "She's the one who knows everything."

CHAPTER FIFTY-FOUR

"I'm so sorry," I tell my daughter as we hear Mick's car back out of the driveway and roar down the street. "I honestly didn't mean for any of this to happen."

"What did you say to him?"

I relay the details of what just transpired.

"Shit," Kleo says, collapsing on the sofa.

"I'm so sorry," I say again, sitting down beside her. "It just all got out of hand so quickly."

"Believe me, I understand," Kleo says. "Things tend to go that way with Mick."

"I shouldn't have said anything. I shouldn't have interfered."

"To be honest, I'm kind of glad you did."

"You are?"

"Saves me the trouble."

"What are you going to do?" I ask.

"Beats the shit out of me," she answers. "What would *you* do?"

"Beats the shit out of me," I echo.

"I know what Vanessa would do. She wouldn't put up with this shit for two seconds."

"No. She probably wouldn't. But you have to do what's right for you."

"But *you* think I should leave him," she says.

"I think only you can decide that. I can't tell you what to do."

"What if I *want* you to tell me?"

I shake my head. "I can't, sweetheart."

"Do you think there's any chance we could be wrong, that there's some other explanation? What the fuck am I talking about?" Kleo says, the two sentences running together as one. "There's no possible explanation other than that my husband is a liar who's been cheating on me with God knows how many women for God knows how long. How can I even consider staying with him?" She bursts into tears. "You want to know the worst part of all this?"

Not really. "Tell me."

"The worst part is that I think I've known all along. Or at least, suspected. Even before we found those magazines. All those late nights. All those charges for expensive dinners on our credit card. The lack of any money coming in. I knew deep down there were no prospective new clients. I just didn't want to face it. And now . . ."

"Now?"

"How can I not face it when he rubs my nose in it?" She shakes her head. "It's ironic. I've spent the better part of the last three years researching and writing this fucking dissertation on the rise of the self-conscious heroine in modern American literature, when what do I know of self-conscious women? I'm as unconscious as they come! I thought I was so smart. I wasn't like Vanessa, who'd been planning her wedding since she was, like, eight years old. Marriage was never a priority. I loved my independence. I certainly wasn't going to settle. And then, what happens? I meet Mick when I'm old enough to know better, and conscious thought flies out the window. I fall head over heels, hook, line, and sinker. I turn into a blithering idiot. I'm every fucking cliché you can think of, every clueless housewife who has no idea her husband has been cheating on her for weeks or months or even years, despite all evidence to the contrary! And what's worse, what's *worse,* is that I can't help thinking that this is somehow *my* fault. Is it something that I've done? Or maybe it's something that I *didn't* do. Maybe I'm not woman enough to satisfy him. Is that why he turns to those awful magazines, to other women? Because I don't turn him on anymore? Because . . . I don't know . . . I don't know anything anymore."

"Sweetheart, no," I tell her. "You are not responsible for Mick's bad behavior. Men's cheating rarely has anything to do with their wives, regardless of what they may try to tell themselves. You could be the sweetest, most understanding, most desirable woman in the world and your husband will still cheat on you, if he's so inclined. The fault is his, not yours."

"You want to know the *most* pathetic part?" Kleo continues, as if I haven't spoken. "The most pathetic part is that, in spite of everything, I still love him!"

"Oh, sweetie."

"You don't just stop loving someone, even when they hurt you, even when common sense tells you they're no good for you, even when they give you a fucking STD! I still love the man I *thought* I married! What kind of idiot am I, that what I want more than anything is for him to come home and somehow convince me that there's been a terrible mistake, that the doctor read the results of the test incorrectly, or that her assistant called the wrong house. I want him to tell me that he knows he's been a jerk these past months, but that he loves me more than anything in the world, that he'll do anything to keep from losing me. That's what's so pathetic. *Me!* I'm what's so pathetic."

I say nothing. What more can I say? There's only so much a mother can do. My daughter has to figure this one out for herself. So I put my arms around her, and she cries against my chest in much the same way I cried into Jenny's chest earlier. We sit like this until the light shifts around us, and the afternoon is swallowed by the night.

It's just past nine o'clock when Kleo climbs into bed beside me. We didn't bother with dinner, neither one of us having much of an appetite. So now we huddle together, watching a repeat episode of *Dateline*, hoping—and failing—to be distracted by a doctoral student in criminology who has stabbed to death four fellow students in the house they shared off campus.

Mick hasn't come home.

Not that we expected him to. At least not tonight. Tomorrow is another story, of course. One I'm not particularly looking forward to. But even if Mick chooses to stay away another day or two, he has to come back at some point. His clothes are here, his computer, pretty much everything he has.

Kleo has asked me to stay close to home until he does. She doesn't want to risk being alone with him, at least until she decides what to do. And depending on her decision, I have some of my own to make.

If my daughter can somehow manage to find it in her heart to forgive Mick, can I?

If she decides to take him back, can I allow them to continue living under my roof after everything that's happened, after all that's been said?

Common sense dictates that they can't stay here.

But when has common sense ever ruled the day?

And where would they go? They have no income, little in the way of savings, no hope of renting a decent apartment.

Can I just toss my daughter into the street?

I know the answer even before I finish asking the question.

I can't.

I don't have a choice. All I can do now is wait, watch, and worry.

CHAPTER FIFTY-FIVE

"Go away," Jenny says when I knock on her door the following week.

"It's me, Jenny," I tell her. "Linda. Linda Davidson."

"I know who it is," she calls back. "Go away. I don't want to talk to you."

"Is something wrong? Are you feeling all right?"

"I feel fine."

"Are you mad at me?"

"Why would I be mad at you?"

"I don't know," I say, although I think I might.

"Could I be mad because you broke your promise? Because you haven't been back to see me since your friend Carol left?" she asks, confirming my suspicions.

"I'm sorry about that, Jenny. I really am. It couldn't be helped. I was dealing with some things at home."

"I don't care. Go away. I don't like you anymore."

I stand outside Jenny's door for another minute, trying to decide whether to stay or leave. Clearly, Jenny doesn't want to see me. I've been dismissed in no uncertain terms.

Except I have nowhere else to go.

I could go home, I tell myself.

Except I don't want to go home.

Mick is there.

"I'll wait in the lounge for ten minutes," I tell Jenny. "In case you change your mind."

I get no response.

"Great," I mutter as I proceed down the corridor. *Now not even serial killers want anything to do with me.*

"I take it she wouldn't talk to you," Selena says as I approach.

"She's mad because I haven't visited in over a week."

"Frankly, I'm amazed you're here at all. Do you mind my asking, why *are* you here? I mean, your friend is gone. You're under no obligation to keep seeing Jenny."

"I know that. The truth is . . . I like talking to her. She's had an interesting life."

Selena's eyebrows squish toward the bridge of her nose. "You do know that she's . . ."

". . . crazy?"

"Well, we're not supposed to use that word. But . . . you really can't put much stock in anything she says."

I nod. "I'll just sit here for a few minutes, if it's all right, in case she changes her mind."

"Suit yourself."

I cross to the visitors' lounge and sit down on one of the purple velvet sofas, noticing that the fabric is starting to fray around the seams. Not the most practical material to have picked, and the color shows every speck of dust and lint, I think absently, trying to avoid thinking of anything else.

To avoid thinking of Mick.

It's been five days since he phoned Kleo, begging her to take him back. He'd stayed away three days and nights, claiming he hadn't wanted to pressure her, that he'd wanted to give her the space she needed to work through her rage and think things over rationally. I suspected his reason for coming home had more to do with being kicked out of wherever he'd been staying by whomever he'd been staying with, but I kept those thoughts to myself. God knows I'd already said enough.

"What do I do?" Kleo asked, although we both knew she'd already made up her mind. She'd been crying for three days and nights. The relief on her face when Mick called was almost palpable.

I stayed in my bedroom for more than two hours while they hashed it out in theirs, emerging only when I heard Kleo's soft knock on my door. "Mom? Can you come out? Mick wants to talk to you."

"Shit. Fuck. Fart," I whispered, taking several deep breaths to slow the rapid beating of my heart. "Shit," I repeated for good measure before opening the door and stepping into the living room.

Kleo and Mick were seated on the couch. Mick stood up the second he saw me, nervously wiping the palms of his hands along the front of his jeans. My first thought was that he looked as exhausted as I felt, as miserable as my daughter had been these last few days. He hadn't shaved and there were deep circles under his eyes that matched the deep circles under Kleo's. He gave a sad little smile and motioned toward the now-empty space beside Kleo.

I sat down beside my daughter, felt her reach for my hand, her icy-cold fingers digging into my flesh as Mick began to speak.

"First, I want to apologize to you," he began.

"It's not me you need to apologize to," I interrupted him to say.

"Mom, please," Kleo pleaded. "Hear him out."

I nodded, understanding that whatever he'd said to persuade her had obviously worked and I had no choice but to listen. "Sorry."

"No," Mick said. "You have absolutely nothing to be sorry for. This is on me. It's all on me." He released a long, deep breath. "I want to apologize for the unkind, totally unwarranted things you overheard me say, for the unbelievable ingratitude I've shown you after all the generosity you've shown me, for the pain I've caused you, for making you feel uncomfortable in what is undeniably your home, and for being an all-around jackass.

"I've already apologized to Kleo for everything—for my thoughtlessness, my disrespect for her work . . . for my affair. Of which there was only one, I swear. And it meant absolutely nothing. And I have no excuse for it, other than that I'm an idiot whose ego needed stroking because my new business hasn't been performing as I'd been expecting, and I was feeling sorry for myself, feeling less of a man because I wasn't able to support my wife the way she deserved, and I was feeling mad at the world and more than a bit entitled, if I'm being honest, and I'm so sorry. I'm so very, very sorry.

"And this is going to sound more than a little peculiar, I know. But in a strange way, maybe getting that STD was the best thing that could have happened, even though, God knows, I'm mortified that I passed it on to Kleo. But maybe it was the wake-up call I needed. It reminded me of how much I love my wife, and of how much I have to lose. And I swear to you, just as I've already sworn to Kleo, that it will never, *ever*, happen again."

So, what could I say? What could I do?

If nothing else, Mick is a terrific salesman. You *want* to believe him, regardless of his past lies, regardless of the voice in your head, urging caution. Even when you suspect, deep down, it's all bullshit.

Besides, the decision had already been made. Mick had said, quite literally, everything Kleo wanted and needed to hear, and she had decided to give her husband another chance. Now her eyes were begging me to do the same.

"I don't expect you to forgive me," he continued, tears filling his eyes, "at least not right away. I understand that I have to earn back both Kleo's trust and yours, and I'm prepared to do whatever's necessary." He took another deep breath, releasing it slowly, as if exhaling smoke from a cigarette. "Kleo has suggested marriage counseling, and she said that you very generously offered to pay for it. If that offer is still open, we'd like to take you up on it."

"Of course," I whispered.

"Thank you." The sigh that followed was one of relief. "If there's anything you want to say to me, now's your chance. Let me have it."

"Just be good to my daughter."

"I will. I promise."

Will he? I wonder now. Promises are easy to make, harder to keep.

Hadn't Jenny just reminded me of that?

I check my watch, note that more than ten minutes have passed and Jenny still hasn't appeared. I push myself to my feet and approach Selena's desk.

"Giving up?"

"Temporarily," I concede. "Look. I'll leave you my phone numbers—both my cell and my landline—and you can call me if she changes her mind about seeing me."

"You sure about this?"

I shake my head. When was the last time I was sure about anything?

CHAPTER FIFTY-SIX

I drive to the Gardens Mall.

The mall is a beautiful upscale enclosed two-story shopping mall on PGA Boulevard in Palm Beach Gardens, a ten-minute drive south of Jupiter. While not as luxurious—or as overwhelming—as the mall in Bal Harbour, it's not only a premier shopping destination but a pleasant and convenient place for people, especially seniors, to walk during inclement weather or when the outside temperature proves too steamy.

I park on the upper level behind Nordstrom, not sure which I'm here to do—shop or walk. About the only thing I'm sure of these days is that I don't want to go home. The last five days have been difficult ones for me. Having Mick around again is a constant reminder of the awful things he said that night and the hell he's put my daughter through.

Not that he hasn't been putting his best foot forward. He's gone out of his way to be helpful, volunteering to do the grocery shopping, to barbecue more often, to tidy up after dinner. He made a show of throwing out his offensive magazines, researched marriage counselors in the area, and even made an appointment with one for him and Kleo for some time next week.

Still . . .

I find myself holding my breath around him, afraid to say or do the wrong thing, to upset our delicate balance. He'd complained about having to tiptoe around me. But now I'm the one walking on eggshells around him.

Despite his seemingly heartfelt apology, experience tells me that it's only a matter of time before he reverts to form. I don't trust him, and I remain convinced my daughter would be better off without him.

Still . . .

I can't sit around waiting and watching for the first hints of cracks in the façade. I've decided that the less time I spend at home, the better for everyone.

Except . . . now what?

Carol has been moved to Miami; Vanessa and my grandchildren are in Connecticut; I've either abandoned, or been abandoned by, my old friends; I've given up the interests Bob and I once shared; Jenny Cooper doesn't want to see me.

So what do I do?

"You get out of your car, that's what you do," I say out loud.

I pull open the heavy glass door at the entrance to Nordstrom, walking briskly through the men's and jewelry sections before venturing into the main part of the mall.

I spend the next hour walking aimlessly around, going in and out of the smaller shops, finding little in the way of fashion that excites me. Everything is too young, too staid, or too expensive. I comb through rack after rack of flimsy little dresses and flouncy short skirts, knowing I'll look ridiculous in all of them, but trying a few on anyway, if only to confirm my suspicions.

"You look so cute!" a salesgirl tells me as I view my dimpled knees in the mirror.

Oh, God, I moan silently. *When did I get cute?*

I see a sweater I like in Chanel. It costs three thousand dollars. I try it on anyway, relieved when it looks like shit.

"Not really your color," the saleswoman offers generously.

I spend yet another hour drifting from store to store. I overhear one customer complaining about the lack of sales help and think about applying for a job.

As if anyone would hire a seventy-six-year-old woman! I'm not exactly the demographic these stores are hoping to attract. Besides, there's no way I could stand on my feet for the long hours required. Not to mention having to learn to navigate a new computer system when I can barely manage my phone.

What the hell am I thinking?

My watch pings.

It looks like you're working out, it tells me.

I lift my wrist to my mouth. "Fuck off," I tell it.

"I'm sorry, but did you just tell your watch to fuck off?" I hear a voice say from somewhere beside me.

I turn to see a man approximately my age, a huge smile on his deeply lined and weathered face. He's of average height and build, with wavy gray hair and an unmistakable twinkle in his gray-blue eyes that I can't help but find attractive. "I did, yes," I admit, sheepishly. "Sorry about that."

"Oh, please, don't apologize," he says, laughing. "I've been tempted to do the same thing myself, many times."

"I'm just not used to inanimate objects offering me their opinions."

"The joys of modern technology," he says, falling into step beside me. "I'm Max Silver, by the way."

"Linda," I tell him. "Linda Davidson."

"Very nice to meet you, Linda. Are you headed anywhere in particular?"

"Not really."

"Well, then. Can I interest you in a cup of coffee?"

I come to an abrupt halt. "Do you always ask strange women you meet in shopping malls out for coffee?"

"Only the ones who tell their watches to fuck off," he replies.

"In that case, yes," I say. "I'd love a cup of coffee."

· · · ·

Over the next half hour, I learn that Max is seventy-five years old and a widower with three grown daughters and eight grandchildren, that he is a retired accountant, that he golfs twice a week, and that he plays bridge as often as possible, mostly online since his former bridge partner died last year.

"I used to love bridge," I confide.

"You don't play anymore?"

"I more or less gave it up after my husband died."

"You should start again."

"I don't know."

"I do," he says. "How about this weekend?"

"What?"

"There's a duplicate game every Saturday night at the Community Center over on North Military. I could use a partner."

"Thanks, but I don't think so. I'm really not very good."

"Neither am I. Who gives a shit?"

"I don't think so," I say again.

"Well, I tell you what. I'm going to give you my phone number, and you can call me if you change your mind." He grabs a pen from his shirt pocket and jots his number down on a paper napkin, then slides the napkin across the small table toward me. "I'd add my number to the list of contacts in your phone, but I confess I haven't got a clue how to do that."

I smile, drop the napkin into my purse.

"Promise me you'll at least think about it?" Max says as he escorts me to my car.

"I'll think about it," I agree.

My cellphone rings as I'm watching him walk away.

"Hello, Linda?" a familiar voice asks.

"Yes?"

"This is Selena Rodriguez, from Legacy Place. I have a message for you from Jenny Cooper."

"Okay." I realize I'm holding my breath.

"She says to remind you that it's her birthday on Friday and that you promised to bring her a cake."

CHAPTER FIFTY-SEVEN

Happy birthday to you. Happy birthday to you. Happy birthday, dear Jenny. Happy birthday to you!

We're gathered in the visitors' lounge—Jenny, me, Selena, Lance, and approximately fifteen of the fourth-floor residents of Legacy Place. Despite barely remembering their own names, everyone knows the words to the song, and they sing loudly and with great, childlike exuberance.

"Hooray!" a white-haired gentleman calls at the song's conclusion.

"Three cheers for . . . three cheers for . . ." another man chimes in.

Jenny leans toward me. She's wearing an emerald-green party dress that is missing its two top buttons and a pair of white ankle socks, trimmed in lace, no shoes. "Who are these losers?" she asks, although she's smiling so hard it looks as if her cheeks might crack. She's clearly loving every moment of this, and I feel a surge of pride that I've been able to provide her with it.

The cake is beautiful—a large rectangular vanilla cake with lemon filling and white icing, lots of soft pink roses, and *Happy Birthday, Jenny* written in red cursive lettering across the top, exactly as requested. Two large red-and-white candles—one in the shape of a 9, the other a 3—sit side by side in the middle of the cake.

"Blow out the candles," Selena urges.

Jenny leans forward, releasing a long, surprisingly strong breath. The fire from the candles flickers, dancing from side to side for several seconds before disappearing in two tiny puffs of smoke.

"Hooray for the Mulligans!" a man shouts as Selena moves the cake to her desk and prepares to slice it.

"I want a corner piece," a woman calls out.

"I want a rose," another chimes in.

"There's lots here for everyone," Selena says.

"Who said they can have any?" Jenny asks, a pout overtaking her smile. "It's *my* birthday and *my* cake. Linda bought it for *me*."

"We discussed this, Jenny," Selena reminds her. "You agreed."

"I never did," Jenny insists.

"Come on, Jenny," Selena whispers. "Do you really want to disappoint all these nice people here to celebrate your birthday?"

"There'll be lots left over," Lance assures Jenny as Selena starts cutting the cake into small squares. "Everyone, grab a paper plate and plastic fork and line up to the left of Selena's desk."

"Who died and made you the boss?" Jenny demands.

"Jenny, be reasonable," he says. "You can't eat this whole cake by yourself. You'll get sick."

"I don't like you," Jenny tells him. "You can't have any cake."

Lance lifts his hands in the air, as if Jenny is holding a gun to his chest. "Okay. If that's what you want. I won't have any."

"Good. I don't like you."

"Come on, Jenny. Be nice," Selena says. "It's your birthday."

"If it's my birthday, where are my presents?" Jenny asks, spinning around. "What's a birthday without presents?"

"I think the cake is present enough, don't you?" Selena asks.

"A cake isn't a present," Jenny informs her in no uncertain terms. "A cake is a cake, and a present is a present. You get cake on your birthday, and you get presents. Who bought me a present?"

"I did," I say softly.

"You see," Jenny shouts. "Somebody here knows what birthdays are all about. You get cake, and you get presents. What did you buy me?"

"Why don't we eat our cake and I'll give it to you in your room later?"

The smile returns to Jenny's face. "Sounds like a plan, Linda Davidson. Sounds like a damn good plan."

"So, what did you buy me?" Jenny asks as we enter her apartment, closing the door behind us.

I reach into my purse and pull out an oblong, brightly wrapped package. "It's just a little something I thought you could use."

"What is it?" Jenny tears off the paper, letting the colorful scraps fly toward the floor, revealing a pair of fuzzy pink slippers.

"Do you like them?"

"I love them!" Jenny pulls them apart, quickly slipping her feet inside them. "They're the best present ever. Thank you, Linda Davidson!"

"My pleasure," I say, and it is.

Jenny plops down on the small sofa and lifts her feet into the air, waving them up and down, admiring her new slippers. "I'm never going to take them off."

"Well, you might want to take them off when you go to bed."

"Nope. Never."

I smile, lowering myself into the chair beside her.

"How's your friend . . . what's her name? Carol! Her name is Carol," Jenny says, proudly. "How's she doing down in good old Miami?"

"Her husband tells me that she's settled in quite nicely."

"Her husband that you're *not* fucking?"

"That's the one."

She laughs. "Hah! You're so funny. I used to live in Miami, you know."

"You did? When was that?"

Jenny shrugs. "A while back. After Sarasota. Before Fort Lauderdale. Or maybe Naples. I rented a little apartment near the beach in Sunny Isles. It was nice. I liked it there."

"Why'd you leave?"

"Pretty much had to."

"How do you mean?"

"I killed the building manager."

"What?"

"He was a meanie-poo."

"Come on," I say. "Now you're just pulling my leg."

She looks from her feet to mine. "Nobody's pulling your leg. Your legs are right there. I'm not touching them."

"You really killed him?"

"He had it coming. Always making excuses to talk to me, rubbing my arm, my back, making suggestive remarks, even though he had a perfectly nice wife. They lived in the building."

"What happened?"

"You mean, how did I kill him?"

"That's what I mean, yes."

"Let's see. His wife was away, visiting relatives in New York, and he invited me to his apartment, said he wanted my opinion on some piece of furniture he'd just bought, because he thought I had great style. Which was true. I *did* have great style. So, I went, brought him a piece of homemade peach pie. Actually, it wasn't homemade," she clarifies. "I bought it in this little bakery down the street." She giggles. "But I added my own special topping." She kicks her feet in the air, as if she's sitting on a dock, splashing her toes in the water. "His wife found his body when she came home a few days later. I heard from one of the other residents that the poor man had suffered a fatal heart attack. Anyway, I moved out soon after that. Moved to Fort Lauderdale. Or maybe it was Naples. Can't remember."

"What was his name, the building manager?"

She shrugs again. "Tony something or other. Who cares? He was a meanie-poo who was cheating on his wife. He deserved to die."

There's a gentle tapping on the door.

"Who is it?" Jenny shouts.

"It's Lance. I've brought you the rest of your cake, along with some paper plates and plastic cutlery."

"You didn't eat any of it, did you?" she asks as he carries everything inside.

"Not a bite."

"Good. You can put it on the coffee table and go."

Lance does as he's been told. "Happy birthday, Jenny," he says on his way out the door. "Always a pleasure."

"You bet your backside," Jenny says.

CHAPTER FIFTY-EIGHT

"That was a little rude, don't you think?" I ask Jenny after Lance is gone.

I recognize the irony. Jenny has just confessed to yet another murder, and here I am castigating her for being rude.

"Was it?"

"He was just being nice, bringing you your cake."

"It's his job to be nice to me."

"Yes, but . . ."

"No buts about it."

"Would it hurt you to be nice back?"

Jenny smiles. "He's still alive, isn't he?"

What can I do but laugh? "Just how many people *have* you killed?" I ask.

She looks up at the ceiling, then back at me. "How many did I tell you?"

"Well, you originally said four, but clearly that was . . ."

"A lie."

". . . not right."

"It was a lie. I didn't want you to think badly of me if I told you the truth."

"So, how many were there?"

Another glance at the ceiling. "I can't remember."

"Try."

Jenny's eyes narrow. "Are you with the CIA?"

"No. Just curious."

"Hmm."

"Hmm?"

"More than four. Less than twenty."

"You're saying you killed between four and twenty people?"

"Closer to twenty."

"I don't believe you," I say, almost certain now that she's playing with me, that she's been playing with me ever since we met.

"What don't you believe?"

"That you killed that many people."

"If you can believe I killed four, why not twenty?"

"How could anyone kill that many people and get away with it?"

"People do it all the time, Linda Davidson. It's really not that difficult when you know what you're doing," she says, matter-of-factly. "Especially if you're a woman. People prefer to see women as victims."

"But surely someone would have suspected . . ."

"People really aren't very bright. And I moved around a lot, remember? Besides, the proof is in the pudding." She looks suddenly confused. "What does *that* mean, the proof is in the pudding? *What* proof is in the pudding? What's pudding got to do with anything?"

"We're getting off track here, Jenny."

"I don't like pudding. Do you?"

"Not really."

"I can't remember the last time I had any. Unless you count rice pudding. I like rice pudding. Especially if it has raisins."

"Jenny . . ."

"You're very nosy today. Are you wearing a wire?"

"I'm not wearing a wire," I tell her. "And I'm not taking off my clothes."

"I should hope not! That would be rude." Her watery blue eyes twinkle. "And we mustn't be rude. That wouldn't be nice."

"Jenny . . ."

"Right. Getting off track." Her eyes circle the room, come to rest on the coffee table. "Is that a cake?"

"It's your birthday cake."

"What's it doing here?"

"Lance brought it in."

"Where's the rest of it?"

"You shared it with the some of the staff and the other residents on the floor."

"That was *very* nice of me," Jenny says, pointedly. "Except you said I wasn't very nice to Lance, that I was rude to him." Tears suddenly fill her eyes. "I should apologize. He's really a very sweet young man. Could you get him for me? Please?" she begs. "I feel terrible."

"All right. Be right back." I push myself to my feet, offer an apologetic smile. "Don't kill anyone while I'm gone."

"Hah! You're so funny." Jenny laughs as I open the door.

I proceed down the corridor, spot Lance coming out of Carol's old room.

"Someone's already moved in?" I ask, approaching.

He shrugs. "Doesn't take long."

I inform him that Jenny would like to apologize to him for her earlier behavior.

"Really? That's a first."

We enter Jenny's apartment to find her standing in front of the coffee table, a paper plate containing a large piece of birthday cake in her hands.

"I'm sorry for being such a meanie-poo earlier," she says, offering the plate to Lance. "You can have a piece of my cake."

The thought suddenly occurs to me that Jenny might have added something to Lance's cake. But I barely have time to process the thought, let alone stop anything from happening, before Lance has popped the whole thing into his mouth, white icing coating his lips as he swallows it down.

"Why, thank you, Jenny. That was very kind of you." Lance winks. "You didn't spit on it, did you?"

"Of course not," Jenny tells him, returning his wink with one of her own. "That would be rude."

CHAPTER FIFTY-NINE

"Hah!" Jenny says as soon as Lance leaves the room. "You should see your face!"

I realize I'm holding my breath. *What the hell just happened?*

"Close your mouth," she tells me. "A bug will fly in."

"Please tell me you didn't poison Lance's cake."

"I didn't poison Lance's cake," Jenny repeats without conviction.

"Jenny . . ." I'd been gone for less than two minutes. Was it possible that, in that short space of time, Jenny had added something lethal to the piece of cake she'd offered Lance? That I'd just witnessed a murder?

"Relax. What's that expression—you don't shit where you eat?"

"You poisoned Ralph McMillan," I remind her.

"Not the same thing."

"How is it different?"

"Ralph McMillan was old and demented. Lance is young and healthy as a horse. Men his age don't suddenly drop dead. It would raise all sorts of red flags. There'd be an autopsy for sure. They'd figure out it was me, even if you didn't tell them. And I like it here. I don't want to leave."

I breathe a huge sigh of relief.

"Hah!" she says again. "What kind of monster do you think I am anyway?"

"Sorry," I tell her. "It's just that . . ."

"I may have put a little something in his cake," she says.

"What?"

"Not enough to kill him."

"What?" I say again.

"Just enough to make him a little sick."

"Oh, my God!"

She bursts out laughing. "Relax. I'm just joking. You really should see your face. You're white as a sheet." She points toward the bathroom. "Go look in the mirror."

I shake my head, sink into the nearest chair. "I'm too old for this."

"Hah! Wait till you get to be my age. It's my birthday, you know. I'm ninety-three."

"Happy birthday," I tell her.

"How old are you?" she asks.

"I'm seventy-six."

"Hah! I'm old enough to be your mother. She's dead, right?"

"What?"

"Your mother. She's dead, right?"

"She's dead. Right."

"Did you kill her?"

"I did not."

We sit for several minutes in silence. "How did you end up here anyway?" I ask.

Jenny plops down into the other chair. "What do you mean?"

"Well, before Lance brought in your cake, you said you were living in Miami . . ."

"Sunny Isles, yes. I liked it there."

"And then you moved to Fort Lauderdale . . ."

"Or Naples. Can't remember which came first. I moved around a lot in those days."

"Because you kept killing people?"

She laughs. "Maybe."

"And you eventually ended up in Jupiter."

"That's right."

"How long ago was that?"

"Ten years ago, maybe. Give or take. I was over eighty. I know that. I'd stopped killing people by then." She laughs. "I retired!"

"So, how did you come to Legacy Place?"

"Through the front door. Same as everybody else."

"No. I mean, what brought you here?"

"Taxicab, probably."

"I mean, what were the circumstances? Did you realize you were starting to forget things . . . that you were . . ."

"Crazy?"

"Are you?" I ask.

"I think I must be, don't you?"

"Did somebody bring you here?"

Jenny closes her eyes. The pause that follows is so long I think she might have fallen asleep. I'm debating whether to leave when she speaks, her eyes still closed.

"Mr. Cooper," she says. "Mr. Cooper brought me here."

"Who is Mr. Cooper?"

"My husband, of course."

"Your husband?"

"Is there an echo in here?"

"Sorry," I apologize quickly.

"Mr. Cooper was my husband. How do you think I got the name Cooper?"

"I never actually thought about it."

"You're looking very pained," she says. "Is there a problem?"

"I just didn't realize you'd gotten married again."

"I was married before?"

"Twice," I tell her.

"I'm sure you're mistaken."

"It's what you told me. To David Huston and Parker Rubini."

"What kind of name is Parker Rubini? You're making that up."

I shrug.

"I've never heard of these men," she insists. "Would you like a piece of cake?"

"No, thank you."

"Why not?"

"I already had a piece."

"Have another."

"No, that's okay. Thank you."

"What's okay? You're welcome."

My head is starting to spin. "I think I should probably head out. Let you get some rest. It's been an eventful day."

"Do you think I'm going to poison you, Linda Davidson?" she asks. "Is that why you won't have another piece of my birthday cake?"

"No, of course not."

"Are you sure?"

"No," I admit.

"Hah! You're so funny. I would never poison you, Linda Davidson. You bought me these wonderful slippers for my birthday."

"I'm so glad you like them."

"I love them. I'm never going to take them off."

I smile, push myself to my feet. "And I'm going to get going."

"*Going* to get *going*. Hah! You're so funny."

"See you next week," I tell her.

"I'll be waiting," she says.

I see Lance on his hands and knees beside Selena's desk as I'm walking down the corridor to the elevators. "Oh, God," I moan, breaking into a run. *Did Jenny poison his cake after all? Just enough to make him "a little sick"?*

"Careful!" Selena calls as I approach. "Don't slip on the cake!"

I come to an abrupt halt as Lance climbs to his feet, a wad of icing-covered paper towels in his hands.

"One of the residents dropped her cake," he explains. "Too

bad, too. It was delicious." He smiles. "Think I could persuade Jenny to give me another piece?"

"I wouldn't push my luck," I tell him, honestly.

"Probably right," he agrees. "She's a real character, that one."

I smile, say nothing.

What else is there to say?

CHAPTER SIXTY

"Hello, Nana?"

It's barely eight o'clock in the morning when the phone rings, waking me from a dream where I'm puttering around in my garden, unaware that a deadly viper is curled up behind a clump of nearby purple impatiens, waiting to strike.

While the phone call has no doubt saved me from being done in by a lethal snakebite, I'm in no mood for more scams that prey on the elderly. At least this caller has hit on the right name, I think, tempted to play along, then deciding that I'm just too damn tired.

"Go fuck yourself," I tell the young man, returning the phone to its charger and falling back against my pillow, hoping to catch maybe another hour of much-needed sleep. I haven't slept well the last couple of nights. Make that the last few weeks.

Kleo and Mick have been fighting again.

What started out promisingly enough—Mick's apology and promises to do better, his willingness to attend counseling—has been steadily losing ground over the past month. His business has come to a complete standstill and his prospects have all but disappeared; he refuses to look for another job; he's turned increasingly surly, often lashing out at Kleo for her perceived lack of support; after three sessions with the marriage counselor, he announced it was a waste of time, that the therapist was always siding with Kleo, and he had no intention of going again.

So, we're pretty much back to where we started, and I'm back to walking around on eggshells, waiting for the next explosion.

The phone rings again.

"Goddamn it! Enough is enough!" I reach for it. "Hello!" I shout into the receiver.

"Mom?" comes the startled voice on the other end of the line.

"Vanessa?" I push myself into a sitting position, trying to clear my head.

"Are you all right?"

"I'm fine," I say. "You?"

"Well, I was okay until my mother told my son to go fuck himself!"

"*What?* Oh, my God! That was Ethan?"

"Who did you think it was?"

"I thought it was a scammer. I'm so sorry. He just sounded so grown up. Is he all right?"

"Aside from being traumatized for life, I'm sure he's okay. You sure *you're* okay?"

"I'm fine," I repeat. "I was at the doctor the other day for my yearly physical and, apparently, for someone my age, I'm in mint condition." I glance at the clock, thinking it a little early for Vanessa to be calling. "Is everything okay?"

"Everything's fine, but something's come up and Brad and I were wondering . . . A client just invited us to his place in the south of France for a week—we'd be flying there on his private plane, no less—and we were thinking we could just tool around for maybe another week after that on our own, you know we haven't had a holiday, just the two of us, for a long time, and so, we were wondering if . . . I know it's a real imposition, and I want you to feel free to say no . . . but I was thinking that you haven't spent a lot of alone time with the kids in a while, and well, they're at camp during most of the day anyway, and a bus picks them up in the morning and brings them home around four, so you wouldn't have to drive them, and there's the housekeeper during the day, so you wouldn't have to do any cooking or housework—"

"Vanessa, stop, sweetheart," I interrupt. "I'd love to look after them while you're gone, if that's what you're asking . . ."

"Oh, my God. That would be so wonderful. The kids are already so excited. That's why Ethan wanted to call himself and ask you . . ."

"Does he still feel that way?"

"Are you kidding? He's fourteen. He probably thinks he has the coolest nana in the world after that outburst."

"When are you thinking of going?"

"Is next week too soon?"

Not soon enough, I think. "Next week is terrific."

"Great. Of course, we'll pay for your flight to Connecticut and everything."

"That's really not necessary."

"It's not up for discussion," she states firmly. "I'll make all the arrangements and get back to you."

"Sounds perfect."

"Okay. Great. Talk later. Love you."

"Love you more."

I hang up the phone and climb out of bed. No point trying to get back to sleep now. Excitement beats exhaustion every time. So I shower and get dressed, make the bed, and cautiously open my bedroom door.

Kleo is already at her computer, although the closed door to her bedroom indicates Mick is likely still asleep.

"Who's been calling so early?" she asks, as I head for the kitchen.

I tell her about Vanessa's plans and her request that I babysit the kids while they're away.

"Are you sure you're up for that?" she asks. "Three kids are a lot to handle, even with a housekeeper and day camp."

"I'll be fine. Actually, I'm looking forward to it."

Kleo grimaces. "I guess it'll be nice to get away from here for a bit."

"You could come, too," I offer. "I'm sure Vanessa wouldn't mind. And the kids would be thrilled to see their auntie."

Kleo smiles and shrugs. The smile says she'd love to; the shrug says she can't. "Already have my hands full with one kid." She glances toward her bedroom.

I nod, heading for the kitchen before she can see the tears forming in my eyes.

"What do you mean, you're going away?" Jenny demands when I visit her later that afternoon.

"It's just for two weeks."

"Two weeks is a long time, Linda Davidson. A lot can happen in two weeks."

"Nothing's going to happen."

"You don't know that." She offers up a sly smile. "People could die."

"Nobody's dying," I tell her, ignoring her less than subtle threat.

"What if *I* die?" she asks. "I'm almost ninety-four, remember."

"You just turned ninety-three a month ago."

"Exactly! How many months do you think a person my age has left?"

"Knowing you, Jenny, you'll outlive us all."

"Hah! Maybe I will. Just for spite. You look tired," she says in the same breath. "I think it's that blouse. Green isn't exactly your color. Or maybe it's the heat. You know what they say, don't you? 'There are only two seasons in Florida—summer and hell.' Guess which one this is."

I think of the ongoing situation with Kleo and Mick.

I don't have to guess.

CHAPTER SIXTY-ONE

I won't lie. I have the best two weeks.

The weather up north is terrific—sunny and warm, without being oppressive; my grandchildren are equally sunny and warm, respectful, and for the most part peaceful. They rarely fight, and even when they do, their arguments are resolved quickly and with relative ease. There is no name-calling, no snide looks or cruel digs, no running to Nana to report on each other's perceived transgressions.

"You've done a wonderful job with them," I tell Vanessa upon her return from the south of France.

"I had a great teacher," she says.

I spend a few days with her and Brad after they return home, and it's a nice reminder that happy marriages can, and do, exist.

I confess I'm not looking forward to returning to Jupiter.

Not that I don't miss Kleo. I do. I just don't miss the ongoing soap opera her life—and consequently mine—has become. I don't miss the ongoing tension, the constant worry, even the welcome relief when, for a few days, things seem to be going well.

Kleo and I speak daily for the first week—brief and casual inquiries about the weather, the kids, our respective plans for the day—until I hear Mick braying loudly in the background: "You're talking to your mother *again*? What are you, two years old?" After that, the calls become less frequent.

"How's it going, living with Kleo and Mick?" Vanessa asks me as I'm packing to go home.

"Great," I lie. No point in both of us worrying.

"What about that woman you were telling me about?"

"Jenny Cooper? She's good."

"Good? Or good and crazy?"

"Not so sure about the crazy."

"You're not still seeing her, are you?" Vanessa asks.

"Occasionally," I tell her, minimizing the amount of time I spend with Jenny so as not to alarm her.

"Because . . . ?"

"I like her," I answer, the first truly honest answer I've given my daughter during this whole exchange.

I arrive at the Palm Beach Airport at just after two o'clock to find no one waiting for me, which is strange because Kleo was adamant about picking me up. I wait around a few minutes, then head down the escalator to the baggage claim area, expecting to see Kleo among the line of limo drivers waiting to pick up their fares.

She isn't there.

Probably stuck in traffic, I tell myself, checking down the crowded inside corridor before stepping outside to make sure she isn't in the long lineup of cars hanging around the no-parking area.

She isn't.

I go back inside, locate my suitcase on the appropriate carousel, and manage to drag it off by myself. I lean against a nearby pillar, assuring myself that Kleo will show up momentarily.

She doesn't.

Twenty minutes later, it occurs to me that she might have left me a message on my phone, which I discover upon retrieving it from my purse is still on airplane mode. "Stupid thing," I mutter, tapping the appropriate little green circle in my settings to undo it, then checking to see if I have any messages.

There is one.

From Mick.

"Please don't be alarmed," the message begins.

My knees immediately go weak; my heart sinks into the soles of my feet.

"Kleo is fine," Mick's voice continues. "She just had a slight accident this morning and we're at the hospital. Not sure how long we'll be, but probably best if you take a cab home. And try not to worry. I promise you she's fine."

"What do you mean, she's fine, you moron?" I shout after he disconnects. "How can she be fine if she's at the hospital?"

"I'm sorry," a voice says quietly from somewhere beside me. "Is everything all right?"

I turn to see a woman around my own age, regarding me with concerned gray eyes.

"Sorry," I mutter. "My daughter was supposed to pick me up, and I just got word that she's in the hospital. She's fine," I say quickly. "At least according to my son-in-law. Who's a moron," I can't help adding.

The woman laughs. "I have one of those," she says.

It's all I can do to keep from hugging her. "Sorry if I scared you."

"Oh, I don't scare all that easily. Do you know what hospital she's in? I could give you a lift."

"That's so kind of you, but no, thank you. Apparently, they're on their way home. And I live in Jupiter, so . . ."

"Then we're practically neighbors. I'm over in Tequesta. My husband is just bringing the car around. I insist you let us drive you home."

"No, really."

"I *insist*," she says again.

"You're sure?"

"Absolutely. I'm Bev Hurley, by the way."

"Linda Davidson."

"Nice to meet you, Linda. Oh, there's my husband now."

Bev, whose chin-length gray hair is a perfect match for her eyes, sits beside me in the backseat of the white Lexus and keeps up a steady stream of chatter as her husband drives. I understand she's doing this to keep me from dwelling on Kleo's accident, and I'm deeply appreciative.

Among the things I learn on the forty-minute drive north is that the Hurleys have been married for fifty-one years, and that they retired to Florida a decade ago from Buffalo, from where they've just returned after visiting the oldest of their four children. They met while working for the local paper, he as a reporter, she as the book editor.

"Do you like to read?" Bev asks as we're approaching Jupiter.

"I do," I answer, although I haven't so much as opened a book in months.

"I belong to a book club," she says. "We could use some fresh blood, if you'd be interested. Here, let me give you my number," she continues without prompting, "and you can think about it and let me know once everything settles down." She reaches for my phone and enters her name and number in my contact list.

Easy-peasy, I think.

"Whatever you decide, please call me and let me know about your daughter," she says as her husband pulls to a stop in front of my house, then hurries to retrieve my suitcase from the trunk.

"I will. Thank you again so much."

"Good luck."

I push open the car door and step onto the pavement, my legs shaking so hard I have to grab the side of the car to keep from falling over. I take a deep breath, then another and another as I wheel my suitcase up the front walkway, waving goodbye to the Hurleys as I reach the front door. Mick's car isn't in the driveway, which means that Kleo and Mick aren't home from the hospital yet.

I don't even know what hospital Mick took Kleo to, I realize as I unlock the door and stumble toward the living room sofa, where I collapse in a flood of tears.

Whatever I'd been expecting to return to, it wasn't this. I look around the empty space, feel the quiet slam against my ears. *Welcome back,* it says.

CHAPTER SIXTY-TWO

I don't know how long I sit there before I hear their car pull into the driveway. I'm immediately on my feet and at the front door, pulling it open and rushing outside even before Mick is half out of the driver's seat.

"What happened? How is she?" I ask, as he comes around to the passenger side and opens the car door, reaching inside to help Kleo out. "What happened?" I ask again.

"It's okay, Mom," Kleo assures me, swinging her legs toward the ground. "I'm okay."

Which is when I see the cast on her right arm.

"Oh, my God. You broke your arm?"

"Linda, please," Mick says. "Can we just get out of this heat? We'll explain everything inside."

I stand back, following behind them and closing the door after us.

"Oh," Kleo says, noting my suitcase just inside the door as Mick guides her toward the living room sofa, sitting down close beside her. "You haven't even unpacked yet. I'm so sorry."

"I can unpack later. Tell me what happened."

"I tripped."

"You tripped? How?"

"It was so stupid. I was at the computer and I got up to get something, and my foot must have fallen asleep, and I couldn't find my footing and I just went flying. I put out my hands to break the fall and ended up breaking my wrist instead."

"I was in my office," Mick continues, without prompting, "and I heard this scream, and I rushed out to find her on the floor, clutching her wrist, and crying that she was sure it was broken, so we hopped in the car and drove to Jupiter Medical Center, and they did X-rays, and sure enough, it's broken all right, and she'll be in a cast for six weeks."

"Naturally, it's my right hand, so I don't know how I'm going to get any work done. Or cooking. Or anything, with this god-damn cast."

"I keep telling her that you and I can handle the cooking," Mick says to me.

"Of course," I agree. "And I can drive you to the library when you need to go, and I can make notes."

Kleo smiles and bursts into tears.

"And the six weeks will fly by in no time," I rush to assure her.

"My dissertation is due at the end of the year," she reminds me. "There's no way I can finish it in time now."

"Then you'll ask for an extension. I'm sure that under the circumstances, they'll understand," I tell her, although I'm sure of no such thing. "And we can hire someone to do whatever typing you need, if it comes to that."

"Which would cost a fortune," Mick says.

"Let me worry about that," I tell him.

"That's very generous of you. As always." He turns his head, although not quickly enough for me to miss the sudden surge of anger flashing through his eyes.

I feel a stab of nameless anxiety.

"I don't know about you," Mick says, "but I think Kleo could use a cup of tea. And I could sure use a beer. If you wouldn't mind, Linda . . ."

"Of course." I move quickly to the kitchen, retrieve a bottle of beer from the fridge and pour it into a tall glass, then drop tea bags into two cups, trying not to allow the uncomfortable thoughts circling my brain to land.

But it's already too late. They've not only landed. They've taken root.

Is it possible that Kleo's broken wrist isn't due to a freak accident but rather is the result of a deliberate act? Could Mick have grabbed her wrist in anger, twisting it to the point that it snapped? Could he have pushed her to the floor when one of their heated arguments got out of hand? Could he be responsible for Kleo's injury?

I fill the cups with boiling water straight from the tap, then pour milk into a small pitcher and arrange everything on a tray. I'm about to add Mick's beer to the tray when I impulsively decide to leave the glass sitting on the counter. I carry the tray back into the living room, noting that Mick hasn't moved from Kleo's side. "Here we go." I place the tray on the coffee table beside the bowl of peanuts and sit down on the other side of my daughter.

"I'm so sorry to put you to all this trouble," Kleo says. "You're probably exhausted after your flight."

"I'm fine."

"Somebody forgot my beer," Mick says.

"Oh, I'm sorry. I must have left it on the counter."

"Surely you don't expect my mother to go back and get it," my daughter says.

"Of course not," Mick says with laugh. He pushes himself to his feet, walks quickly from the room.

"Did Mick do this to you?" I whisper as soon as he is gone.

"What? No! Of course not!" Kleo says.

But her eyes say otherwise.

"Tell me the truth, sweetheart."

"I fell," Kleo insists. "That's the truth . . ."

Mick is quickly back at Kleo's side, one hand cradling his beer, the other falling protectively across her shoulders.

Who exactly is he protecting? I wonder, sensing that his reluctance to leave his wife's side stems less from a concern for her welfare than from a fear of what she might say while he's gone.

Please let her be telling the truth. Please let her broken wrist have been an accident.

"So, tell us about your trip," Mick says, grabbing fistfuls of nuts between sips of his beer.

"Yes," Kleo agrees. "How are Vanessa and Brad? How was it looking after three young kids?"

"Vanessa and Brad are great," I tell them. "The kids are wonderful. We went swimming in their Olympic-size pool, and I took them to a few movies, and Ethan showed me how to play some of his favorite videogames, and . . ."

"You do go on," I hear Jenny say.

". . . and?" Kleo prompts.

"And Taylor and I played with her Barbies, and Scott showed me these extraordinary drawings he's made," I continue, not really paying attention to the words coming out of my mouth, my concern for Kleo overriding my desire to share the details of my trip. I babble on for several more minutes, about Hartford, Vanessa's beautiful house, some of the funny things the kids said, anything to keep my mounting suspicions at bay.

Didn't Kleo just assure me that her fall was an accident, that Mick had nothing to do with her broken wrist? Why am I so quick to assume the worst? Do I really think Mick is capable of such violence?

"And now I think my wife is right," Mick says, swallowing the last of the beer and leaving his empty glass on the table. "You must be exhausted after your flight, and I'm pretty sure Kleo could use a nap after her ordeal. So, why don't you go get organized and we'll order pizza or something for supper and make it an early night. Sound like a plan?"

"Sounds like a plan," Kleo says.

"Sounds like a damn good plan," I hear Jenny say.

I nod as Mick helps my daughter to her feet.

"Would you mind bringing my suitcase into my room?" I ask him, eager for a few more seconds alone with my daughter.

"Of course." Mick hesitates. "Just let me get Kleo settled first, then I'll be right there." He guides Kleo toward their bedroom.

She turns briefly toward me. "It's okay," she mouths. "I'm fine."

But her eyes say otherwise.

CHAPTER SIXTY-THREE

I don't leave my house for two weeks. Partly because I'm still hoping for some alone time with my daughter and partly because I'm afraid to leave her alone with Mick.

Unfortunately, Mick doesn't leave the house either. He's never far from Kleo's side, playing the role of solicitous husband to near perfection. And while I try to buy into his act, I can't help feeling that he's enjoying his role as caregiver to his injured wife a little too much, that his eagerness to be of service is more about control than about concern.

Unless that concern is about himself.

I try to convince myself that I'm being unfair, that Mick's motives are pure, that my daughter would never tolerate such abuse.

And I can't help wondering if this is somehow my fault, that my failure to protect my daughter from my mother's caustic tongue has laid the groundwork for her acceptance of Mick's mistreatment.

What about my own behavior? Hadn't I usually deferred to Bob's wishes, often putting his interests above my own? Wasn't I usually the one to give in, go along, concede an argument I should have won?

Is this the legacy I've passed on?

I remind myself that abusers are experts at transferring the blame from themselves onto others, making you feel responsible for the abuse you suffer at their hands. Is this how Kleo feels—as if she deserves what happened? Is that why she's lying?

Is she lying?

These thoughts consume me, filling my every waking hour and interrupting my sleep. I lie awake for hours, worrying about her, wondering what I can do.

Except . . . maybe they're telling the truth. Maybe Kleo's foot really did fall asleep and she fell and broke her wrist. Maybe it really *was* an accident. Maybe Mick's concern is as genuine as it appears.

Except . . .

Maybe . . .

Except . . .

"Good morning, Linda," Mick says as I emerge from my bedroom to find him sitting beside his wife at her computer. "How'd you sleep?"

"Great," I lie. "You?"

"Off and on," he says. "This one almost clocked me a few times with her cast."

What a good idea, I think. "How about you, sweetie?"

"Off and on," Kleo repeats.

"Well, just another month to go. How's the work coming along? Typing getting any easier?"

Kleo waves the fingers peeking out from the end of her cast. "Slowly but surely." She smiles at her husband. "And Mick's been a big help."

I smile. "What about your own work?" I ask him. "Don't you have a business to run? I can help Kleo with whatever she needs."

"My stuff can wait. Kleo's what's important here."

"Yes, she is," I agree.

Is it possible Mick's telling the truth? That his concern is real? That I'm doing him a terrible disservice?

"What about you?" Mick asks.

"Me?"

"Don't you have places to go? Things to do? You haven't been to visit your psycho friend since you came home from Connecticut."

"Her name is Jenny and she's not a psycho."

"Sorry," he says. "Your perfectly normal friend Jenny, who claims she kills people. How many is it now, anyway?"

The phone in the kitchen rings, and I excuse myself to answer it, grateful for the interruption, even as I suspect it's another scam. Scammers are pretty much the only people who call my landline these days. "Hello?"

"Is this Linda Davidson?" a woman asks.

"It is."

"This is Bev Hurley. I don't know if you remember me. We gave you a lift home from the airport . . ."

"Of course, I remember you. I can't thank you enough."

"Please. No thanks necessary. And I hope you don't mind my calling, but when I didn't hear from you, I got concerned, so I looked you up. I was just curious . . . Your daughter, is she okay?"

"Oh, you're so sweet. Yes, she's fine. Well, not fine, exactly. She broke her wrist. But she's okay, thank you so much for asking. And I'm sorry I didn't get back to you. I remember now that you asked me to call and let you know. It's just been kind of hectic—"

"*You do go on,*" I hear Jenny chastise, causing me to break off midsentence.

"I understand completely," Bev says. "No need to apologize."

"*You apologize way too much,*" Jenny says.

"I actually have another motive for calling . . ."

"Yes?"

"My book club, the one I told you about? We met last night, and, well, I was wondering if you've given any thought to joining us?"

"I'm so sorry. I forgot all about it," I confess.

"Well, of course you did. You've obviously been way too busy. I don't know what I was thinking . . ."

"Actually, I'd love to join," I hear myself say. *Really? When did you decide this?*

"You would? That's wonderful. We meet once a month. Our next meeting is at my house on October sixteenth. We do a mix of classic and contemporary. I can text you all the details."

"Sounds good," I say, deciding that I've been housebound for far too long. Not just the last few weeks, but ever since Bob died. Maybe it's time I reclaim what's left of my life.

"Who was that?" Kleo asks when I return to the dining area.

I tell her about Bev Hurley and how we met.

"So, looks like something good came out of Kleo's accident after all," Mick says.

Kleo smiles. "What is it you always told me? Things have a way of working out?"

I return her smile. Maybe she's right.

Maybe . . .

Except . . .

I go to see Jenny.

"How's she been?" I ask Selena when I arrive.

"Not so great," Selena informs me.

"Is there a problem?"

"Other than that she's ninety-three and suffering from dementia?" Selena asks.

"I guess that about covers it," I concede.

"She's just very low energy, which is so unusual. She's been sleeping a lot. Especially the last few weeks." Selena shakes her head. "I guess we can't expect them to last forever. Even when they're as feisty as Jenny."

"Can I see her?"

"Of course."

I proceed down the corridor to Jenny's room. Her door is unlocked, and I peek inside, then quietly approach her bed. "Jenny?" I whisper, watching the barely visible rise and fall of her chest under the covers.

She opens her eyes. "Linda Davidson!" she says, her voice weak, my name barely audible. "Where've you been?"

"I went to visit my daughter in Connecticut. Remember? I told you. And then, my daughter Kleo fell and broke her wrist, so things have been a little hectic . . ."

"*You do go on,*" I think I hear her say, but Jenny's eyes have closed and she's drifted back to sleep.

My watch pings as I'm leaving the room. *You didn't make it happen!* it scolds me in bright orange lettering across its face.

Great, I think. *Just what I need: a guilt trip from my watch.*

I unsnap its leather band as I proceed to the elevators, dropping the damn thing into the trash on my way out.

CHAPTER SIXTY-FOUR

I return to Legacy Place the following afternoon to find Jenny sitting up in bed, on top of the covers, three pillows propped behind her head. She's wearing floral flannel pajamas underneath a ratty-looking black-and-white mohair sweater, a pair of heavy argyle socks stuffed into the delicate pink slippers I bought her for her birthday, her hair hidden inside a blue-and-white plastic shower cap.

"Did you just get out of the shower?" I ask her, dragging one of the chairs from the sitting area to the side of her bed.

"Why would you ask me that?"

"Because you're wearing a shower cap."

"I am?" She pulls off the cap, arthritic fingers moving to fluff out the matted gray hair beneath. "No wonder I was so hot."

I laugh. "How are you feeling today?"

She shrugs. The shrug says, not so great.

"Is anything in particular bothering you?"

"Like what?"

"I don't know. Does something hurt?"

"I'm almost a century old. Everything hurts."

I laugh again. "Selena tells me you've been sleeping a lot lately."

"Not much else to do. You weren't around."

"I know, and I'm sorry. I went to visit my daughter in Connecticut, and then my other daughter fell and broke her wrist . . ."

"You told me that yesterday," Jenny snaps.

"Sorry—I didn't think you heard me."

"Of course, I heard you. I'm demented, not deaf." She picks at a loose strand of wool on her mohair sweater. "How is she? The one who broke her wrist."

"Getting better."

"How'd she break it?"

"She says it was an accident, that she fell . . ."

"What do *you* say?"

I count silently to ten before answering. "I don't think it was an accident," I tell her, voicing such thoughts out loud for the first time.

"Hmm," Jenny says, closing her eyes.

Several minutes pass. Jenny's eyes remain closed. I wait, hoping she'll open them again, regale me with her tall tales of murder and revenge, anything to take my mind off my suspicions, but her eyes remain stubbornly closed. I sit for five more minutes, until it becomes obvious that she's fallen into a deep sleep and isn't about to wake up anytime soon. I stand up, wait another minute, then return my chair to its previous position in the small sitting area and head for the door.

Her voice stops me as I'm about to exit. "You know what you have to do, don't you?" she says.

I gasp and spin around. "What did you say?"

But Jenny's eyes are closed and her breathing is as it was when I left her side. I leave the room, not sure if the voice I heard was hers or my own.

"Mr. Marshall?" I ask, peeking my head into the office of the manager of Legacy Place. "I was wondering if I could speak to you for a few minutes."

He motions me inside. "Please, have a seat."

I sink into the chair in front of his desk. If he remembers me from our previous encounter, he gives no indication. "I was wondering if you could tell me anything about Jenny Cooper."

"Jenny Cooper?"

"The resident in room 415."

"I'm sorry. Who are you, exactly?"

"My name is Linda. Linda Davidson. I'm a friend of Jenny's. Well, I was actually a friend of Carol Kreiger, but her husband moved her down to Miami . . ."

"Yes. How is Mrs. Kreiger adapting to her new environment?"

"Very well, apparently." I feel a pang of guilt that I haven't been to see her since her move. One more pang to add to my growing collection. "Anyway, I've become very close to Jenny over the past months, and she's been telling me some pretty wild stories about her life, but of course, I recognize she's . . . well, that she's . . . suffering from dementia . . . so I don't know how much of what she's told me is real . . ."

"I'm not sure how you think I can help you," Henry Marshall says.

"Well, I know that she hasn't had any visitors in years, but I was wondering if you knew if she has any family, or anyone really, whom I could possibly get in touch with?"

"Well, let me see," he surprises me by saying. "Jenny Cooper," he repeats several times, punching her name into his computer. "Jenny Cooper. Jenny Cooper. Yes, here she is." He studies the information on his screen. "It appears she came to us seven years ago, brought in by her husband, Wilfred Cooper. Yes, I remember now. A sad story, really."

"How so?"

"Well, if I'm remembering correctly, they'd met and married late in life. In their eighties, as I recall. It was a real love story, according to Mr. Cooper. And then, unfortunately, after a few years, Mrs. Cooper started showing signs of dementia and Mr. Cooper was diagnosed with Parkinson's and wasn't able to continue caring for her at home, so he wisely brought her here, made all the necessary arrangements, and then passed away soon after." Henry Marshall continues reading through the file on his computer screen. "There doesn't appear to be any other family listed, no one to notify when Mrs. Cooper passes on." He looks from his screen to me. "Would *you* like to be notified?"

"I would, yes." I provide Henry Marshall with my name and phone numbers. "Hopefully, that won't happen anytime soon."

He smiles. "Is there anything else I can help you with?"

"No. I think that's it. Thank you."

"Take care," he says as I'm leaving his office. "Be safe."

I don't go home. Instead, on impulse, I drive to Miami.

I'd told Henry Marshall that Carol was adjusting well to her new environment, but the truth is that I've only spoken to Lorne once since the move, and I have no idea how she continues to fare.

The traffic along I-95 is surprisingly light, due partly to the time of day, mostly to the time of year. September is a relatively light month for tourists, the majority of snowbirds waiting until October or November to start flying south. January through April see the busiest influx, the population of South Florida almost doubling in size. It won't be long before the roads become as clogged as residents' arteries, I think, and laugh, catching a look of concern on the face of the driver in the next lane.

I pass the northern suburb of Miami known as Sunny Isles, recalling that Jenny said she liked living there. "She also told you she killed her building manager," I remind my reflection in the rearview mirror.

Just how much of what Jenny has told me is actually true? Is any of it?

I spend at least twenty minutes trying to locate the facility where Carol now resides. I know there's a way to program the GPS in my car, or use the app Mick installed on my phone, but I've never used either, so there's no point in trying to figure them out now. After another ten minutes, I manage to stumble onto the right address.

I find Carol in the beautiful plant-filled atrium off the main lobby. She sits in a wheelchair among at least a dozen other wheelchairs, the chairs' occupants staring vacantly toward the outside world, their blank faces lit by the sun.

"Carol, hi," I say, kneeling in front of her chair and fighting back the tears I feel forming. This is the first time I'm seeing my friend in a wheelchair, and it breaks my heart. "It's me, Linda."

She stares at me for a few seconds before returning her gaze to the wall of glass behind me. We stay this way until I feel the light shift, and an orderly approaches to return Carol to her room in time for dinner.

"Take care," I tell her as she's being wheeled away. "Be safe."

CHAPTER SIXTY-FIVE

"Where have you been all this time?" Kleo asks as I walk through the front door. "I was worried. I phoned you half a dozen times. Why didn't you return my calls?"

I reach into my purse for my cellphone. "Sorry," I say sheepishly. "Looks like the battery's dead."

"That's because you have to remember to charge it."

"Sorry," I say again, feeling like a wayward teenager.

When did our roles reverse? At what age did my daughter become the parent and I the child?

"I drove into Miami," I tell her.

"You what?"

"To see Carol. It was a spur-of-the-moment decision."

"Since when did you become a spur-of-the-moment kind of person?"

I shake my head. I have no answer for that.

"Well, next time, I'd really appreciate it if you'd give me a heads-up."

"I will definitely do that."

"And remember to charge your phone."

"Yes, ma'am."

"Thank you."

"Where's Mick?" I ask, suddenly aware he isn't hovering.

"He went to pick up something to eat. There's this new place he's been wanting to try, and we didn't know what time you'd be getting back, so he thought he'd just run over and get something—"

"How did you break your wrist?" I interrupt, seizing the opportunity to ask.

"You know how I broke it."

"I know how you *told* me you broke it. I want to know what *really* happened."

"I don't understand," she says, although the look in her eyes tells me she understands perfectly.

There seems little point in beating around the proverbial bush. Who knows when I'll get this chance again. "Did Mick do this to you?"

Kleo pales instantly. "No! I've told you that!"

"Tell me the truth, sweetheart."

"We've been through this. I *am* telling you the truth."

"Mick had nothing to do with you breaking your wrist?"

She hesitates. Not long, but long enough.

"Tell me," I say again.

"I can't."

"You can."

"It's complicated."

"How is it complicated? Either he did or he didn't."

She looks toward the front door. "It's not what you think."

"Then tell me what it is."

"He begged me not to say anything. He said you wouldn't understand."

"What won't I understand?"

"That it was an accident, that he didn't mean for it to happen."

"You're trying to tell me that he 'accidentally' broke your wrist?"

"I'm trying to tell you what happened."

"Okay. I'm listening."

Kleo starts pacing back and forth, her eyes never leaving the front door.

I realize I'm holding my breath, my ears tuned to the sound of approaching tires.

"This is more than a little embarrassing," she begins.

"We're way past being embarrassed."

"Okay. Okay. But you have to promise not to overreact."

I nod.

"Out loud."

I nod again. "I promise."

She looks toward the ceiling, then the floor, then from side to side. Anywhere but at me. "I was trying to get some work done," she finally begins, "and Mick was a little hungover from his night out with the guys, and shit . . . How do I say this? He was feeling a little . . . frisky . . . and he kept at me, trying to drag me away from the computer, playing with my hair, kissing the back of my neck, doing everything he could to distract me. And I kept telling him that I was right in the middle of something important, to just give me twenty minutes to finish what I was doing, but he wouldn't stop. He kept pawing at me, and I was starting to get irritated. So, I slapped his hand to get him to back off, and he grabbed my wrist. And, I don't know, it just . . . snapped."

"Dear God."

"It was an accident. He didn't mean to grab it that hard. And he felt sick about it. Honestly. He was crying and saying over and over how sorry he was, that all he'd wanted was to make love, that he certainly never intended to hurt me . . ."

I shake my head, trying to control the rage building inside me.

"And when you think about it, think about it rationally, not emotionally," Kleo says, "it was my fault as much as his."

"What the fuck is rational about that? How is any of this your fault?"

"Mom, please. You promised you wouldn't overreact."

"You listen to me. *None* of what happened is your fault."

"I never should have slapped his hand."

"He should never have let it get that far. He should have backed off when you told him to stop."

"Yes. He acknowledges that. He swears it will never happen again."

"And you believe him?"

"I want to."

"Why?" I ask, simply.

"*Why?*" she repeats, her eyes filling with tears. "He's my husband."

I know I should stop. But I can't. "What are you getting out of this relationship, Kleo?" I ask. "Mick lies. He cheats. He has no respect for your time or your work. What is this man contributing to your life? Other than broken bones and STDs."

"That's not fair. He's just going through a hard time. Things will get better. Once his business picks up . . ."

"Things like this don't get better," I tell her.

Which is when we hear Mick's car pull into the driveway.

Kleo pushes the tears out of her eyes. "Please don't say anything to Mick. He begged me not to tell you. He said you wouldn't understand."

I nod. She's right. I don't understand.

The door opens and Mick steps inside, a bag of takeout Thai food in his hands, a wary look on his face. "Hey, Linda," he says. "When did you get home?"

"Just walked in the door two minutes ago," I say. *Mick isn't the only liar in the family.*

Kleo smiles with relief. "Something smells delicious." She takes the bag from Mick's hands, carries it into the kitchen.

"Where were you all afternoon?" he asks me. "Kleo was getting worried."

"Yes, sorry. I drove into Miami to see Carol."

"You should call next time."

Really? You're lecturing me on how to behave?

"How is the old girl, anyway?"

"Same." *The less I say, the better.*

"Yeah, from what I understand, her condition's only going to get worse."

I nod. He's right.

It's only going to get worse.

CHAPTER SIXTY-SIX

"I just don't get it," I say to Jenny when I visit the following week.

We're sitting in the garden, under the shade of a sprawling banyan tree. A slight breeze floats around our heads, providing only a modicum of relief from the heat. Despite the humidity, Jenny is wearing her mohair sweater over her flannel pajamas and seems unaffected by the outside temperature. I, on the other hand, am perspiring profusely in my white cotton T-shirt, despite my bare arms and legs.

Jenny looks toward the pink slippers on her feet and says nothing.

"I mean, I'm not a psychologist or anything," I continue, although judging by the blank look on Jenny's face, I doubt she's even listening. "But I think it might have something to do with her sister." I pause, waiting for Jenny to tell me that's a stupid idea, continuing when she doesn't.

"It's just that Vanessa has always been the more outgoing, the more self-assured of my two girls. She's succeeded in everything she's set her mind to. She has a great marriage, a great career, she's a terrific mother, she makes a ton of money, she can afford to buy me expensive gifts." I point toward the Louis Vuitton bag she bought me for Mother's Day, which rests at my feet. "And Kleo has always been a bit in her shadow, despite the fact that she's the elder. Not that she hasn't been successful in her own right. Not that she isn't as smart as a whip. She is. About everything except men." I pause, waiting for Jenny to interrupt to tell me I'm boring her, as she would have done only a few short weeks ago.

But she says nothing. So I keep talking, not because I expect to gain insight into my daughter, but more to fill the ever-widening space I feel is developing between Jenny and me, to assure myself that nothing has changed, that she's still the same senile old crone of whom I've grown so fond. "Unfortunately, Kleo has always picked guys who were more like wounded birds," I rattle on, "the kind who need fixing. But at least she was smart enough not to marry any of them. Until Mick."

"I always preferred Keith Richards," Jenny says suddenly.

"What?"

"Keith Richards," she repeats. "I always preferred him to that one who was always prancing around with his boas and tight pants."

I smile, grateful for the return of a familiar glint in Jenny's eyes. "Not that Mick."

"What Mick are we talking about?"

"My daughter's husband."

"Your daughter is married to Mick Jagger?"

"No."

"Then why are we talking about him?"

"We aren't."

"You aren't making any sense," she tells me.

It's all I can do to keep from throwing my arms around her neck and hugging her. I've missed this so much. "I was just saying that I think the reason my daughter stays with her husband is that she doesn't want to fail."

"Stupid reason," Jenny says.

"I agree."

"She should just kill him."

I laugh out loud.

"What's so funny?"

"I'm sorry," I say. "It's just so nice to have you back."

"Where have I been?"

"It's an expression."

"What does it mean?"

"That you haven't been quite yourself lately."

"Who else have I been?"

"You've just been a lot quieter than usual." *Weaker,* I think, but don't say. *I was afraid I was losing you. Like I lost Bob. Like I've lost Carol.* I look around the garden, note two elderly residents sitting in silence, side by side, on a nearby bench, their words having largely deserted them. So much of growing old is about loss, I think. Our worlds get smaller and smaller. Our memories are the last holdouts. Is it fair we have to lose those, too? "Did you really kill anyone, Jenny?"

"Did I? How rude." She stares at me for several long seconds, the mischievous glint slowly disappearing from her eyes, like liquid from a straw. "I think I'd like to go inside now," she says.

I stand up, reach for her elbow, guide her inside the building. We ride the elevator to the fourth floor, her head resting heavily against my shoulder.

"Everything okay?" Selena calls as we turn down the corridor.

I wait for Jenny to holler back that it's none of her damn business.

"She's tired," I say when she doesn't.

I open the door to Jenny's apartment, and she heads immediately for her bed, lying down on top of the covers and closing her eyes. I lower myself into one of the corduroy chairs, my eyes drifting aimlessly around the room, from Jenny to the paintings on the walls, from the window to the end table beside her bed, back to Jenny's pale face, her lips parted in sleep. "Please don't die," I whisper, my own eyes closing.

Which is when I see my mother.

We're standing in her spotless, all-white kitchen, the only color in the room coming from a collection of copper pots that hang above the center island and the dozen amazingly lifelike plastic plants that line the countertops. She is berating me for another of my perceived shortcomings, as a daughter, as a mother, as someone who has never failed to disappoint.

The torrent of angry words trip over themselves as they rush to escape her mouth, collapsing in a verbal heap that no longer makes sense. Like snow melting, her words have turned to slush. It's then I notice that her face has gone slack, her mouth tilting ominously to one side, her lips like Play-Doh, sliding toward her chin.

"Mom?" I shout. "What's wrong?"

She stares at me through eyes struggling to focus, and it's then I understand that she's having a stroke.

"Mom!" I shout as she crumples to the floor.

I stand frozen to the spot, unable to move.

I command my feet to push forward, but it's as if I'm slogging through wet cement. When I'm finally able to reach the phone to call 911, my fingers stumble repeatedly over the numbers, and I barely manage to inform the operator of what is happening. She tells me an ambulance is on its way.

So I sit down on the cold tile floor, cradling my mother's head in my lap, watching helplessly as her lips turn from pink to blue. Minutes later, the ambulance arrives, but she is already dead.

I ask the paramedic if there was anything I could have done, if I should have performed mouth-to-mouth or CPR while I was waiting, but he assures me that my mother was likely dead before she hit the floor, and that in any event, nothing I could have done would have saved her. He says he's sorry for my loss.

You can't lose what you never had, I'm tempted to tell him. But I say nothing.

You just sat there and watched me die, my mother says now.

Did I? I've often wondered. Could I have moved faster, tried harder, done something—*anything*—to save her?

Despite what the paramedic said, I'm honestly not sure.

My mother's image fades as I push myself out of the chair and walk to Jenny's bedside, leaning forward to whisper in her ear. "Turns out you're not the only one with secrets," I say.

CHAPTER SIXTY-SEVEN

Jenny continues to deteriorate over the next few weeks.

I visit almost daily. Mostly she's asleep, but even when she's awake, she doesn't say much. I'm not even sure if she knows who I am most of the time. Occasionally, there are flashes of the old Jenny, and this is what keeps me coming back.

"How's that old guy you were fucking?" she demands one afternoon.

I remember how I used to be appalled by such outbursts. Now I welcome them. "We weren't fucking," I remind her.

"No? Too bad. He was a good-looking man. I bet he'd be great in bed."

"He was—at least, according to Carol."

"Who's Carol?"

"My friend. He was her husband."

"You were fucking your friend's husband? Not very nice, Linda Davidson!"

"We weren't fucking," I say again.

"No? Too bad. He was a good-looking man. I bet he'd be great in bed."

"I heard he's fucking someone else," I offer as consolation.

She sits up in bed, swings her feet toward the floor, the slippers

I bought her dangling from the tips of her toes. "The scoundrel!" she exclaims.

I laugh at the old-fashioned word.

"And how do you feel about that?"

"Truthfully?" I ask. "Relieved."

Her turn to laugh. "So, who's the lucky girl?"

"I don't know her name. I hear she's a lot younger than he is. But I don't know if that's true," I admit. "It's just a rumor . . ."

"Rumors are good," Jenny says. "You know what they say, don't you? 'Where there's smoke . . . ' "

"There's fire," I say, finishing the thought.

"There's a fire?" she gasps.

"No, there's no fire," I assure her quickly.

"Then why'd you say there was?"

"I was just finishing the expression, 'Where there's smoke . . .' "

"There's fire!" she exclaims triumphantly. "Everybody knows that. Keep up, Linda Davidson!"

Another morning finds her on the love seat in her small sitting room, totally naked except for the now-tatty pink slippers on her feet.

"I think we should get you back into these," I tell her, retrieving a pair of discarded pajamas from the floor and helping her into them, trying not to notice the loose, motley-colored flesh hanging from her brittle bones. "Weren't you cold?"

"I was a little, yes. Thank you, dear," she says. "Are you new here?"

"New?"

"I don't think we've been introduced. My name is . . ." She looks to me to give voice to her identity.

"Jenny," I whisper, my voice breaking upon contact with the air.

"That's my name, too," she says, brightly. "Why are you crying, dear? Is something wrong?"

Two days later, the old Jenny is back.

"How's that daughter of yours?" she surprises me by asking. "Still with her husband?"

"She is, yes."

"She is what?"

"Still with her husband."

"I had a husband," she says.

"I believe you had several."

"I did?"

"David Huston, Parker Rubini . . ."

"What kind of name is Parker Rubini? You're making that up."

"Wilfred Cooper."

"Ah, yes. Willy. He was a lovely man."

"Tell me about him."

"He was kind. Not much of a looker. But kind. He was kind."

I smile. "Anything else I should know?"

"I didn't kill him," she says.

"Did you kill any of them? Your husbands," I qualify, before she can ask.

"I don't think so," she says. Then seconds later, "I may have."

"But not Willy."

"No. He was nice. He was kind."

"How did you meet him?" I ask.

Jenny gives my query a moment's thought. "I can't remember," she says finally. "I think he was just . . . there."

"There?"

"Where he was."

"I understand you were both in your eighties when you got married," I continue, trying a different approach.

"You understand correctly, Linda Davidson."

"And you were happy?"

"I must have been. I didn't kill him!"

I laugh. "But you killed the others?"

"What others?" she asks.

"And 'so it goes,'" I say, quoting Kurt Vonnegut.

"So what goes?"

"It's a quote from an old novel. *Slaughterhouse-Five*. The author uses the refrain repeatedly in the book: '*So it goes.*'"

"I don't understand. Where does what go?"

"Life, I guess."

"Life goes," she repeats, taking a moment to let this sink in. "And this is a real book you've actually read?"

"The first time when I was in university. The second time just last week."

"Why would you read the same book twice?"

"It was last night's selection at this book club I joined recently."

"And at this book club, you talk about life and where it goes," Jenny says.

"We talk about life and where it goes," I repeat.

Her eyes close. "Let me know when you find out," she says.

CHAPTER SIXTY-EIGHT

I'm straightening up around the house, fluffing errant pillows, attacking stray crumbs on the kitchen floor with my Dustbuster, waiting for Mick and Kleo to come home from the hospital. It's six weeks since the "accident," and Kleo is having her cast removed.

It's been a period of relative peace. I feel my breath catch painfully in my chest. I know what comes next.

It's become an all-too-familiar pattern. Things between my daughter and her husband will go along smoothly for a few days, maybe even a week. Mick will be on his best behavior. Then a minor quibble will escalate into a major blowout. Angry words will be exchanged. The house will reverberate with the sound of slamming doors. Mick will stay out late, come home smelling of too many beers. There will be more tears, more angry words, more slamming doors, more fraught silence, eventually leading to the calm before the next explosion.

So it goes.

Despite Mick's promises to Kleo, and her assurances to me, I know it's only a matter of time before the next "accident," the next broken bone. I feel powerless, useless, exhausted from the constant dread and anticipation. There are days I can barely rouse myself from my bed, nights where I go to sleep almost praying I won't wake up, unable to stomach the thought of my daughter in harm's way.

I've thought of asking them to move out, to offer to pay for an apartment until Kleo goes back to work and Mick's business finally gets on its feet. I've even contemplated moving out of my own home, giving them the house. Maybe a little space is all that's needed, I try to convince myself.

And yet, I know that without the safety net my presence provides, there's no telling what Mick might do, what he's capable of, that I'm the only thing keeping my daughter safe.

I can't abandon her now.

I can't, and I won't.

I hear a car turn in to our driveway, and I rush to the door. But it's only someone backing up, turning around, heading back down the street. I look toward my wrist to check the time, but I no longer have a watch. *Should have thought of that before you tossed me in the trash,* I can almost hear the discarded watch berate me as I march into the kitchen to check the time on my microwave oven.

Kleo's appointment was at ten, and it's almost noon, so they should be back anytime now. I glance around the kitchen, notice a few coffee stains in the basin of the white porcelain sink. I retrieve some cleanser from the cupboard beneath the sink and scrub the offending marks until they disappear, then wipe down the counter and the cupboard doors. I look out the small kitchen window at the house next door. *Maybe they have something that needs cleaning,* I think. *Maybe I should hire myself out as a housekeeper.*

It would certainly give me something to do. I've already finished reading my book club's selection for next month, and made two trips to Miami to see a woman who no longer has any clue who I am. And there is only so much time I can spend with Jenny, who is getting weaker by the day. Her heart is slowing down, Selena tells me. It won't be much longer.

What do I do when I no longer have our conversations to look forward to, when Jenny, too, deserts me?

I decide to clean out the purse Vanessa gave me for Mother's Day. Its fine leather and metal hardware make it heavy to begin with, and I've filled it with so many things—my wallet, a metal holder for my credit cards, my house keys, my car keys, sunglasses, reading glasses, a small bottle of hand sanitizer to keep the germs at bay, a smaller bottle of aspirin in case I suffer a heart attack while out, some breath mints in case I run into someone I know, a packet of tissues in case I need to blow my nose, my cellphone in case of an emergency—that my arms and shoulders are starting to ache from lugging the damn thing around.

Dear God, what is all this shit?

I turn the purse upside down, shaking its contents onto the coffee table in the living room, the credit card holder knocking over the small bowl of peanuts sitting in the middle of its glass top. I quickly corral the nuts, returning them to the bowl before giving the bag a final shake. I watch as some loose change tumbles out, followed by a black Sharpie, along with several old receipts from long-forgotten purchases.

One last crumpled piece of paper clings stubbornly to the bottom of the bag. I reach inside and pick it out, note the name written boldly across its crumpled surface: Max Silver. Followed by a phone number.

Who the hell is Max Silver?

And then I remember. The man from the mall. The man looking for a bridge partner. I'd forgotten all about his offer. *Should I call him? At the very least, it would give me something to do, provide me with a much-needed distraction.*

But I haven't played duplicate bridge in years. It would be a disaster.

Who gives a shit?

I reach for my cellphone in the middle of the items now littering the coffee table and press in Max Silver's number before I can talk myself out of calling him, listening as his phone rings, once . . . twice . . . three times.

"This is Max Silver," a recorded voice announces after ring number five. "Please leave a message."

I immediately disconnect. "Stupid idea," I say, dropping my belongings back inside my purse one by one. I leave out the old receipts. "Because that will make all the difference," I tell the empty house.

An unfamiliar ring fills the air.

My cellphone, I realize, my hand fishing frantically back inside my bag to retrieve it. *Almost no one has this number. It must be Kleo or Mick, calling to say they're running late, a problem has arisen, there's been another accident . . .*

"Hello? Hello?" I all but shout into the phone.

"Hello?" a strange voice answers back. "Who's this?"

"Who's *this*?" I demand.

"This is Max Silver. I believe you just called me. You hung up before I could get to the phone. Who is this?" he asks again.

"It's Linda Davidson."

"I'm sorry . . ."

"Linda Davidson," I repeat. "We met at the mall a while back. You mentioned you were in the market for a bridge partner . . ."

"The woman who told her watch to fuck off!" he exclaims.

"That's me," I admit, sheepishly. "Listen. I'm sorry to bother you. I know I should have called before, and I don't know if you're even still interested. You've probably found someone else by now . . ."

"I'm still interested," he says. "If you promise not to tell *me* to fuck off if I misplay a hand."

I realize I'm smiling. "You have my word."

"Is this Saturday night too soon for you?"

"This Saturday night is fine."

He's providing me with the time and place when I hear a car pull into the driveway. My smile disappears. "Listen. I have to go . . ."

"Until Saturday," he says.

"Until Saturday," I repeat as my front door opens and Kleo and Mick walk through.

CHAPTER SIXTY-NINE

"Well?" I ask, pushing myself to my feet.

"It's off!" Kleo holds out her right arm, triumphantly.

"How does it feel?"

"Strange. Like it belongs to someone else."

"You should sit down," Mick tells her. "She almost fainted when the doctor was removing the cast."

"He says it happens all the time," Kleo elaborates as I sit down beside her on the sofa. "Something about the shock to your body, the blood rushing to your head . . ."

I'm reaching over to take her hand when I notice a series of small, fading purple blotches on her upper arm, as well as a larger, fresh bruise just above her elbow. "What's this?"

Mick looks over and laughs. "Must be from when I grabbed her to keep her from falling," he says. "Your daughter was headed straight for the floor and a major concussion."

"It was very embarrassing," Kleo says.

"Well, I don't know about you guys," Mick announces, "but I'm starving. Any of that delicious lasagna left over from last night?"

"There should be some in the fridge."

"Great," Mick says, leaving the room.

"How did you get these bruises?" I whisper as I hear Mick puttering around in the kitchen.

"Mick just told you. He grabbed me when I was about to pass out . . ."

"And these?" I ask, indicating the smaller, faded ones.

She shrugs. "These are nothing. I don't even remember how I got them."

"Kleo . . ."

"Mom . . ."

"If Mick did this . . ."

"Leave it alone. Please. Who were you on the phone with when we walked in?" she asks, in an obvious effort to change the topic.

I recognize I'll get nowhere if I continue to badger her, so I drop it. She's been badgered enough. "No one."

"No one?"

"Just this man I met at the mall."

"You met a man at the mall?"

"Are you going to repeat everything I say?" I hear Jenny ask.

"Who met a man at the mall?" Mick asks, returning from the kitchen with a full plate of lasagna in one hand, a beer in the other.

"It's just someone I met who was looking for a bridge partner . . ."

"A *man* she met," Kleo corrects.

"Way to go, Linda!" Mick says, sitting down at the dining room table and depositing his plate of lasagna dangerously close to Kleo's papers.

I watch the color drain from my daughter's face. "Please be careful with that," she warns, her back stiffening.

"Maybe you should eat in the kitchen," I say.

"And miss hearing about your latest conquest?"

"No conquest. Just a man looking for a bridge partner." I watch as Mick guides a heaping forkful of lasagna into his mouth, a few errant drops of sauce dripping onto the front of his black T-shirt. "And I don't know about my daughter," I add, "but I would certainly feel a lot more comfortable if you'd get that food away from Kleo's papers."

"Well, I certainly wouldn't want to make anyone uncomfortable . . ." Mick gives a little bow as he lifts his plate off the table with one hand, the dish tilting precariously to one side as he pushes himself to his feet.

The lasagna is already sliding off the plate toward Kleo's papers by the time Mick reacts, his arm reaching out to sweep the papers out of harm's way, knocking over his beer in the process, the glass shattering upon contact with the floor, a combination of sauce, glass, and liquid spraying across everything in its path.

"Oh, my God!" Kleo jumps to her feet.

"Shit!" Mick shouts. "Shit!"

I run into the kitchen to retrieve a roll of paper towels and return to find Kleo on her hands and knees, trying to wipe the mess from her papers with the bottom of her skirt. "Here, let me," I say, joining her on the floor.

"What am I going to do?" she cries. "Everything's ruined."

"If you'd just let me eat in peace," Mick is shouting, pacing back and forth in front of us, the now-empty plate still in his hand, "this never would have happened."

"If you'd eaten it *in the kitchen*," Kleo corrects, "this never would have happened."

"Shit!" Mick waves his free hand in the air. "Nothing I ever do is right! It's not enough that I organize my entire day around you, that I drive you to the hospital, wait there for hours when I could be working . . ."

"For God's sake, Mick," I say, rising to my feet, my patience at an end. "This isn't about you."

"Well, it's certainly not about you, is it? So why don't you keep your damn mouth shut."

"Don't talk to my mother like that!"

"I'm telling you it was a goddamn accident."

"And I'm telling *you* that there have been a few too many *accidents* around here of late," I hear myself say.

"Excuse me?" Mick says.

"Mom, please . . ." Kleo scrambles to her feet.

"What the hell is that supposed to mean?"

"Let it go," Kleo urges.

"First, my daughter's wrist. Now her work . . ."

He turns menacingly toward Kleo. "You told your mother I broke your wrist?"

"I explained it was an accident . . ."

"You bitch!"

"Accident or not," I say, quickly maneuvering my body between them, "the result is the same. Kleo's wrist got broken, there's lasagna and beer all over the goddamn place, and don't you dare call my daughter a bitch, you miserable piece of shit!"

I hear Kleo gasp as Mick's eyes fill with fury. His fist clenches at his side, and not for the first time, I think he might actually hit me. Instead, he spins around and hurls the plate in his hand at the far wall. The plate shatters, sending shards of china and tiny bits of meat sauce shooting in all directions.

"Mick, for God's sake!" Kleo cries. "Stop this! What are you doing?"

"I'll tell you what I'm doing. I'm going out to get something to eat. You can come with me or you can stay here with your miserable cunt of a mother . . ."

"Whoa. Just a minute . . ."

"Moment of truth, Kleo. Who's it gonna be? Your husband or Mommie Dearest?"

My breath escapes my lungs in a series of short, painful bursts as I wait for my daughter's response.

Kleo looks from me to Mick. "Get the fuck out of here," she tells him.

CHAPTER SEVENTY

"First time I've ever been called a cunt," I tell Jenny.

I'm sitting beside her bed. Her eyes are closed, as they have been since I arrived over an hour ago. I've been telling her about what happened yesterday with Mick, how quickly the situation developed, escalated, then spiraled out of control.

"Consider it an honor," she mutters, the words sliding from between barely parted lips.

"You're awake," I say.

"Hard to sleep with you nattering on."

I laugh. "How are you feeling?"

"I've felt better."

"Can I get you anything?"

"Like what?"

"A glass of water? Another blanket?"

"I'm not thirsty and I'm not cold."

I smile.

"I'm dying," she says.

My smile disappears.

"So where is this miserable piece of shit now?" Jenny asks, repeating my words.

"Who knows? He didn't come home last night."

"He'll be back," she says.

"I know."

"What will your daughter do then?"

"I'm not sure."

"Will she take him back?"

"God, I hope not. We obviously can't keep living in the same house if she does."

"You may have to kill him," Jenny says, opening her eyes.

I laugh.

"I'm serious."

"Don't tempt me."

We sit in silence for several minutes.

I try not to fantasize about murdering my son-in-law.

"So," she says, "tell me about this man you met."

"Max Silver?"

"I don't know. How many men have you met recently?"

"He's the only one."

"I like the name Max. It's short and to the point."

"What point is that?" I ask, knowing that's what she'd have said.

She smiles. "I don't know. You tell *me*."

"What do you want to know?"

"Is he handsome?"

"I guess. I mean, he's my age, so . . ."

"Young," she says.

I laugh again.

"Married? Widowed? Divorced?"

"Widowed. Three daughters. Eight grandchildren."

"Boring. What else?"

"Not much."

"You're going out with a man you met in a mall, a man you know almost nothing about? What's the matter with you, Linda Davidson? He could be a serial killer, for God's sake."

"Some of my best friends are serial killers," I remind her.

Her turn to laugh.

"You don't think I should go?"

"What do *you* think?"

"I don't know what to think anymore . . . about anything."

She laughs again. "Maybe you think too much, Linda David-son. Ever consider that? If you want a happy life, maybe the best thing is not to think so much. Maybe that's the real secret."

"*Psst,*" I hear her say. "*I have a secret.*"

"Did you really kill all those people?" I ask.

"Do you really want to know?" she asks in return.

I smile. "Maybe not."

"Good answer. Uh-oh."

"Uh-oh?"

"You're thinking again. I can see it on your face. It goes all squishy . . ."

"Squishy?"

Jenny crosses her eyes and puckers up her mouth, sucking her features into the middle of her face. "Like your nose got caught in a door."

"Charming." I do my best to unsquish my face. "How's that?"

She shrugs. The shrug indicates I've been only partially success-ful. "So, what were you thinking about?" she asks.

I debate making something up, telling her that I was thinking about Kleo, Mick, Max Silver, ultimately opting to go with the truth. "That I'm going to miss this," I say.

"This what?"

"This *this*. What we do. *Us*."

"Me, too," she says. "Or at least I would . . . if I weren't dead."

Tears fill my eyes.

"No. No. You can't cry, Linda Davidson. Death is part of life. You're old enough to know that."

"Doesn't make it any easier for those of us who are left be-hind."

"I guess not." She reaches for my hand. "But you'll be all right. You have your daughters and your grandchildren. And now you have your book club and your bridge and your Max Silver. You'll make lots of new friends, Linda Davidson. You'll forget all about me."

"I don't think that's possible, Jenny Cooper."

"Hah! You got that right!" She laughs as our arthritic fingers intertwine. "You know that you're the closest thing I've ever had to a friend. What do you think about that, Linda Davidson?"

"I consider it an honor," I say, using her earlier words.

She closes her eyes. "I'm going to sleep now. Will you stay awhile?"

"Absolutely."

"And stop thinking. I can feel your little brain twitching and it's keeping me awake."

I smile and lean back in my chair, forcing my mind to go blank. Within minutes, Jenny and I are both asleep.

CHAPTER SEVENTY-ONE

"You came!" Max Silver declares, his face all but lighting up when he sees me.

"You look surprised."

"Honestly, I wasn't sure you'd show up."

"Honestly," I admit, "neither was I."

We're standing just outside the front door of the Community Center on North Military Trail, a squat white concrete building that has seen better days. *Then again, so have we all,* I'm thinking as I watch the steady stream of elderly bridge players file inside.

"It's really nice to see you again," he says. "You're looking well."

"Nice to see you, too." He's handsomer than I remember, in his navy pants and open-necked blue shirt, a sweater draped casually around his shoulders.

"That's a lovely blouse. Mauve suits you."

"Thank you."

"And I can't help noticing you have a new watch." Max points to the old-fashioned Timex on my wrist.

"An oldie but a goodie." *Like me,* I think, but don't say.

"Right. What was that saying? 'Timex. It takes a licking . . .'"

". . . and keeps on ticking,'" I say, finishing the once-famous tagline. "It was my husband's, actually."

"You wear it well," Max says, with a smile.

"Thank you."

"Shall we go inside?"

A blast of ice-cold air greets us as we step into the wide hallway. "It's freezing in here!"

"I should have told you to bring a sweater," Max apologizes. "Here. Wear mine." He transfers the sweater from his shoulders to mine.

"No, really. That's not nec—"

"I insist."

We enter the equally frigid gymnasium to our right. I do a quick count of twenty-four card tables spaced appropriate distances apart.

"It can actually get pretty heated in here," Max says with a laugh. "Bridge players are a notoriously touchy group. I heard there was this woman one time who got so mad at her partner she upended the table, threw her cards in his face, and stormed out, screaming that he was a fucking moron who wouldn't know his ass from the ace of spades." Max cocks his head to one side. "That wasn't you, was it?"

I laugh, glancing around the rapidly filling room.

"Sorry. I couldn't resist." He leads me to an empty table. "Which position do you prefer—north-south or east-west?"

"I really haven't played much duplicate," I confess. "Whichever you'd like."

"Well, north-south stays put and east-west moves after every third hand, so let's go with east-west. Gives us a chance to stretch our legs."

"Good idea." I sink into the appropriate chair.

"Should we discuss our strategy?"

"Do we have one?"

Max chuckles. He fills out the form on the table, alerting one's opponents to the various systems one plays. "Basic bridge, it is."

The next three hours fly by. I discover Max is right about the temperature. Within the first half hour, I've already shed his sweater, undone the top two buttons of my blouse, and witnessed

two near blowups by opponents. To my surprise, I discover that
while I may have forgotten many of the finer points of the game, I
still know how to play a hand. And Max makes an excellent partner, complimenting me when I do well, keeping his mouth shut
when I don't, giving me only the odd questioning look at my ten-
dency to overbid.

"I think we did very well," he tells me as he walks me to my car
at the end of the evening.

"We came in second to last."

"We'll do better next time," he says. "If you'd be interested in
a next time, of course."

"I would, yes."

"Great. And maybe dinner beforehand? We didn't really get much
chance to talk."

"Dinner would be lovely."

"Great. I'll call you in a few days, firm things up."

"Sounds good. Thanks again for a fun evening."

"My pleasure. Talk soon." Max stands to one side to allow me
to back my car out, then watches as I drive away. I see him waving
to me as I turn onto Military Trail.

Did I just agree to a second date?

It's not a date.

It's definitely a date.

And I'm definitely too old for this nonsense.

What would Bob think? I find myself wondering.

He always said he hoped I'd find love again, even as I insisted
that his love was all I'd ever need. What would he think of Max
Silver? What do *I* think?

"*Maybe the best thing is not to think so much,*" I hear Jenny
say. "*Maybe that's the secret.*"

"I'll miss you, Jenny Cooper," I tell her, turning up the country
music on the radio, listening to Chris Stapleton wail melodically
about starting over. Maybe it's time I started listening.

What is it they say about country music? *Three chords and the
truth?*

Moving on doesn't have to mean forgetting what was.

Hopefully, Kleo is also ready to move on.

My hopes die the minute I turn onto my street and see Mick's car in the driveway.

"Shit," I mutter, parking on the street. I'm walking up the front path and taking out my key as the door opens.

"Mick's here," Kleo says.

I step inside, take a look around. "Where is he?"

"Passed out in the bedroom. He showed up about an hour ago, drunk out of his mind, crying that he's sorry, that he loves me, that he'll do anything to make things right. The usual."

"What did you say?"

She smiles. "I told him it was over."

I breathe a deep sigh of relief. "How'd he take it?"

"He stared at me for a while, like he couldn't quite believe it. Then he just shrugged, asked me to give him a few minutes to clean his stuff out of the bedroom. I said okay. Then I waited and waited. Finally, I went in to see what was taking him so long and found him passed out on the bed. I tried waking him up, but it was no use."

"You'll sleep with me tonight," I tell her. "We'll get him out in the morning."

I put my arms around her and lead her to my bedroom, closing the door behind us and offering up a silent prayer that getting Mick out of the house in the morning will really be that easy.

CHAPTER SEVENTY-TWO

The phone wakes me up at just after eight o'clock the next morning.

I grab at the landline beside my bed, hoping to reach it before it can ring again and wake Kleo, who I suspect didn't get a whole lot of sleep last night. I know I didn't.

I lift the phone to my ear, preparing my body for outrage. *If this is another recording telling me that my Netflix account is about to be disconnected or that there have been some suspicious charges on my Visa . . .*

"Hello?" I whisper, not bothering to disguise my annoyance.

"Linda Davidson?" the voice asks.

Not a recording.

"Who's this?"

"It's Selena Rodriguez, from Legacy Place."

I push myself up in bed, my body stiffening. Early morning phone calls are almost as bad as ones that come in the middle of the night. They rarely contain anything good. "What's wrong?"

"Who is it?" Kleo asks, sitting up beside me.

"I'm afraid I have bad news," Selena begins. "You asked to be notified in the event of . . ."

I hear the rest of what Selena is saying as if she's speaking into a malfunctioning microphone. The words fade in and out, some loud, some barely audible. *Died peacefully . . . the staff . . . slippers . . . left you something . . .*

"Okay. Thank you. I'll try to stop by this morning," I mumble, returning the phone to its charger.

"Who was that?" Kleo asks again.

"One of the nurses from Legacy Place. I'd asked to be notified in the event of . . ." I hear my voice crack, then break. I clear my throat. "Jenny Cooper died in her sleep sometime during the night. The staff found her when they did their morning rounds."

"Oh, Mom. I'm sorry. I know how fond you were of her."

"Apparently, when they took off her blankets, they found that she was wearing the slippers I bought her for her birthday. Selena said that she never took them off."

Kleo leans her head against the rounded slump of my back, the warmth of her cheek permeating the thin cotton of my nightgown. "Are they having some sort of ceremony later?"

"I don't think so. Why?"

"I heard you say you'd try to stop by."

"No, no ceremony. Apparently, Jenny left something for me."

"What?"

"I have no idea." I shrug. "I guess I'll find out."

We look toward the bedroom door.

"Do you think the phone call woke Mick up?" Kleo asks.

"I guess that's something else we'll find out." I climb out of bed, throwing a robe over my nightgown. I walk to the bedroom door, open it and peek out as Kleo comes up behind me to peer over my shoulder. She's wearing the pair of pajamas I lent her last night, her feet bare.

The house is eerily quiet.

The door to her bedroom is closed, as is the door to Mick's office. I tiptoe toward them and gently push open the bedroom door. The blackout blinds are down. The room is dark. I can't see a thing. I flip on the overhead light.

The bed is empty.

I check the closet, then his office. "He's not here," I tell Kleo, returning to the main part of the house.

"His car's gone," she says, opening and closing the front door.

"Unfortunately, his clothes and his computer are still here."

"Which means he'll be back," Kleo says.

I nod. "We can get his stuff packed up in the meantime."

The look on Kleo's face troubles me.

"Having second thoughts?"

"No," she says. "Just wondering what comes next."

I don't have to ask what she means. It's not like Mick to give up so easily, to take no for an answer, to give up without a fight, a nasty one at that. She's right to wonder what comes next.

I guess we'll find out, I think again.

I arrive at Legacy Place a little after ten and go directly to the fourth floor.

There is the familiar charge in the air, the silent signal having been circulated among the other residents, alerting them to what has happened and warning them their time is fast approaching. I hear moaning from behind a closed door, see a woman wandering the halls with tears falling from her blank eyes, although I doubt she knew Jenny.

Selena is sitting behind her desk and she offers a little half smile when she sees me. "Sorry if I woke you up this morning," she says. "I wanted to make sure I caught you before you got busy with your day."

"I appreciate it. Thank you."

"For what it's worth," Selena tells me, "it was a good death. Jenny didn't suffer. We don't all get to be ninety-three and die peacefully in our sleep."

I nod. If even half of what Jenny told me is true, she'd suffered enough during her lifetime. She deserved a good death.

Although I'm not sure the people she claimed to have killed would agree.

Had she really killed anyone?

"Is she still here?" I ask.

"No," Selena says. "Her body has been sent to the cremato-rium, as per the instructions we had on file."

I nod, finding it impossible to imagine Jenny reduced to a pile of ashes. "You said she left something for me?"

"She did." Selena reaches into the top drawer of her desk, re-trieves a sealed envelope, and extends it toward me. "Here it is."

I take the envelope from her hand. LINDA DAVIDSON is printed in bold letters across its front. PERSONAL AND CONFIDENTIAL.

I smile as I tear open the envelope, carefully extricating the sin-gle sheet of paper inside and lifting it to my eyes.

JENNY'S SPECIAL RECIPE is scrawled across the top of the page. Directly below is written STIR TOGETHER WELL, followed by a list of familiar over-the-counter pharmaceuticals, along with how much of each is required.

"Some final words of wisdom?" Selena asks.

I return the piece of paper to its envelope and drop it inside my bag. "You got that right," I say.

CHAPTER SEVENTY-THREE

I go to the beach, spend the next hour sitting on the sand, watching the waves splash against the shore. *The ebb and flow of life,* I think.

"Don't think," I hear Jenny say.

I laugh, attracting the attention of a group of young women in bikinis, arranging their bodies on towels, exposing their firm flesh to the unforgiving rays of the sun. I think of telling them that they'll pay for such irresponsibility when they get older, that wrinkles and age spots are already lurking just below the surface, not to mention potentially deadly cancers, and that prolonged exposure to the sun could result in skin as leathery as my expensive new handbag.

"Don't think," Jenny warns again.

Again, I laugh. Louder this time.

Again, the young women look warily in my direction.

"Sorry," I say. "A friend of mine just died." It's only after the words have left my mouth that I realize how insane they must have sounded.

I'm about to explain, to provide context for my remarks, but the women are already gathering up their towels and moving farther down the beach.

They think I'm crazy.

They may be right.

Who else comes to the beach to mourn the death of a demented old lady with delusions of being a serial killer?

Is there even a slim chance that any of what she told me is true?

I reach inside my purse, pull out the envelope Jenny left me and remove her "special recipe." I scan the list of ingredients, smile at the instructions to STIR TOGETHER WELL.

Whether this is, in fact, a recipe for a lethal cocktail or the ravings of a damaged mind, whether Jenny actually poisoned a multitude of victims with her so-called special recipe, one thing is indisputably true: I'm going to miss her. "I'm going to miss you, Jenny," I say out loud, returning the envelope to my purse. I brush the sand from its bottom as I scramble to my feet, thinking that Monsieur Vuitton wouldn't be too happy to see his fine leather treated in such a cavalier fashion.

"Don't think," Jenny warns again.

"Rest in peace, Jenny," I mutter, crossing the busy highway to where my car is parked.

Ten minutes later, I'm home.

"Hello?" I call as I walk through the front door. "Kleo? Hello? Anybody home?"

There is no response.

I'm a bit surprised. I'd offered to drive Kleo to the library after lunch, and she hadn't said anything about going out beforehand, especially now that Mick has their car and getting anywhere without one is something of a chore. Of course, it's possible that she got restless, decided to take a walk, get some exercise and some air before spending the afternoon trying to make up some of the work she lost to Mick's carelessness.

Carelessness? Or sabotage?

"Bastard," I say out loud. "Jackass."

I walk into the kitchen, check to see if my daughter has left me a note telling me where she's gone and when she'll be back. But there's no note on the counters, nothing on the dining room table, nothing on the coffee table in the living room except the familiar bowl of nuts.

Which is when I realize that the door to her bedroom is closed.

Shit! She probably went back to bed, desperate for a few more hours of uninterrupted rest, and here I come barging in, yelling her name, probably waking her up from the best sleep she's had in days. *Shit, fuck, fart!*

And then I hear it.

"Mom? Mom?" More moan than actual words.

Coming from behind the closed bedroom door.

"Kleo?" I hurry toward the door and throw it open.

The blackout blinds are still down, as they were this morning, and I have to flip on the overhead light to see anything. A loud gasp escapes my mouth as I view the chaos that greets me. The room looks as if a hurricane has swept through it, lifting bedside lamps from their small tables and tossing them to the floor, sending clothes scattering in all directions, upending drawers and emptying their contents. The voluminous white comforter that normally covers the king-size bed is now more off the bed than on. I follow the bottom of the comforter to the floor.

Which is when I see her.

My daughter is sitting on the floor on the far side of the bed, her eyes staring vacantly into space, her legs stretched out in front of her. Uncombed hair falls into her face, not quite hiding the dried tears staining her cheeks. A line of dried blood runs from the bottom of her split lip to the quarter-size bruise on her chin.

"Oh, my God!" I cry. "Kleo! Sweetheart! What happened?"

But even as the words escape my mouth, I know the answer.

Mick.

Mick happened.

"He showed up just after you left," she tells me, her voice a dull monotone. "He must have been watching the house, waiting for you to leave. He knocked on the door, told me he was here to collect his stuff, so I let him in. At first, he was being really sweet. You know how he can be. He said he understood that he'd fucked up big time, and he knew it was over, that he was truly sorry, and that he hoped one day we could be friends. I offered to help him get his stuff together, which is when we came into the bedroom, and he asked if he could hug me one last time." Her voice catches in her throat. "I said I didn't think that was a good idea, and he just lost it, started screaming, throwing things, telling me that I'd be sorry, that he was never going to let me go, that he'd ruin my reputation, ruin *me*."

"We'll go to the police . . ."

"No! We can't go to the police."

"Why not? For God's sake, look what he did to you!"

"You don't understand."

"What don't I understand?"

Kleo's eyes close. "He has pictures."

"Pictures? What do you mean? What kind of pictures?"

Kleo pauses long enough for what she is saying to sink in.

"Pictures of you?" I say, pushing the reluctant words from my mouth. "Like the kind we saw in those awful magazines?"

"No, nothing like those, but . . . We were playing around one night; he took a bunch of pictures; I'm naked; they're pretty graphic. Of course, he promised me he'd erase them later. But now he's threatening to send them to the school, to my students, their parents, to the doctoral committee, that he's going to post those pictures online, that they'll live on the web forever, that I'll be a laughingstock, that I'll never get another job, that I can kiss my PhD goodbye! Oh, God, Mom. How could I have been so stupid! What am I going to do? I'm so ashamed."

I sit down beside her, take her shaking body in my arms, absorbing the terror in her eyes and the bruises on her beautiful face, knowing those bruises are the least of the damage Mick has done. I look toward the closet, see Mick's clothes hanging stubbornly inside. *We'll never be rid of him*, I understand in that moment. *That monster will never leave my daughter alone.* "Call him," I tell her.

"What?"

"Call him and tell him that I want to talk to him, that I have a proposition I think might interest him."

"What kind of proposition?"

"Mick needs money. I *have* money. I'm sure we'll be able to work something out."

"I don't think that's such a good idea . . ."

"Don't think," I tell her. "Just do it. Tell him to be here at six o'clock. That will give us enough time to get all his things boxed up and ready." In the next instant, I'm on my feet, moving toward the front door.

"Where are you going?" she calls after me.

"Call him," I repeat, opening the door and stepping outside. "I'll be back soon."

CHAPTER SEVENTY-FOUR

Mick arrives at exactly six o'clock.

"Linda," he says warily, as I open the front door. He steps inside, looks around, notes the large cardboard box I picked up earlier standing by the door. "Where's Kleo?"

"She went out. I thought it best that she be elsewhere while you were here." I motion toward the living room sofa. "Sit down. We need to talk."

"I understand you have a proposition for me."

"I do. Sit down," I say again.

"Oh, I like it when you get all bossy. It might turn me on, if you weren't so . . . what's the word? . . . old."

I smile. "Well, I guess old age has its perks after all."

He laughs, plops down on the sofa, crosses one leg over the other, grabs a handful of peanuts from the bowl and pops them into his mouth. "Is this going to take long?"

"It might," I qualify, hearing traces of Jenny Cooper in my voice.

"Okay. Well, then, in that case, I could probably use a beer. There should be some in the fridge. If you haven't already packed them up with the rest of my stuff." He grins. "You wouldn't mind getting me one, would you?"

"It would be my pleasure," I say, not bothering to disguise the sarcasm in my voice. I walk into the kitchen, retrieve a bottle of beer from the fridge, pour it into the tall glass waiting on the counter, and return with it to the living room, holding it out toward him. "Here you go."

He downs almost a third of the glass in one long gulp. "Aah. Nothing like an ice-cold beer."

"If you say so."

He swallows another handful of peanuts, takes another long sip of his beer.

I watch and say nothing.

"So, what's this proposition you have for me?" he asks after a minute's silence.

"Kleo told me about the pictures you took of her, that you're threatening to post them online."

"Yeah, there's some pretty racy stuff. Not sure how well it'll go over in the halls of higher learning. Would you like to have a look?" He pulls his phone from the back pocket of his jeans.

"No, thank you," I say quickly.

"You sure? There's some pretty good ones." He extends the phone toward me.

I grab at it, but he snatches it back before I can reach it, returns it to his pocket, takes another sip of his beer, leans back, smiles, and says nothing, waiting. "I assume there's some sort of offer coming," he says finally.

"How much is it going to take?" I oblige him by saying.

"You tell me. You're the one throwing this party."

I give my answer a moment's thought. "Ten thousand dollars?"

He frowns.

"Twenty?"

"I don't know. I think these pictures are worth a lot more than that." He wolfs down another handful of nuts and finishes the last of his beer. "It's awfully hot in here. You think you could lower that thermostat?" He wipes a sudden line of perspiration from his forehead.

"How much more?" I ask, ignoring his request.

He pushes some hair away from his forehead, now bathed in sweat. "Well, it seems I've kind of maxed out my credit cards, and motels are pretty expensive these days. I can't really keep living in them. I'm gonna need to rent an apartment sooner than later, which is gonna require first and last month's rent, plus security, that sort of thing." He takes a deep breath, then another, stretches his neck from side to side.

"How much?" I ask again.

"Well, ballpark, I'd say . . ."

"*Yankee Stadium!*" I interrupt. "*Camden Yards!*"

"What?" The color drains from Mick's face. He looks at me as if I've gone completely mad.

"Sorry. You were going to tell me how much you want."

He swallows, blinks, blinks again. "Well, I don't want to be greedy. I was thinking that fifty thousand dollars should just about do it."

"Fifty thousand dollars," I repeat.

"For starters." He pushes himself to his feet, sways unsteadily. "Look. I'm gonna go now, give you some time to think about everything, and call you in the morning. How does that sound?"

"Oh, I don't think we have to wait till tomorrow. I can give you my answer right now."

"By all means."

"I'm not giving you a fucking cent."

Mick grimaces. "I really think you need to reconsider, Linda. These are the type of pictures that aren't going to do Kleo's career any favors. Shit!" He swipes at the sweat now dripping down his face. His hand reaches for his chest.

"What's the matter, Mick? You don't look so good."

He grabs his left arm with his right hand. "Sharp pain," he says, gasping.

"Maybe you should sit back down."

"Call 911."

"I will." I don't move. "Soon."

He stares at me, the reality of his situation starting to sink in. "You bitch! What have you done to me?"

"I may have poisoned your beer."

"What?"

"I did," I admit, channeling Jenny. "I poisoned your beer."

"*What? Are you crazy?*"

"Maybe. Maybe not."

"You'll never get away with this."

"Oh, I think there's a good chance I will."

I smile as I watch Mick fall to the floor, his eyes rolling up into his head. I sit down on the sofa, wait until his lips have started turning blue. Only then do I walk slowly to the kitchen and place a call to 911. "Hurry," I tell the operator, my voice catching in my throat. "I think my son-in-law is having a heart attack!"

CHAPTER SEVENTY-FIVE

Jenny was right.

It's remarkably easy to kill someone and get away with it. Provided, of course, that you have the right recipe.

The paramedics who showed up at my door were unbelievably dedicated and efficient, and I confess to a few anxious moments after the ambulance arrived. They worked for over twenty minutes trying to revive Mick, and I found myself holding my breath in the event a miracle occurred.

Fortunately, there were no miracles.

I breathlessly related what happened as they went about their business: that Mick and my daughter had recently separated and that Mick had come over to collect his belongings while Kleo was out, that I smelled beer on his breath and suspected he was intoxicated, that I didn't think he should be driving in that condition, that he didn't look well, how I urged him to sit down for a few minutes before trying to load the heavy box containing his clothes and his computer into his car, that he stubbornly waved away my concerns, insisting that he was perfectly all right.

At this point in the story, I actually managed to squeeze out a few tears. My son-in-law and I had always enjoyed a good relationship, I told the paramedics. He and my daughter had been living with me ever since my husband passed away; Mick had been like a son to me; I was devastated by their decision to go their separate ways.

I explained the tremendous pressure Mick had been under to get his struggling business off the ground, that his behavior was becoming increasingly erratic, and that this, no doubt, had contributed to the breakdown of his marriage.

I cried as I described how Mick had clutched his left arm, then his heart, complaining of a sharp pain, before falling to the floor. I described how I ran into the kitchen to call 911, how I tried desperately to revive him by doing the chest compressions I'd seen on countless TV shows, but that, unfortunately, at my advanced age, I just wasn't strong enough, and my efforts fell tragically short.

I left out the part where I'd gone to the drugstore earlier in the day and purchased the ingredients for Jenny's special recipe, the part where I combined those items and stirred them well, as per her instructions, the part where I left the lethal mixture in a tall beer glass on the counter, then waited for Mick to arrive, how I watched him drink every last drop before collapsing to the floor, how I then took that glass into the kitchen and washed it thoroughly by hand before loading it into the dishwasher, how I flushed what remained of Jenny's special ingredients down the toilet, although there was probably no need, as all the items are available over the counter and, I suspect, a common sight in medicine cabinets across the country.

Of course, I had no way of knowing for sure that Mick would ask for a beer, but I had a pretty good idea. And if he hadn't asked, I would have offered. It's unlikely he'd have turned me down. Those peanuts are awfully salty, and contrary to Mick's inflated opinion of himself, he wasn't all that complicated.

"You did everything you could," the female paramedic assured me as she and her male partner loaded Mick's body into the ambulance.

I'd already disposed of his cellphone, dropping it into the garbage disposal and humming as the machine ground its contents into dust.

"Your son-in-law suffered a massive heart attack. There was no way you could have saved him."

I smiled at the familiar words.

Maybe not, I thought. But I could save my daughter.

As soon as the ambulance drove off, I called Kleo. I'd sent her to the movies, told her to save her ticket stub, a precaution I took in the event the police were called in to investigate Mick's death.

I needn't have worried.

Mick's death was ruled a heart attack. There was no investigation.

Kleo was granted an extension on her dissertation, due to her husband's untimely passing. We spent Christmas in Connecticut with Vanessa and her family. We're planning another, longer visit there next summer to celebrate Kleo getting her doctorate.

Since we've been back, I make regular visits to Carol in Miami, meet once a month with my book club, spend an increasing amount of time with Max Silver. I've gotten to know a few of our neighbors and have agreed to tutor some of their teenage offspring in English. I've even started volunteering at Legacy Place one afternoon a week. Selena tells me I have a soothing effect on the residents, and I have to admit that helping out there in whatever small way I can makes me feel useful, as if even at my ripe old age, I still have something valuable to contribute.

Life goes by too quickly to waste time worrying what it's all about. Life is about living.

Maybe that's the true legacy of Legacy Place.

Maybe the name isn't so ironic after all.

Occasionally, I think about Mick and what I did; then I hear Jenny's voice in my ear.

"Don't think," she says.

Kleo has never asked for the details of what happened that night, although I sense she has a pretty good idea. "Did he suffer?" she asked me as we settled into bed that night.

"It was over pretty quick," I said, not quite answering the question.

"I love you," she's told me every night since.

"I love you more" comes my immediate response.

"Impossible," we say together.

Acknowledgments

There are always so many people to acknowledge: my regulars—Larry Mirkin, Beverley Slopen, and Robin Stone, whose advice is invaluable. Much as I think that I've got it right this time, that there's not a word that needs changing, in the immortal words of Roseanne Roseannadanna, aka the late, great Gilda Radner of *SNL*, "There's always a-something."

What hasn't changed is my ever-wonderful agent, Tracy Fisher of WME, who has been steadfastly in my corner for more years than I care to think. ("Don't think," as Jenny Cooper would undoubtedly say.) I would also like to thank her various assistants over the years—Sam Birmingham, Celia Rogers, and Megan Murray—for all their efforts on my behalf.

Many thanks and a sad goodbye to Anne Speyer, the editor I've worked with on my last several books at Ballantine and who oversaw much of the work on this one, but has now moved elsewhere, leaving me in the welcoming hands of Jesse Shuman, who assures me that while he is young, he is good and he is "scrappy," which I love. His advice on bringing this novel to its completed form has been spot-on. Thank you to the rest of the production crew at Ballantine: Jennifer Hershey, Kim Hovey, Kara Welsh, Derek Walls, Dennis Ambrose, Michelle Daniel, Angie Campusano, and Emma Thomasch.

Thank you to everyone at Doubleday Canada: Kristin Cochrane, Amy Black, Val Gow, Kaitlin Smith, Robin Thomas, Christine Vecchiato, Maria Golikova, and Martha Leonard. And to anyone I may have inadvertently left out, please accept my apologies as well as my sincere thanks.

Thanks also to my various publishers throughout the world and their wonderful translators—a special shout-out to Milena Havlova, who is not only my Czech translator but has become a valued friend and pen pal.

Thank you to Corinne Assayag for her continued support and everything she has done for me over the years.

My love and appreciation to Mary Castillo for making sure my condo is clean and I get enough to eat, and especially for never complaining when I invite people over for dinner and everyone requests something different.

And finally, to my family: my husband, my daughters and their husbands, my grandchildren, and my sister, as well as my friends. I love you more.

About the Author

JOY FIELDING is the *New York Times* bestselling
author of *The Housekeeper, All the Wrong Places,
The Bad Daughter, She's Not There, Someone Is
Watching, Charley's Web, Heartstopper, Mad River
Road, See Jane Run,* and other acclaimed novels.
She divides her time between Toronto and Palm
Beach, Florida.

joyfielding.com
Instagram: @fieldingjoy
Find Joy Fielding on Facebook